The Evolution of
Annabel Craig

The Evolution of Annabel Craig

A NOVEL

Lisa Grunwald

RANDOM HOUSE
NEW YORK

The Evolution of Annabel Craig is a work of fiction whose main characters often interact with both famous and lesser-known historical figures. All incidents and dialogue that occur between and among them are thus products of the author's imagination and are not to be construed as real. For trial scenes and speeches, however, the author frequently quotes from or condenses official transcripts and printed materials. Please see the source notes at the back of the book if you are interested in more detail.

Published in the United States by Random House,
an imprint and division of Penguin Random House LLC, New York.

RANDOM HOUSE and the HOUSE colophon are registered trademarks
of Penguin Random House LLC.

Library of Congress Cataloging-in-Publication Data
Names: Grunwald, Lisa, author.
Title: The evolution of Annabel Craig: a novel / Lisa Grunwald.
Description: New York: Random House, [2024]
Identifiers: LCCN 2023005267 (print) | LCCN 2023005268 (ebook) |
ISBN 9780593596159 (Hardback) | ISBN 9780593596166 (Ebook)
Subjects: LCSH: Self-realization in women—Fiction. | LCGFT: Novels.
Classification: LCC PS3557.R837 E86 2024 (print) | LCC PS3557.R837 (ebook)
| DDC 813/.54—dc23/eng/2030206
LC record available at https://lccn.loc.gov/2023005267
LC ebook record available at https://lccn.loc.gov/2023005268

Printed in the United States of America on acid-free paper

randomhousebooks.com

2 4 6 8 9 7 5 3 1

First Edition

Book design by Jo Anne Metsch

In memory of four strong and glorious women:

BEVERLY GRUNWALD,

DONNA ASH,

BARB BURG,

and SUSAN KAMIL

A certain light was beginning to dawn dimly within her—
the light which, showing the way, forbids it.

—KATE CHOPIN, *The Awakening,* 1899

The Evolution of Annabel Craig

In the famous, hell-hot summer of 1925, three thousand people snaked their way through the muddle of my hometown. Men at makeshift stands on the streets hawked lemonade, wrinkled hot dogs, watch fobs, Bibles, pamphlets, and palm-leaf fans. Hand-painted signs saying READ YOUR BIBLE were nailed to buildings, fence posts, and privy doors. Total strangers called each other infidels and atheists, zealots and fools.

Until that summer, I had never questioned a miracle, witnessed a gunfight, or seen a dead body. I had never met an agnostic, a scientist, or a Jew. I had thought I knew exactly what I wanted and what I didn't. But before the summer was over, all that and much more would change. I would listen to a preacher who insisted the earth was flat—and to a zoologist who compared the teeth of humans to the scales of sharks. I would pour bootleg liquor for Yankee lawyers and scientists. I would shake hands with two of the country's most famous men, as well as with a piano-playing chimpanzee named Joe Mendi. I would ask myself the kinds of questions I'd never had to ask before. And I would bear witness as Dayton, Tennessee—the quiet mountain town where I'd been born, baptized, orphaned, and married—was crazily transformed into a raucous, divided, and infamous world.

By chance, I was present at this world's creation.

Part One

||||||||||||||||||||||||||||||||||||||||||||||||||||||||||||||||||||||

1

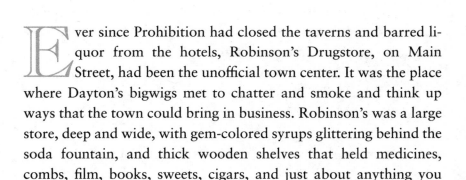

Ever since Prohibition had closed the taverns and barred liquor from the hotels, Robinson's Drugstore, on Main Street, had been the unofficial town center. It was the place where Dayton's bigwigs met to chatter and smoke and think up ways that the town could bring in business. Robinson's was a large store, deep and wide, with gem-colored syrups glittering behind the soda fountain, and thick wooden shelves that held medicines, combs, film, books, sweets, cigars, and just about anything you could want. Folks tended to linger at the tables in back—tippy round tables on wrought-iron legs with looped feet that looked as if they could walk.

On an afternoon in early May of 1925, I'd gone in to buy some buttons for my husband's shirts and to pick up a fresh roll of film, but Hank Dawson, the boy at the counter, told me my new batch of photos had just arrived, so I sat down to see how they'd turned out and to drink a cherry Coke. Two tables in front of me, under a ceiling fan stirring their cigarette smoke, a half dozen of the town leaders were hatching a plan. The men wore wrinkled pale linen jackets, and wide ties that ended about three inches up from their belts. They wore straw boater hats that they kept pushing back from their foreheads in greater and greater excitement.

Their topic was a brief article that had just come out in the *Chattanooga Daily Times,* and George "Rapp" Rappleyea, a short, frenetic thirty-year-old engineer who ran Dayton's failing coal and iron works, stood up to read it aloud. It seemed that in New York, a group called the American Civil Liberties Union was offering to back any Tennessee teacher willing to test a new law in court. This law, which Rapp said the governor had just signed, was called the Butler Act, and it was meant to protect our state's children by forbidding the teaching of evolution in Tennessee's public schools. When Rapp finished reading the article, the men murmured and called for more fountain drinks. Then they did a small thing that would turn out to be monumental. They sent Hank to find John Scopes, the coach of the high school football team. Not ten minutes later, John came in from playing tennis, wearing a sweat-drenched white shirt and an unsuspecting smile, and in less than half an hour, they had talked him into being arrested.

They started with things like

"You filled in for Mr. Ferguson when those boys and girls were studying for their final exams, right?"

And

"You taught them all about Charles Darwin, right?"

And

"You don't have any particular plans for this summer, do you, John?"

Frank "F.E." Robinson was the drugstore's owner and also head of the Rhea County school board. Eager and affable, with a tidy, wide side part in his hair, he pulled up a chair for John and handed him an orange soda. Once more, Rapp read the article aloud. The Butler Act made it illegal to teach "any theory that denies the story of the Divine Creation of man as taught in the Bible, and to teach instead that man has descended from a lower order of animals."

Rapp was originally from New York, and he had the kind of energy I imagined all citified people did. His wiry brown hair stuck both up and out, like the hair of a cartoon character with his finger in an electric socket. He put the paper down, took a step back, and thrust an arm toward John as if calling him up to receive a medal.

"They need a Tennessee teacher. We want *you* to be that teacher," he said.

Before John could respond, the other men chimed in:

"If Dayton doesn't do it, some other town will."

And

"Some other town will get the glory."

"And the attention."

"And the business."

I was curious, so I stayed put, just sifting through my photographs, though by now I'd seen them all many times. A few were portraits I'd been hired to take, but most were still lifes I'd done for myself. A field of sunflowers. A cloud formation. My gray cat, Spitfire, somehow looking annoyed.

With all those men talking over each other, it was hard to figure out if they were more worked up about defending the Bible story or about becoming famous for defending the Bible story. It seemed that at least three of them were truly in favor of the Butler Act, and that Rapp himself was firmly against it. But gradually, I realized it didn't matter what each man believed about creation or evolution or what should be taught and where: They all agreed emphatically that testing the law in Dayton would be sure to bring in business—maybe even revive the blast furnace that had once helped the town thrive.

"Whattaya say, John?" Rapp finally asked.

John reminded them that he wasn't the regular biology teacher and had only filled in for him during review classes.

"But you had them review that science textbook, right?"

"And evolution's *in* that textbook, right?"

"It's the state's own textbook," John said matter-of-factly. "And yes, of course evolution is in it."

"Then that's that," Rapp said. "Are you willing to be our Tennessee teacher?"

Both he and John wore round horn-rimmed glasses, and they happened to take them off and wipe them at the same moment. They laughed in unison and, in unison, put their glasses back on.

John Scopes said he was willing.

Frank Robinson looked newborn. He shook John's hand, clapped him on the shoulder, strode to the telephone at the counter, and asked the operator to connect him to the *Chattanooga Times*. He said, "This is F. E. Robinson in Dayton, Tennessee. I'm chairman of the school board here. We've just arrested a man for teaching evolution."

Even decades later, that very same little table where the men had sat would be ensconced in the Tennessee State Museum and would feature, under glass, a card that read:

AT THIS TABLE, THE SCOPES EVOLUTION
TRIAL WAS STARTED, MAY 5, 1925

Here is what I knew about evolution on that day in May of 1925: Nothing. Sure, I must have studied it on at least one day in high school, because the textbook hadn't changed since I'd graduated five years before. But if you'd asked me about evolution then, all I would have told you is that folks who believed in it thought men had come from monkeys, and so we should pray for those folks. I'd have told you I'd heard that evolution was a conspiracy hatched by godless Yankee highbrows to turn good Christians away from the Bible and therefore destine us to spend eternity in hell.

What I didn't know about evolution was anything close to the reasoning or the facts behind the science. And I didn't know that, when confronted with even the word alone, some people who were otherwise decent and faithful would lose their decency in order to protect their faith.

But I did know John Scopes. He'd come to Dayton the year before to teach some science and math classes and to coach the Yellow Jackets, the Rhea Central football team. Just a few weeks earlier, I'd photographed him with the boys for the yearbook. John's face was shaped like a spoon, and his pale hair was already thinning. He was twenty-four, just a year older than I was, close in age and spirit to the boys—and it had taken me a while to settle them all down to pose for the picture. They'd been tossing footballs at John and swiping cigarettes from his shirt pocket, and he'd been saying, "Now, boys," but smiling just the same.

John Scopes seemed like a shy but popular fellow, and I'd spotted him at church and church functions. I was sure I'd seen him singing hymns without having to read from a hymnal. And I knew I'd seen him bow his head when Reverend Byrd said, "Let us pray."

At Robinson's, I paid for my cherry Coke, gathered my photos, and then went outside to wait for John. I stood next to the tall white porcelain scale that I'd always thought looked like a large lollipop. I noticed the wavy shimmers on the mesh of the screen door, torn and patched in many places and floppy from all the hands and elbows that had pushed against it for so many years. I tried as always to tuck my hair back into the bun that was forever unraveling and falling against my neck.

"Why'd you say yes?" I asked John as soon as the screen door banged shut behind him.

I was genuinely perplexed.

"Howdy to you too," he said. If he was rattled by what he'd just agreed to do, it didn't show in the slightest. His eyes were blue and calm.

"Howdy," I said. "Why'd you do it?"

"Seems like a worthy cause," John said.

"To break the law?"

"To break *this* law."

"But it's the law."

"But it's a bad law."

I wondered how he could be so sure.

It was late afternoon, with barely a hint of a breeze. John and I had to sidestep a knot of youngsters—just out of school for the summer—as they jostled each other on purpose, pretending they couldn't all fit through Robinson's door.

"Then don't you have to go to jail now?" I asked John.

"No. I have to go finish my tennis game."

Dayton, the seat of Rhea County in East Tennessee, was settled snugly between the knobby blue Appalachian Mountains and the wide Tennessee River. The town occupied just six square miles, and a lot of that was farmland. Houses were low and lonely, and the only buildings that really mattered were the courthouse and the churches. It took at most ten minutes to walk from Robinson's on Main Street over the unpaved roads to our house on Walnut. Today I dawdled. On my way up Cedar, I stopped to study Loula Hodge's prized red camellia bush. Color film wasn't around then, so composing a photograph meant I would squint and stare until the colors disappeared, and I could change them in my mind to a palette of black, white, and gray.

It simply made no sense to me that John had agreed to test this new law. Maybe, as a school employee, he felt pressured by Frank Robinson and the school board. Or maybe, as a teacher, he thought there shouldn't be a law telling him what he couldn't teach. But did he actually believe that evolution was true?

Genesis said God had created the heavens and earth and the land and water and the trees and grass and the fish and fowl and every animal, and only after all that, on the sixth day, had He created man in His own image. If you knew the Bible, how could you ever believe that man was anything but a special, a unique creation? And if you didn't hold to the Bible on Creation, what else might you not believe? I had never thought to ask. There had been no need to. The sky was blue, the hills were purple, the summers were long, and the Bible was true.

There was a large oak tree at the corner of North Cedar and Third, wide enough for a child to hide behind, and as I neared the corner, I saw half a dozen children playing tag, using the tree as home base. They shouted and laughed and wiped their mouths on their sleeves; their pigtails flew; their caps fell off. They were so muddied and breathless and young. What could be so bad about a law that was meant to protect our children—to protect all of us—from doubting our faith and losing our way?

2

The first time I left Dayton I was eight years old. My mother woke me up at dawn with a kiss, a biscuit, and a sip of black coffee, and at six we boarded the train and rode almost all the way to Kentucky. A thin, cheerful woman with eager eyes was waiting for us at Emory Gap and drove us in a hay-filled cart over barely drawn roads to her family's farm.

My mother had made many such trips, all around the Tennessee countryside. She was like an itinerant preacher, except her gospel wasn't the Bible; it was self-sufficiency, practicality, independence—and canning. It's hard to imagine now how a simple thing like canning tomatoes could ever have been so exciting. But my mother understood. If you were a girl in the rural South in the early twentieth century, joining a canning club meant getting a taste of freedom from your school, your church, and all the little and lofty things that people were always expecting of you. Canning also meant you could do things people didn't expect you to do: learn crop cultivation; work steam pressure cookers; use math to figure out acreage and profits; use science to enter the modern world. The motto of the canning clubs was "Grow more perfect tomatoes, and you will grow more perfect women."

For months, I had been begging my mother to let me come along with her. Now, bumping down the road in the cart, I nestled against her gingham shirt, which already smelled of the hay and the sun.

SEE HOW WE CAN

That was the home-sewn banner—the *see* an invitation, the *we can* a description but also a declaration—that my mother hung at the canning club exhibitions. Today I got to hold the front of it for her while she tied its fraying ropes around the craggy trunk of a thick poplar tree. The girls were arriving steadily—on mules, in carts, even in one Model T. Puffs of dirt and dust flew up from the road as they hopped out. Most were carrying wooden baskets filled with the tomatoes they'd grown—shiny tomatoes of every color from deepest purple to nearly white. I ran down to look into the baby carriage that one young woman had brought, and I laughed along with the other girls when we saw there was no baby inside, just a mound of bright orange tomatoes.

On a cracked gray wooden table in front of the farmhouse, my mother spread out a plaid tablecloth, lined up supplies for the demonstration, and asked me to build a tower of large empty cans. There were two boxes of them sitting in the sun by the farmhouse steps, and though they were already so hot that they seemed to singe my fingertips, I laid out a first row, carefully spacing them so I could balance each new row over the others. When I got as high as the fourth row, I needed to stand on a stool to reach. For the eighth row, someone brought me a ladder, and the other girls watched as, at last, I stood on tiptoes to crown the tower with one last can.

I remember looking down on about twenty faces, poking up like pink flowers from a meadow of faded denim coveralls and dresses, straw bonnets and pale kerchiefs tied into rabbit-ear points. Everything was earthy and raw except for the tin cans that blazed in the sun and seemed to be painted with vibrant stripes and zigzags of white light.

I watched the canning for an hour or so, then settled a few yards from the farmhouse in a field of clover and timothy grass. The blue and purple hills of Kentucky were on the far horizon, and for a while I just listened to the chatter of the girls and to my mother's voice, the voice my father had always said could talk the Devil into prayer.

Soon another girl, a bit younger than I was, came over and sat down. Like me, she had long brown braids and was wearing a white cotton shirt, but hers was missing two buttons, and her smile was missing a tooth.

"Your mama sure knows a lot," she said.

Her name was Freddie, short for Frederica.

"Do they call you Annie for Annabel?" she asked.

"Just my parents," I said.

We stretched out our legs and leaned back on our elbows, our faces in the sun. Against a perfect, flat blue sky, strips of long, thin clouds looked like small ripples on the surface of a pond. The smell of blanching tomatoes mingled with the odors of the farm: the earth, the manure, the black-eyed Susies, the apples that had fallen nearby and were rotting sweetly in the grass.

"Y'all from farming?" Freddie asked.

I nodded. "Dayton," I said. "Strawberries."

I sat up and reached for a wide blade of grass, lined it up carefully between my thumbs and the heels of my palms, and then blew into it, making a high sour whistle.

"How'd you do that?" Freddie asked.

"Easy," I said, though I'd only recently learned how myself. Freddie tried blade after blade, her fingers turning yellow-green with the juice of the grass and her spit. Finally, she blew hard enough for the blade to make at least one rude sound, and for the next ten minutes we sat making grass music and laughing. Then, in the field in front of the farmhouse, the boys showed up. There were six of them, wearing coveralls that all seemed too short or too long for their legs.

Freddie and I got to our feet.

"What're *they* doing here?" she asked indignantly. Her eyes narrowed. "They've got their old corn clubs, don't they?"

At first the boys just seemed to be laughing and chasing each other around, but soon they started singing. There was a canning club song that went—barely—to the tune of "Dixie." The boys were making it sound bawdy and mean:

> *The canning girl you'll not forget her*
> *Makes the best a little better*
> *Can away, can away, can away, tomato girls.*

They sneered and waggled their hips as they went on:

> *Come, customer, step up and try 'em*
> *Taste 'em once, you've got to buy 'em . . .*

They tumbled around the outskirts of the yard, popping up like gophers now and then from the tall grass and alfalfa. It seemed they'd chosen to play at reenacting the War Between the States, but they couldn't settle on who would be the Union, so one of them hit on a different idea.

"Hey!" he shouted. "Y'all watch this!"

In one motion, he reached into his coveralls pocket, pulled out a tattered baseball, and hurled it at my beautiful tower. The ball fell a good yard short but roused inspiration in the other boys.

"That your best?" one of them shouted. He pushed the others aside and took aim with his own baseball. It hit the cans dead center, and he and the other boys jumped and hooted as if they were at the Rhea County Fair and he'd just knocked over the wooden milk bottles.

I didn't think. An instinct I'd alternately question and relish seemed to come over me. I ran to the table and plunged both hands into a pail of slimy discarded tomatoes, grabbing the first two I could get my fingers around. Then I dashed forward into the yard and launched first one and then the other at the boys who'd fired the first shots. I caught one of them square on the shoulder and another on the knee. Tomato juice, like the blood of battle, dripped down their clothing.

The boys were so startled to see a little girl coming at them that for a moment they didn't move. Then Freddie caught up with me and threw another tomato. I ran back to get two more. It was war.

Neither my mother nor the women helping her stopped more girls from joining in. The boy who'd aimed the first ball found a crab apple and seemed to be winding up again, and another used a slingshot to launch one that hit Freddie's throwing arm. Once the boys ran out of crab apple ammunition, they tried to throw some of the tomato pulp back, but it didn't travel. Finally, they bent down to wipe their hands on the grass, and they walked away, faking indifferent laughter, pretending they didn't care.

Triumphant, we licked and swiped the tomato juice from our hands and forearms and then went down to the well to wash off the rest.

That evening, my mother and I took the train back to Dayton, and I leaned my head against her, just as I had that morning. I started to pick dried tomato seeds from her gingham sleeve.

"That's all right," she said. "They'll come straight off in the washing tomorrow."

"Mama," I said.

"Hmm," she said. She had just closed her eyes, exhausted.

"I got so angry at those boys—"

"You surely did."

"Did I do wrong?"

Now she looked at me and winked. "Well, they did knock down that pretty tower of yours," she said.

She tugged gently on one of my braids and brushed the hair from my forehead so she could kiss me there.

"So, I didn't do wrong to fight them?"

She said, "You made your stand."

She said it with a smile. A proud smile, I thought. And then she bestowed on me what I would come to cherish as a unique and powerful blessing.

"You led the charge in the Tomato War of 1911," she said.

3

In December of 1918, I used a pair of rusted shears to lop off my two long brown braids. It was the same week I buried my mother. I figured: No point looking like a girl if you have to live like a woman. I was sixteen.

The grocer, Miles McCaleb, had been the first person in Dayton to die of the Spanish flu. The postman, Marcellus Granger, went next, and then two boys and one girl from my high school class. Somehow, I'd believed that the fresh air and wide fields of our farm would protect us. But the flu, which would kill something like 50 million people around the world, ricocheted all through our county like a bullet in a quarry. It had hit my father in early November, and even as I stood beside my mother at his grave, I had felt a wild fever seeping through her old brown jacket. She died just two weeks later. A farmhand came to the high school to give me the news.

I wore her jacket all that winter. I wanted its sleeves to be her arms.

People said God's arms would be around me, but I couldn't feel them.

People said, "Well, your mama just went and followed your papa. Seems like nothing could keep those two apart." As if the thought of them being happy in heaven was enough to make me happy on earth. Did I mention that I was sixteen? Even in 1918, sixteen wasn't that old, and my parents weren't supposed to be in heaven. They were supposed to be in the kitchen, talking over coffee in their sweet, low voices, unaware that I was already awake and listening to their every word. Or they were supposed to be out in the fields, overseeing the planting and picking, coaxing our dark red strawberries from the lavish green leaves, their fingertips always stained pink as prairie roses.

Some of our neighbors and old Reverend Dowling helped me pack up my parents' things to auction off at church. Mr. Murray, from the Dayton Bank and Trust, took me and the money straight there and helped me set up an account with that and my parents' savings. Mr. Murray found a family from Rockwood to buy our farm, and it would be years before I'd go back.

Dayton in those days was home to fewer than two thousand people. Only Main and Market Streets were paved, and horses and wagons were still a lot more common than cars. But most of the buildings had indoor plumbing, electricity, and telephones. There were tidy lawns, a movie house, a car dealership, a German bakery, a Coca-Cola bottling works, and a depot along the Southern line. There were eight churches—ten if you counted what were then called the colored churches; eleven if you counted the Catholic one. Compared to the farms, the town had always seemed downright cultured to me, and even putting the loss of my parents aside, it took me a long time to get used to living there. I missed the early risings and the early-to-beds of life on a farm. I missed the sounds: the low hum of bumblebees working the strawberry blooms, the scattered but pristine birdsong. When you grow up on a strawberry farm, you probably always miss the smell too—the sweetness that, even before the fruit blooms, seems to sit like a mist on the air.

More than a decade after my parents died, I learned that my father had had a half sister living in Omaha. But at the time I knew of no relatives, and none seemed to know about me. I moved to the W. C. Bailey Boardinghouse on Market Street, bringing a few precious relics from home. I kept my parents' wedding rings, cushioned and coffined in a small red Mellomints tin. I kept four dishes, variously chipped, that would always remind me of the subtle way my mother had managed to serve my father his suppers on the least damaged one. I kept my father's Bible, my mother's wristwatch and sewing box, and the SEE HOW WE CAN banner, now threadbare, stained, and hallowed. I also kept my father's prized camera, which, though I didn't know it yet, held a tiny bit of my past and a huge part of my future.

One Sunday soon after I had moved to town, Major Thomas McClure, a veteran of the War Between the States, stopped me before church. The major was a town legend. He was eighty-one years old and had had four horses shot out from under him during the war. His gunshot-shattered face had been sewn together with crude cross stitches that looked like the ties on a railroad track. He had always terrified me, but now he smiled so deeply that his scar almost disappeared. He stretched his hands out sideways, palms up, and asked me to squeeze them as hard as I could. When I did, he winced dramatically.

"See how strong you are?" he said. "I reckon you'll be all right."

I had no reason to believe him.

I felt stingingly, heavily, helplessly alone. The road I'd been traveling with my parents had had all sorts of turns and signposts that I'd never needed to notice in order to find my way back home. Now I knew only that there was no way back, and that somehow, though I walked through the valley of the shadow of death, I was supposed to fear no evil.

But I was filled with fear, the fear that comes with bewilderment. I had already wondered what sort of God would punish the whole earth with so much war and sickness and loss. Now I wondered why God wanted me to be an orphan—or whether He just didn't care that He'd made me one. I nearly winced every time someone told me that God worked in mysterious ways. Or when they told me He just needed two more angels in heaven. As if He hadn't made angels in the first place and couldn't make as many more as He wanted, whenever He wanted, without having to take away anyone's parents.

I had been kneeling by my bed to pray every night since before I could remember. And of course I had gone to church almost every Sunday. ("If you can walk, you can worship," my father had often said.) But I had never had an image of the Lord in my head. Now I struggled harder to reach Him. Sometimes, I might get the sense of being immersed in a Dayton summer of emerald- and lime- and blue-green leaves. Other times, I couldn't get the words "let there be light" out of my head, and I imagined Him as all the light: the sun high in the sky or shimmering on the pond; or even the moon throwing down a beacon to show a path in the dark. More often, everything was in shadow.

On Christmas Day, old Reverend Dowling gave me a beautiful lamp with a base for holding a wide candle and a rosy glass globe etched with delicate six-point stars. At night, in the darkness, the candlelight slipped through those stars, a hint of heaven. Along with the lamp, the reverend gave me a note, written shakily in his old-fashioned, inky, squared-off letters. That lamp would be broken—perhaps on purpose—just a few years later, but I've never lost the note.

The Lord is my light and my salvation; whom shall I fear?
—Psalm 27

Naturally, when I was growing up, I'd read the Bible in Sunday School, and I'd heard it casually but frequently quoted by one parent or the other. There had always been the official Lessons during service, taken from the Old and New Testaments, but intoned by Reverend Dowling at a pace so numbingly slow that it made God-fearing men sneak guilty looks at their watches. But I had never tried to—I had never needed to—seek out the Bible for consolation.

Now, reading Psalms every night, I started to find it.

> *The Lord is nigh unto them that are of a broken heart.*

And

> *Weeping may endure for a night, but joy cometh in the morning.*

Until that incomprehensibly sad winter, faith had simply been the universal, ancestral music of my childhood. Now I strained to hear it better, realizing I already knew both the melody and the words, just that they had never sat in my own voice.

By that smoky pink lamp, and with the help of the Psalms, I finally learned to pray—not the prayers we said in church, with their pomp and remorse. But prayers of my own, another song entirely, a song of condolence and, occasionally, of peace.

Mr. and Mrs. Bailey, who owned and ran the boardinghouse, were never nasty or mean to me, never cursed or said an unkind thing. But I never felt at home there. Part of the reason may just have been the nature of a boardinghouse, with so many people coming and going, people whose names I tried to learn before realizing I didn't have to. Other than Mr. and Mrs. Bailey, there was only one person—Meriwether Tate—who was, like me, a full-time resident. But Mr. Tate was slovenly and scary, rarely shaved, and rarely spoke; when he looked at me, he did so in a way that made me feel he was thinking sinful thoughts. I did everything I could to avoid him, and that included spending most of my time at the Aqua Hotel, where I worked.

If I could have afforded to live at the Aqua, I would have. People generally agreed it was the finest place in town. It was known for its three stories, its thirty-six rooms, its vast banquet hall, and the mystery of its name—oddly misleading in a town carved out of hills. Despite its own constantly changing visitors, the large staff at the Aqua remained nearly as fixed as the two columns framing its entrance, with their bold white capital letters spelling A-Q-U-A, from top to bottom.

Fred Whittle, the Aqua's manager, was much kinder than the Baileys. He called me Sunshine, which was laughably inaccurate. But he gave me confidence, having me do just about every job that the other women did: I made the beds and washed the dishes; folded the hand towels and ironed the sheets. And Fred encouraged me to learn other things as well: how to do a bit of bookkeeping, typing, scheduling, and keeping guests mollified. There were forty people, men and women, who worked at the Aqua, but Fred, who knew I loved reading, always insisted I get first dibs on any books the visitors left behind.

So I spent a lot of time with them—whether heavy volumes about fishing; sticky, torn-up children's books; or novels I knew some people in my church, and plenty from other churches, had banned. I decided not to worry about what was supposed to be wrong with these books. I went through quite a few of them more than once. There was an old copy of *The Awakening* by Kate Chopin, which told the story of a married woman who realizes she's not living the life she needs to live. I read and reread *This Side of Paradise* by F. Scott Fitzgerald, a novel about a decadent college student and his many failed attempts at love.

My favorite was a book by Amy Bell Marlowe called *The Girl from Sunset Ranch*. In it, a sixteen-year-old girl named Helen whose father has just died ends up moving from the wilds of Montana to the wilds of New York City, where, Marlowe wrote, Helen's first reaction was "Why! There are so many people here one could *never* feel lonely!"

Eventually I realized that this book suffered greatly in style and quality by comparison to Chopin's and Fitzgerald's. It was part of a series of "books for girls" and very simple. But at the time, it awed me. On just about every page, Helen showed what my mother would have called *gumption*. Helen didn't cry when she was insulted by nasty relatives. She didn't shrink from the newness of the city streets. She wasn't put off by the strangeness of the Jewish families she met and, in fact, found them kinder than her wealthy Christian relatives.

I marveled at Helen's courage and outgoingness, but I had neither the chance nor yet the temperament to be that bold. Besides reading, I didn't do much with my spare time. There actually wasn't that much to do. When I was off from work, my friends at the Aqua were usually on. The Gem didn't show movies except at night. And shopping, for me, was strictly practical. I was managing to get by on my earnings from the Aqua, and I didn't want to dip into the savings from my parents. The girls at the hotel sometimes teased me about my clothes, which were pretty much limited to a few dresses and skirts. But there was no reason to dress up.

Often on my days off I would walk to the cemetery to visit my parents' graves. Buttram Cemetery was about two miles from the center of town, and it was rich in history even then. Most of the headstones had been chiseled the century before. The lettering on them was uneven, and the markers themselves were as different in height, width, and girth as people; like people, too, some of them leaned toward each other, the decades that had passed making them look as if they were stuck in eternal arguments or conversations.

My parents' graves were marked only by the simplest footstones: just their names and the dates of their births and deaths. Reverend Dowling had arranged for the stones. In other parts of the cemetery, some headstones were carved with sheep or cherubs or flowers. But nothing about my parents had been showy or fancy in life, and in death, I figured, it should be no different. I used to bring two single flowers—whatever was in season—and lay them across the stones, the blooms meeting between them like hands. I knew I wouldn't see my parents again unless and until I had lived as faithful a life as theirs and we could meet in heaven. But I kept thinking there must be a way to feel their presence, their reassurance.

Sparrows and blue jays frequented that graveyard, and there were two cardinals—one male, one female—that I often saw hopping on the grass just up a hillock from where I'd sit. Sometimes I let myself pretend they were my parents. I'd say "Hi, Papa" and "Hi, Mama." It's not like I ever expected them to answer. But I felt that the birds had somehow come because of me, that somehow they carried my parents' spirits.

I wish I'd understood then that I wouldn't always feel what I did—about life, about love, about God, about the whole sad world around me. But it didn't seem possible that I would ever feel safe or carefree again. I didn't realize that I was still mourning.

It helped to find comfort at the Aqua, where for the most part the staff was lively behind the scenes, collecting and trading the magazines, sayings, and sometimes even the clothing that visitors from bigger towns and cities left behind. When the guests weren't around, we practiced using the slang we'd overheard, like *all wet!* and *and how!* Eva Jenkins, late great head of the Aqua's kitchen staff, could be motherly and kind when she wasn't snapping out exhortations from Proverbs. Eva fed me generously so that I wouldn't have to eat at the boardinghouse. And a maid named Zipporah McGovern, who was even younger than I was, gossiped with me about the visitors, making up whatever stories we could.

One autumn day, I was passing Room 11 when Zippy called out to me. There she stood, in front of the tall oval mirror, swanning around in a green silk robe with a fringed belt.

"The missus left it!" Zippy said.

"It goes to the lost and found," I told her.

"I know. But don't you want to try it on first?"

The robe was silky and decadent. The fine tassels on the ends of its belt fell like water running through my fingers, and for a moment in that mirror I saw an entirely different version of myself. I wondered: Was this what I would look like, what I would wear, in some Yankee city where women were called flappers, smoked cigarettes, and rouged their cheeks? For what it's worth, I have never owned a green silk dressing gown or, for that matter, a dressing gown of any color or fabric. But from the Aqua Hotel, I took not only skills, friendships, and a shelf full of mismatched books but also—however fleetingly—an image of myself as a fashionable, modern woman.

Still, I think I was waiting for something to change around me before anything could change inside.

Four years later, in 1922, old Reverend Dowling had finally retired, young Reverend Byrd had come to take his place, and I'd stopped praying for impossible things—that my parents weren't really dead, for example, or that I had a hidden twin sister somewhere. Now I prayed for the sick neighbors I visited on Sundays after church. I prayed for my friends. I prayed for Reverend Byrd and Major McClure, for Eva Jenkins and Zippy McGovern. And sometimes—as a reward for all the praying I'd done for others—I let myself pray that I wouldn't always be alone.

I was twenty that year. Almost all the girls I'd gone to school with were already promised or married, and quite a few were even mothers. One of my best friends, Margaret Rush, had married a man from Knoxville and moved away. My oldest friend, Caroline, was engaged to Willie Quinn, the smartest boy in our high school class. Even Zippy talked about having a boyfriend—though with Zippy it was never clear how much was real and how much was wishful thinking. Other girls were settling down into the strawberry-specked landscape of my childhood. Word from some of the hill folk was that if I slept with a beef bone under my pillow, I'd be married in no time at all.

I had never come close to having a beau of my own. I was reminded, kindly but too often, that many of the men who would have been eligible husbands had died in the Great War or from the flu. Despite those explanations, I sometimes wondered if I was simply being punished for something I had done, or something I wanted to do. In a world where bliss and blessedness were so often mentioned together, it was difficult to believe that sadness and sin weren't also linked.

More than I would have admitted to anyone, even to Caroline or Zippy, I worried, too, that my looks were the problem. I was tall, with long legs and thick wrists, and I always fretted that, even though my hair had finally grown back to a girlish length, I looked too much like a boy. When I looked into a mirror, it agitated me. My eyes were blue—admittedly rare for someone with brown hair—but my face was dimpled in uneven places, and on my most uncertain days, I thought I looked like a russet potato. I knew I wasn't as pretty as my mother had been. But girlfriends said that when my eyes looked merry or wise, I could be beautiful. I didn't really believe them. I didn't know then that I would be loved. And I didn't know that even love might not be enough to make everything right.

4

My mother and father taught me many things, but they didn't teach me how to swim. Looking back, I'm not even sure that they knew how. But one day, when I was two or three, I'd toddled into Oak Tree Pond, hit a steep drop-off, and gone under. I had never forgotten the tug of the muddy bottom and the yank of my mother's hand on my ankle as she rescued me. At twenty, I was still afraid of the water. On Saturdays in the spring and summer, and sometimes even after Sunday church, young people would gather to picnic and swim, but even on the hottest, most motionless days, I would only stand on the brown, gritty shore of the sunlit green pond. I actually owned a bathing suit—the black-knit kind that girls wore then—and I always put it on hopefully. But despite even the kindest coaxing from my friends, I never managed to wade in farther than my knees. On either side, on the far banks and close in, people would plunge into the water one after another, the young men popping up to whip the water from their hair like dogs, the young women dunking their heads back to emerge as glossy as seals.

One Saturday morning in July of 1922, a tall young lawyer named George Craig who had just moved to Dayton from Knoxville marched over to me and looked me straight in the eye.

"I've been watching you stand by this pond every Saturday for four weeks," he said.

Without another word, he scooped me up and carried me in.

I was panicked and I was thrilled, and I squirmed and protested in George's arms until he had waded in so far that even if I'd managed to get free, my feet couldn't have touched the bottom.

"Pipe down, Little Fish," George said, with an intimacy nearly as shocking as his lifting me up had been.

I said, "I've already been baptized once."

He laughed.

I said, "Don't you let me go now."

"I've got you," he told me, and those three words, pronounced with such warmth and certainty, overwhelmed me in an instant and became, for better and eventually for worse, the refrain of a new life.

George's arms were thin but strong—certainly stronger than my protests, and stronger than my fear.

In those arms, hands clutching his neck, lips nearly touching his smooth wet shoulder, I felt myself starting to float, and we were married three months later in Dayton's First Avenue Methodist Episcopal Church.

"Smile at me with those eyes, Annie," George said to me, reaching for my hand across the heavy damask tablecloth at the Read House in Chattanooga, where we spent our honeymoon week. He said it, too, when he lay beside me in our hotel bed, the whole business of having relations changing in one night from a mystery to an adventure. In this room, every surface was layered with decoration: intricate patterns of rosettes in the plaster ceiling; flecked red velvet on all the walls; only a few planks of natural wood peeking out, un-

adorned, from beside the heavy, rich carpets. Not even the best
rooms in the Aqua boasted this kind of luxury. I thought I'd been
rescued. I felt cocooned.

Walking beside George on the wide, paved streets of downtown
Chattanooga, I would catch our reflection in the thick, wavy glass
store windows, surprised every time that there was someone beside
me. There was finally someone beside me. And oh, how it felt to
look at him. His straight, fine hair never seemed to fluff with the
heat or humidity. His hair and his eyes were the identical shade of
light brown, as if an artist had run out of paint or simply fallen in
love with the color he'd mixed on his palette.

Sometimes, after we lay together, I would cry unexpectedly.
Four years of loneliness had been vanquished by gratitude and relief. I'd prayed to find George, and he was here. He called me Little
Fish. He called me Flossie ("Why Flossie?" "Why not?"). He called
me Annie, and I let him, though I'd never let anyone besides my
parents.

"That's my Annie," George said when I smiled back at him. The
way he said my name made it seem like a synonym for *wife,* and to
me that was a magnificent, even a mighty, word.

> *Therefore shall a man leave his father and his mother, and*
> *shall cleave unto his wife: and they shall be one flesh.*

George's mother had died in childbirth, and he had been away
at law school when his father, like my parents, had died from flu.
Like me, too, he was an only child. I knew he had been lonely.

He said I was the bee's knees, the cat's whiskers, the tiger's spots.
He called me the dog's fingers, the snake's ankles, the rabbit's wings.

Nothing—except hope and other people's stories—had prepared me for such love. The impishness in his eyes, which seemed
to promise a joyful lifetime. The way he seemed to listen to me with
his whole body, leaning forward as if I was speaking softly, though
with him I almost never did. From the brisk November morning
when we moved into our rented house on Walnut Street, every last

detail of our new life—the wide maple tree that shaded and dappled our small bedroom; the two pillows against the headboard of our bed; the sight of George's seersucker jacket hanging in the closet—seemed a private but perfect miracle.

I loved our house. I loved *saying* "our house." The white ceilings were low, broken up by wide dark beams that barely cleared George's head but made the place feel sturdy and cozy. The unmatched planks of the wooden floors were the colors of whiskey and molasses. In the bathroom upstairs, above the large porcelain sink, there was a section of square white tiles, many fractured by age or heat, and in one tile, the cracks seemed to form the letter G. *George.*

He was working for the law offices of Baxter and Baxter, right down the street from the Aqua and Robinson's Drugstore. For decades, the Baxters had handled all manner of issues, from courthouse to contracts, but by now the elder Baxter was too feeble, and the younger Baxter had never been overly blessed with brains. Their need for a more active partner was the reason George had come to Dayton in the first place, and the Monday after we moved in together, he was heading back to his office. Sitting up in the bed that had come with the house—its flowery white iron headboard was equally beautiful and uncomfortable—I watched eagerly as George got dressed. Boxes of each of our belongings were lined up, mingled, against our bedroom wall. There were others downstairs in the parlor.

"Should I unpack your things?" I asked him.

"I'll do mine later," he said.

For now, he slid his straw boater from the top of our dresser, whipped it once around his finger, and angled it, just so, on his head. "See you this evening, Small Fry," he said, and he bent down to kiss me, just the way my father had kissed my mother whenever he'd left the house.

A minute later, I heard the front door close. Still barefoot, still wearing my thin white cotton nightgown, I ran down the stairs and inched open the door to see my husband walking down Walnut

Street toward Third Avenue, the sun already so bright that it washed out the yellow ribbon that rimmed his straw hat.

Mercy Applegate, who lived next door, had already introduced herself the day we moved in, gleefully presenting me with a well-thumbed copy of Lippincott's *Housewifery,* a different kind of bible, which she would quote nearly as often as the real one. Before this, I'd never even met Mercy, who belonged to one of the town's Baptist churches. But now, within half an hour of George's leaving, she planted herself, an exuberant, self-appointed guide, right in the middle of my kitchen. In addition to her four children (whom she called "the Puppies") and her husband, Tim (whom she called "the Big Dog"), Mercy had wisdom. Ten years' worth of marital and household experience had apparently been stored up, just waiting to be shared. Most of it began with her asking incredulous, boisterous questions.

"You mean you've *never* made your own curtains?"

"You've *never* roasted a Thanksgiving turkey?"

"You've *never* planted a garden?"

"Living in a boardinghouse?" I finally said. "Working in a hotel?"

"No. 'Course not, Lamb," she said, a bit ruffled. "It's been a long time since you've had a regular home, hasn't it?"

"I learned some things at the Aqua," I said.

"'Course you did, Lamb, bless your heart. But you have to learn a whole heap more now, don't you? You have to learn what he best likes to eat. Eggs wet or dry? Toast burnt or pale? What's he always hanker for?"

Mercy was portly. Her midsection was so round that it made her arms look short, even shorter when she raised a preaching finger, as she did for me, for the first of countless times, that morning. " 'Wives, submit yourselves unto your own husbands, as unto the Lord.' " I nodded, torn between a sincere belief in the instruction and a rogue doubt that its strident messenger had ever submitted herself to anyone except God.

Nevertheless, I was excited by the promise of Mercy's lessons.

My mother hadn't sheltered me from hard work on the farm, and my parents' deaths had made even harder work essential. But I'd never been given a single lesson in how to run a household, stock a pantry, or please a husband.

"With a house, you know," Mercy said, "always remember, 'You've got to keep up, so you never have to catch up.'"

I nodded.

"But listen to me, getting ahead of things," she said. "First let's get you settled."

The possessions that had crowded my small room at Bailey's Boardinghouse now all but disappeared into the ample closets, bureaus, and shelves of our new home. It took just minutes to unpack my clothes, my shoes, my pink lamp, and the things of my parents I'd saved. I used the drawers of an old pine nightstand for my mother's sewing box and my father's camera. I placed his Bible on top, beside a brass reading lamp with an ivy-green glass shade that was part of the house's furnishings. I placed the lamp Reverend Dowling had given me, the one with the pink star-etched shade, on the bedroom's mantel shelf. Then, with Mercy looking on, I unfolded my mother's SEE HOW WE CAN banner. For the last four years, it had hung across the wall behind my boardinghouse bed—an ever-fading reminder of the day of the Tomato War: the girl I'd been then, and the woman I hoped to be.

"Was your mama a canning demonstrator?" Mercy asked.

"Yes," I said proudly. "Yours too?"

"No. My mama wasn't one for traveling around. But she did let me go and join a club with my cousin up the road. 'Course I practically wore her bones down begging her to let me go. Never forgot a single one of those lessons. I still have my pin!"

I was holding the banner by its corners. "I still have this," I said.

"And what are you fixing to do with that?"

I looked around at the bare white walls.

"'See how we can'?" Mercy asked, laughing. "Think that's a proper thing to hang over a marriage bed?"

I was embarrassed. "I reckon not," I said, and I folded the banner carefully, then rolled it around the little tin box that held my parents' wedding rings.

After Mercy left to make lunch for her children, I went back downstairs to unpack the books Fred had let me cadge from the Aqua. Proudly, I lined them all up on the painted white shelves in the parlor. I arranged them, alphabetically by author, and I imagined how it would feel to have George's books—and everything they represented—mingled with mine. I would have unpacked all his boxes. I would have folded and hung up all his clothes. I would have done anything for him.

Wrinkles formed at the corners of George's eyes when he smiled or laughed, scrunching up like the folds of a Japanese fan. With other people, his eyes could widen with curiosity, squint with anticipation, dance when he was teasing. But for me, and me only, his eyes could stay fixed, so fixed that they were a tether from which I never wanted to be released. While I was still devoted to helping my neighbors if they were in need, I no longer had to work at the Aqua, and nothing made me happier now than walking around town with my husband: thrilled by how gracious, steady, and clever he was.

Just a few years later, after George was desolate and broken, it would be difficult for anyone who hadn't known him before to understand what had been so wonderful about him.

For now, there was the sorcery of his charm. While he never ceased to find new nicknames for me—Summer Squash, Wool Gatherer, Sadie ("Why Sadie?" "Why not?")—he called other women by their full names until they'd insisted at least twice that their first names alone would do. He always had a pouch of tobacco to offer the other pipe smokers, and like Mercy, he seemed to be very clear about how things ought to be done. He was tidy— maybe too tidy. By strange habit, he folded his undershirts before he put them into the laundry hamper. If I left even one fork or cup out in the kitchen, he would make sure to clean it, or eye it until I did. In the attic, where we would keep things for repairs and cleaning, he and a young clerk from the court had carried up several large old dressers for holding paintbrushes, nails, and tools. He believed in routine. Breakfast at seven. To the law office at eight. Lunch at noon. Supper at 6:30, unless he was running late. Reading before bed. Sometimes more. And then, leaning on our elbows with the moon lighting his face on clear nights, we would tell each other about our days.

The first winter of our marriage was the coldest in Dayton that anyone could recall, and on at least three Saturday mornings in December, we went back up to Oak Tree Pond. On borrowed ice skates, inside the woven embrace of bare trees, we glided in steel-chiseled circles, with George saying "I've got you" every time I started to fall.

5

George had gone to college in Nashville, studied law in Knoxville, and started on the bottom rung of a stodgy firm there. George was five years older than me and better educated than anyone I'd ever met. He wasn't the type to flaunt it, but he seemed to know a little bit about everything. He knew who was running for Congress and the pros and cons of the new Dodges and Fords. The right way to hold a fork and how much to tip a waiter. He knew about engineering, transportation, medicine, and all sorts of things that were happening in cities and countries far away. On religion, he had less to say. I knew he'd been raised a Methodist like me, but when Reverend Byrd asked us to pray aloud, George often fumbled the words.

I knew, though, that he liked Reverend Byrd, who made his sermons less about sin and more about salvation. Our new pastor had young children, a sense of humor, and a love of music. He tapped his thumb on the pulpit—I think without knowing it—whenever the choir or congregation sang. Reverend Byrd was thirty-one, a fledgling by comparison to Reverend Dowling, but it had taken no time at all for our congregation to embrace him.

Our church, built in 1887 from uneven red bricks, held at most a hundred people and was notoriously stuffy and hot. Despite our new pastor's cheeriness, the heat could make it hard to concentrate. One Sunday in the new year, right in the middle of the sermon, George started to nod off. When I nudged his knee to wake him, he took my hand, eyes still closed, and smiled as if we were just sitting back home in the parlor, listening to the radio.

I loved it when he held my hand, so I smiled too. But after church, walking home, I kept glancing at George sideways until he caught my expression.

"What?" he said then.

"You fell asleep."

"I did not."

"I thought you were going to start snoring."

"Well, maybe I did catch a wink or two."

"You're lucky Mr. Bailey didn't see you."

"From the boardinghouse?"

"Don't you know? He collects little pencil stubs," I told him. "Keeps them on his desk in a big glass jar, the type you'd use for penny candy."

"That's what today's sermon was about?"

"Oh, you do like to razz me, don't you?" I said. I bent to pick up a small twig, testing the sharpness of its point. "Walk on," I told him. "And don't look back."

"Oh," he said. "This is that old pillar-of-salt problem, is it?"

"Hush. Go on, now," I said.

George took three exaggerated steps forward, and I launched the twig at his neck, my aim every bit as true as it had been on the day of the Tomato War.

"Hey!" George said, slapping his neck as if he'd been stung.

"That's what Mr. Bailey does when he spots anyone who's falling asleep in church," I said. "Only he does it with his little pencil stubs. And he whittles the points till they're sharp as tacks."

George laughed and scooped me off the ground to kiss me, though anyone could have seen us. I felt a shudder of pleasure.

Back home, he took off his jacket and sat at the kitchen table, watching with contentment as I wrapped up the strawberry cookies I'd baked the evening before.

"Don't you usually make gingerbread for the major?" he asked.

"I do," I said.

I'd visited the old man often in the years since he'd first asked me to squeeze his hands and show him my strength. Gingerbread was his favorite, as he'd made sure to tell me every time I'd brought him something different.

Smiling, George took out his cherrywood pipe. "So, can we stipulate from the evidence of the empty cookie sheet on the counter and the package in your hand that you have hatched a different plan?"

He had taught me a lot of what we called *court jabber.*

"I object to the use of the word *hatched,*" I said.

"Objection overruled."

"Exception," I said.

"So noted. You may proceed."

I laughed. "Please the court, I am taking the cookies to Opal Murray. She has kin coming in this morning, and her foot's bad with gout, and she didn't have time to bake. I'll be back in two shakes."

"And how exactly would you define a shake?"

"You could come with me and find out," I said.

"You could give me a cookie."

"George," I said. "Why don't you come with me?"

"And why would I do that?"

"Because it's a kindness," I said.

He stood up. "Give me a kiss," he said and put his arms on my shoulders, pulling me in. "That is also a kindness."

As I left a few minutes later, I saw that, suspenders down and feet up on a stool, he had already settled into the parlor, happily opening the pages of the *Chicago Tribune.*

George was always scrambling for city newspapers from Chicago, New York, or Boston. Sometimes, that made me fret. What if he decided he wanted us to move to one of those newspaper cities? Of course, one of the reasons he'd come to Dayton in the first place was that he'd wanted to be a bigger fish in a smaller pond than he could be elsewhere, and no city was going to let him be that, at least not for a while. Still, walking toward Opal's house, I did worry. I tried to picture myself in a Yankee city. Despite the gumption of Helen, the Girl from Sunset Ranch, the only thing I could imagine was myself being trapped in F. Scott Fitzgerald's New York, as it glittered with promise and sin. Could I become a city girl if that was what George needed?

I knew that he liked modern things. When we moved into the Walnut Street house, he bought us a new-model telephone and replaced the house's old icebox with an electric refrigerator. He shaved with a double-edged razor and ordered a new kind of toothpaste he'd seen advertised in the newspaper.

One Saturday morning a few weeks after my visit to Opal, George disappeared with a wink and a smile and didn't come back for hours. I was hanging out laundry in the backyard, but neither I nor anyone on Walnut Street could have missed his return, heralded by the honking of a loud, *ah-oo-gah,* car horn. I ran around to the front of the house and found him standing before a shining new black Model T roadster, his smile nearly as sparkling as the brass hood ornament.

"Get your pa's camera, Flossie!" he called.

"I don't even know if it still works!" I said. "And anyway, I don't have film!"

"Well, then, that'll be our first errand. We can drive right over to Robinson's and buy you a whole heap of it."

Excited, I ran into the house and up the stairs, not bothering to tend to the laundry I'd left out back. I retrieved the camera from the nightstand on my side of the bed. It was called a Brownie and was about a foot long and six inches high and wide. It had a short leather handle, a key for winding film into position, and metal levers, the purposes of which were then a total mystery to me. My father had let me take a few pictures way back when, but I had no idea how the camera worked—not even how to load the film. I loved that George had said the film would be for me, though, suggesting a skill I didn't yet have but showing no doubt that I could acquire it. I ran back downstairs and brandished the Brownie.

George was standing at the front of the car, somehow looking even more dapper than usual.

"Shutterbug!" he declared, a nickname I would come to love.

I had ridden in cars before. There had been my parents' funerals, of course. And once, Reverend Dowling had driven a few of us over to Evansville to help out when a freak windstorm had destroyed a dozen houses in the same neighborhood. Another time, our math teacher, Mr. Dalton, had snuck three of us girls over to Harriman to root for the Rhea Central Yellow Jackets. But I had never been in a car's front seat, and the roadster didn't have a back seat. After George had cranked the engine, he slid in behind the big steering wheel and grinned like Christmas morning, motioning me to get in beside him.

"Do you really know how to drive this thing?" I asked.

"Would I be asking you to get in if I didn't know how to carry precious cargo?"

I may have blushed.

"Get in!"

Mercy had come out to see us, two of her boys jumping at her side.

"You going to get into that rig?" she called to me.

"Watch me!" I said, though I was a little bit nervous.

George waved at the boys. "You fellas can get a ride later if your mama says it's okay," he told them.

The top was down. The seat was warm in the afternoon sun. The short, thick windshield was clear as water. And at that moment, my whole life—my whole self—felt new and full of adventure.

"Ready?" George asked, and by way of an answer, I leaned over to kiss his cheek.

We started off down Walnut Street, and it took all of two minutes to get to Robinson's.

"You mind hopping out?" George asked. "I want to stay with the car in case someone asks me to move it."

Inside, Hank Dawson had his elbows on the glass counter, and he was just folding two gray sticks of chewing gum into his mouth.

"You know anything about cameras?" I asked him.

"Try me," he said, as his mouth worked to tame the two sticks of gum.

"What about this kind?" I asked, hefting the Brownie onto the counter.

"Easy as pie. Got any film in it?"

"No, that's what I need," I said. "And I don't know how to load it."

He grabbed a marigold-colored box from the shelf that said "Kodak" in red letters on the side.

"Come on. I'll show you how."

In the windowless back room, we stood between rows of canned goods and boxes of combs, toys, and perfume. Hank looked down at the camera, pulling the key from its side.

"There *is* film in here," he told me.

"Really?"

"Look. It's on number eight."

He pointed out the tiny round window that showed how much film had been used.

They'd be pictures my father had taken.

"How many years do you think film can last inside a camera?" I asked Hank.

He shrugged. "We'll send it to Kodak and find out."

Then he showed me how to wind the film gently with the key, making sure the protective paper was wrapped around it.

"Is that it?" I asked him.

"That's it. Now just pull it out."

I extracted the spool proudly, feeling almost as if I'd rescued something—which, indeed, I had.

With Hank as guide, I loaded my first roll of fresh film and returned triumphantly to the car.

George was still sitting where I'd left him.

"Come on, Shutterbug," he said. "Let's see what you can do with that thing."

For practice, I took one shot of George, his hands proudly on the steering wheel, but he moved at the last minute when a bee swooped down and startled him.

"Sorry," he said. "We'll try again after our ride."

Then we started covering ground. I knew I should have been looking at the roads—or at least at the scenery we were passing. But those things weren't new to me.

What was new—and so exciting—was the sight of George's hands on the wheel. These were the same hands that had held me up at Oak Tree Pond, had lifted my wedding veil, had combed back my hair that first night in bed. His fingers were always careful, and his nails were always clean, and there was something especially thrilling about how he was holding that wheel. He was so much in charge, so precise in his movements, coordinating the levers on the steering wheel with the pedals on the floor. I didn't ask him a thing. I didn't need to. I understood he knew exactly where we were going and exactly how to get there.

6

Even before the appearance of George's roadster, folks in town knew that he had what they liked to call *modern ways*. But that never seemed to make them wary. His manners and warmth were so genuine that an aura of trust quickly attached itself to him, like a pleasant scent. By the end of his first year in Dayton, he'd stood up in court for clients arrested for theft, vandalism, and Saturday-night joyrides. And he'd handled the office clients too: men who were seeking everyday services for wills, contracts, or deeds of sale.

George was so successful with the Baxters that in March of 1923—little more than a year after he'd joined the firm—they let him handle the defense in the biggest, most celebrated, most notorious case that Dayton, Tennessee, had ever seen. Not the Scopes Monkey Trial. That would come later. This was the Walton P. Allen murder trial, and it was what made George a star.

The defendant, one of the town's few doctors, came home late one night to find his wife, Mary Sue, canoodling in the kitchen with a man named Burch Gardenhire. Both men were blind drunk on corn liquor—and also on Mary Sue Allen's charms. Gardenhire, who had fought in the Spanish-American War, was a descendant of Dayton's founder, which was one of the reasons his murder got so much attention. The other was the way he was killed. There had been no guns or knives at this crime scene. No, as the headline in the next day's paper put it:

Former Army Officer Said to Have Been Battered with Household Utensils

Driven for self-protection into a corner of the Allens' house, Mary Sue had witnessed the whole thing. In his rage, her husband had used, among other objects, a cut-glass pitcher, a fireplace poker, a pot, an eggbeater, and the broken-off handle of a wooden spoon. Burch had gotten plenty of his own shots in too. But among the words the paper used to describe his dead body were *brained, crushed, mangled,* and *pulped.*

Anyone who'd met George by now had no doubt that his steadiness made him an ideal choice to defend the man responsible for the town's most scandalous crime. I was fluttery with pride, even though I knew it was wrong to feel so happy when George's success was fastened to other people's miseries. But didn't that come with being a lawyer? Trouble made for laws, and laws made for trouble.

Trouble also made for gossip, which by the morning after the murder was racing around Walnut Street like a frightened mare. This was the biggest thing that had happened in years; no one could even remember a murder, let alone a murder as shocking as this.

"What I heard," said Mercy over her peeling picket fence, her youngest boy straddling her left hip and sucking the thumb of a dirty hand, "was that Walton Allen walloped that cheating son of a gun on the head. From behind. From behind, mind you. With a glass pitcher, for the love of Mike." (*Son of a gun* and *for the love of Mike* were the closest to profanity I'd ever heard Mercy come.)

Kathy Gattis was a widow who lived across the road and usually kept to herself. Like Mercy, she was a Fundamentalist and a member of Dayton's First Baptist Church, South. So, to see her hustle over and speak with such bawdy interest was a first for me.

"Well, what I heard," she said, "was it was a bowl, not a pitcher. And it knocked him out cold on the first blow, so Walton didn't even have to use the fireplace poker, but he bashed in Burch's brains anyhow."

It was Tuesday, a baking day for all three of us, and all our loaves and muffins would be slightly singed that week.

George had been at the jail all morning, getting the lowdown from Doc Allen himself, and didn't come home until eight that night. I'd kept a ham steak and sliced potatoes warm in the oven for him, and now I bent to take them out.

"You should have seen him, Annie," he said, shaking his head and draping his seersucker jacket across his usual kitchen chair. "It was gruesome. Truly a gruesome sight. The doc's face was so banged up, one side was already purple, and the other was almost green. I swear his face looked like an eggplant."

I put the food in front of him and saw him inhale deeply: ham, cloves, brown sugar. He grabbed one of my hands and kissed it as I sat down across from him.

"Napkin?" he said, and it took me a moment to realize it wasn't another new nickname.

"Everyone was talking about it all day long," I told him as I handed him a fresh cloth.

The district attorney had set Allen's bail at ten thousand dollars, George told me, but men started jockeying to put up the bond. They all seemed to think they'd have done the same thing if they'd come home to find some man having his way with their wife.

"There was practically a riot," George said. "Twenty-nine men lined up. Twenty-nine men wanted to guarantee him personally. And the judge turned away another twenty. He said, 'Look here,

I've got no room for any more names on this paper, and if I add up all the money y'all have promised, it's already half a million dollars, and so thank y'all very much for your concern, but I think this'll do.' "

"So, he's out on bail?" I asked, and George nodded.

"But he's a murderer," I said.

"Allegedly, Counselor," George said in his court jabber voice. "Besides, he was stone drunk, and Burch had no business being there with Mary Sue."

"I object," I said.

"On what grounds?"

"On the grounds that aren't folks going to fret about a murderer just walking free?"

George laughed at me, which stung a little. I didn't like it when he made me feel dim.

"*Alleged* murderer, Counselor," he said. "And they'd fret a lot more if they thought any one of them could get locked up just for defending the sanctity of his home."

Major McClure was less interested in the outcome of the hearing than he was in what had led to the crime, which he saw as just one more example of civilization's decline.

His house, way up on Ninth Avenue, was about half a mile from ours. And while the center of Dayton wasn't exactly manicured, the major's street was almost its own neighborhood, where the vines and birds' nests seemed to be taking over, along with a marshy smell that no one liked to mention. The major's front door was green with moss and white with lichen. I'd learned I had to kick it in just the right spot in order to get it open.

The Sunday after the murder, the ache of the major's many old war wounds had kept him from church, and I brought him his favorite gingerbread. No matter how well or poorly he felt, he always greeted me the same way, making me squeeze his hands to show my strength, as he had after my parents died. Today, though I could tell he was in pain, he couldn't seem to sit still. Railing about the wages of liquor and licentiousness, he paced the length of his kitchen, trailing gingerbread crumbs and outrage. His denim shirt, though tidily tucked into his old dungarees, covered a chest that looked nearly concave.

"I never touched a drop of liquor in my life, even the times I got shot and the field docs stitched me up and said the whiskey would dull the pain."

"Well, you're a tough bird," I said. "We all know that. Why don't you sit down, Major?"

He ignored me.

"When I was a tad," he said, "there was this miserable wretch, he was Dayton's worst drunkard. He was only thirty years old when he lay down to meet his Maker, but our Sunday School teacher, he thought it was a good idea for us to see this man before he departed earth. So, Mr. Powers, he lines us up to walk right past the straw pallet where this devil was lying in the basement of the church. Just as I reach to where he's lying, he starts in to thrashing and moaning, and then he screams, 'I'm dying! I'm in hell! Can't you see the blue blazes of smoke and brimstone coming out of my mouth and nose?'"

The major stopped, finally fumbling for his kitchen chair, exhausted by telling the story—and perhaps also by reliving the memory.

"I'd never make a child see that," I said.

"Think again," the major said. "You reckon Burch Gardenhire would be dead today if Walton Allen had ever seen what liquor did to Blue Blazes?"

He took a belligerent bite of his gingerbread. "People today," he added vaguely.

I knew I could have argued with him. I didn't believe the time we were living in had much to do with the drinking habits of Dr. Walton Allen. And for that moment, frankly, I didn't much care.

The trial wasn't scheduled to start until autumn, and for that whole spring and summer leading up to it, George and I were celebrities.

I think there's a certain kind of attention—a mix of pride and curiosity—that goes along with small-town success, especially if the small town, like Dayton, has seen better days. George immediately became as well known as the victim or the killer, but he handled all the fuss as if he'd defended a dozen murderers, though of course Allen was his first.

Neighbors and friends began dropping by on Saturday mornings. Naturally I knew they were coming to dig up all the dirt they could about Mary Sue and Doc Allen. But our Westinghouse was another draw. Radios back then were a lot like cars had been a couple decades before. Both gave us proof that the world was wide but within our reach. Listening to the radio while drinking lemonade or cider, nibbling on cookies, apple cake, or whatever Mercy and I had baked or others had brought, we all stepped out of Dayton for a while. The world opened beyond the two paved streets and dusty roads of a town where there was only one drugstore, one bakery, one movie house—in fact, only one of just about everything except churches.

On the radio, we heard the twisty, bouncing sounds of the Paul Whiteman orchestra; the quivering, quavering voices of Marion Harris and Nora Bayes; and any number of singers taking on the ridiculous but catchy "Yes, We Have No Bananas." (George frequently rewrote the lyrics for my benefit: Yes, We Have No Bandannas; Potatoes; Galoshes; Excuses . . .) We heard news, too, and it came from all over the country. Blizzards in Minnesota. Machine guns in Georgia. Women meeting in upstate New York to write an amendment for equal rights.

On some Saturday afternoons, George and I would get in the car, and he'd drive us into the hills. He always asked me to bring my camera. I'm still not really sure why. Maybe that modern streak in him made him like the idea of me being good at something other than housework; maybe he wanted me to share his love of gadgets; maybe he thought it would distract me from the fact that I hadn't yet gotten pregnant. Whatever the reason, he encouraged me to try to capture the landscape around us.

Having never lived anywhere but Dayton, I didn't think it was all that special; things I'd read about—snow and skyscrapers and oceans—seemed infinitely more magical than East Tennessee. But, spurred on by George, I kept taking pictures, and even those early photographs showed me that there were some things even close to home that were extraordinary. The cloud formations, for example. In no other place I've lived or traveled since have I seen a sky criss-crossed by straight lines of clouds—as if God had thrown down a net; or stacked in rows, like the steps in a staircase; or side by side, like piano keys.

People saw me at Robinson's buying film or picking up envelopes of prints from Kodak, and some asked me to take pictures for them. I photographed three different brides, as well as the Frazier family, recently arrived from North Carolina and wanting to assure their kin that they were still thriving. I took a photograph of the Sunday School class. Even the major asked me to take his picture ("for your practice and my posterity"), and when I showed up with my camera, I was touched and surprised to find him waiting for me on his front porch, not only shaved, but dressed in his Easter jacket and a thin black tie, what was left of his hair neatly combed and pomaded. Most ambitiously, I photographed the entire strawberry picking crew at the Broyles Farm: fifteen adults, a dozen children, and the owner of the farm with his foot up on top of one crate turned on its end.

I began to love the way the camera could absorb a tiny moment and later allow it to expand. Each envelope of photographs seemed to hold a set of clues. I would sit at Robinson's in one of the chairs with the wrought-iron feet. I would drink a cherry Coke slowly and study each picture in turn, discovering all the details I'd missed when I pushed the lever on the shutter—how the tall pines across the pond had grown so close together that not one of them seemed to bend in any direction; how Mrs. Kincannon's eyelids fell like drapes over her rheumy eyes; and how one of the small children in the Broyles Farm photograph turned out not to be a child at all but rather a tall basset hound. Peering at the photographs, discovering the minutiae and the grandness of a moment, I allowed myself to wonder if this was how God got to see all the world all the time.

7

Easter Sunday that year was overcast and humid. In church,
Reverend Byrd read from Peter about the glory of new
birth. He had us sing "Crown Him with Many Crowns"
and "Christ the Lord Is Risen Today." Then, while he started the
congregation on a third hymn, Caroline Quinn and I snuck outside
to hide the eggs that, as in many years past, the Women's Easter
Committee had dyed and left for us the night before. Caroline was
probably my best friend from high school, and we had been hiding
Easter eggs at church at least since then. But this Easter was different. For years she and I had watched longingly as the church
mothers coaxed smiles from their infants or held their toddlers'
fingertips, letting them lurch one chubby leg forward at a time. But
now Caroline had become one of those mothers, and today, she
and her husband, Willie, had brought Charlie, their three-month-
old, to church for the first time. Nestled in the crook of her arm, he
had a pink triangle nose and blue eyes that seemed sublimely wise.

George and I had been married for half a year now, and I hadn't
yet conceived the first of what I hoped would one day be a houseful

of children. Caroline, by contrast, had gotten pregnant on her honeymoon. I ached with envy and, subsequently, with shame.

"Are you sure you can handle the eggs *and* the baby?" I asked her.

"I'll manage," she said. "You'll see when it's your turn. You can do almost anything with just one hand."

I had no idea why I wasn't pregnant yet, but I told myself that God did, and that until He changed His plan for me, all I could do was pray—and try. Trying turned out to be a lot more fun than praying. (George sang, "Yes, we have no pajamas . . .") Still, once a week for the last few months, Mercy had placed a stubby hand on my stomach and said, "You're flat as a washboard. Anyone in there yet?" Just last week, she had asked, "You sure you're doing it right?"

It started to rain just as Caroline and I hid the last eggs in the corner between the church's stone steps and its wall of rough red brick. Then we waited inside the open vestibule for the children to come out. Little Charlie freed one tiny hand from his wraps to yank on Caroline's stringy hair, an act that of course seemed to charm more than bother her. Together we watched as the rain kept on, and the eggs began to bleed their rich, bright colors into the indifferent earth.

It was only a month later—on another rainy Sunday—that I had to bring Epsom salts to Caroline's house because I'd heard that Charlie was suffering from grippe. This was Willie Quinn's childhood home, and I'd been here plenty of times in high school. Stepping in now, though, I felt I'd entered an entirely different place. The shades were drawn in the parlor, where the baby's wood cradle was standing. Caroline's mother, Ellen, moved to greet me but didn't say hello.

"Fever" was all she said.

The room was so ripe with fear that she didn't need to say more.

I put my arms around Caroline, who seemed about to tip over. Hugging her felt like hugging a piece of cloth.

"When did the doctor come last?" I asked her.

"Just this morning," she said.

I followed her to the cradle, where Charlie was lying still. His eyes were closed, his face almost entirely white except for one swath across his forehead that was slightly purple. His tiny chest and thin arms were covered with bruises where the doctor had used hot glass cups to suck out his infection. Charlie no longer had just grippe, Caroline told me. Charlie had pneumonia.

For a long time, the three of us stood by the boy's cradle, Ellen rocking it needlessly. We bowed our heads while she said a prayer.

Willie Quinn came heavily down the stairs and wordlessly took Caroline's place by the cradle. He looked as exhausted as she did.

I asked if there was anything I could do for them.

Willie shook his head no, but Caroline took me aside. "I want you to take Charlie's portrait," she whispered.

Our eyes filled with tears. Even in the 1920s, a family portrait was still usually a formal thing, and sometimes still, as in the past, a dead child would be propped up, creepily, on someone's lap. With Papa's Brownie, I had the chance to capture Charlie while he was alive.

Outside, Caroline's porch was dotted with rain puddles where the wood had warped. A leaf, folded over on itself, looked like a pair of praying hands, Today, there was nothing special in the clouds, which were low, gray, and opaque. A few yards away, I stopped at a white fence and wrapped my hands over the post ball, then rested my cheek against my hands. The rain was a drizzle now, and I could feel it on the back of my neck.

What had Caroline done to deserve this? She had done nothing wrong, as far as I knew. If anyone deserved punishment, I thought, it would be me, as if the sin of my own envy was proving literally deadly.

A flock of chimney swifts flew by. I watched as they swooped and swirled into the distance. The clouds were still dark, and the telephone poles along the road were a line of crosses. I hurried back home.

The next morning, as soon as there was enough light, I ran to Caroline's to take Charlie's photograph. I made it with just a day to spare.

I knew there were some old folks who believed it was sinful to take photographs—folks who gloried in the past as a pure, uncomplicated, better time, a time when we'd all been more favorable in God's sight. But I felt sure the Lord wouldn't mind if I could use my father's camera to leave Caroline with more than a memory of her son.

It usually took about ten days for prints to come back from the Kodak company. During those ten days, I spent as much time as I could helping at Caroline's house of mourning. I cooked for them, prayed with them, tidied and scrubbed. I used Mercy's special cleaning solution of lemon, water, and soap shavings; I opened all the windows and boiled all the bedding. But the place still seemed suffused with liniment, witch hazel, and grief.

It was only May, but the heat pressed down like a physical weight. Walking home each day, I saw full wheelbarrows in backyards, presumably abandoned midtask. Daisies and fleabane drooped so heavily that their faces were obscured. Men mopped their necks with handkerchiefs and squinted against the sun.

"Are you her only friend?" George asked me one evening as I came through the door.

He had just gotten home from the office and was looking around the untouched kitchen. It wasn't the first time he'd sounded peevish, but I was surprised, given that he knew where I'd been and why I'd been there.

"'Do all the good you can by all the means you can in all the places you can,'" I said. It was part of a Methodist creed. I thought it was all the explanation he'd need.

He sighed. "Little Fish," he said. "I just think you're wearing yourself out."

"George, she needs me," I said.

"She does have a husband and a mother."

"They need me too," I said.

While he went upstairs to change, I hustled to put up a pot of coffee and make sandwiches from a leftover roast. I was tired, and he'd criticized me, and it was the very first time I cried because George had made me sad, not happy.

I saw my mother cry only twice. The second time was when I was sixteen and we were at my father's bedside and it was clear that he was going to die.

The first time was four years earlier than that. On a beautiful morning at the end of April, I'd gotten dressed for school but found neither parent in the kitchen; no food on the table; no coffee in the pot. By now, at this time of morning, at least one of them would usually be out in the fields; April was the month when strawberries started to ripen, and extra men and women would be on hand to pick them. But I heard both my parents' voices from their bedroom.

Alarmed, I knocked on their door. There was silence, then whispering that was too soft to understand. Some sharp words from my father followed, and I couldn't make those out either. But then my mother said: "Come in, Annie."

She was propped up in bed on both their pillows, the patchwork quilt that I think had been her own mother's pulled up above her waist. Her hands were on her stomach. Her face was red.

"What's wrong, Mama?"

"I'm all right, Sweetheart."

"Your mother just needs some rest."

"Why?"

"She had a little accident," my father said.

I followed the stare my mother gave him as if it were hanging, visible, in the air.

"Come here, Sweetheart," she said to me.

I walked over to her bedside, and she took one of my hands.

"I'll explain it all to you later," she said. "Grab yourself a hunk of bread and run off to school now."

She wasn't crying then. She was crying later, after school, when I came back home and found both parents in the kitchen. They each said hello but otherwise didn't acknowledge me. My mother was standing across from my father, her back to the stove, her arms crossed tight over her chest. She looked beautiful even with tears on her cheeks.

"I won't go through this again, Bertram," she was saying.

"You'll feel different with time, Bethany."

"That's what you've said every time."

"And it turned out to be true," he said.

My mother's eyes were swimming, her grip around her own arms tighter. I saw a tear fall straight from her eye to darken the wood on the kitchen floor.

I went to my bedroom but left the door open enough so that I could overhear them.

"It won't be true this time," she said. "I can't. I won't go through it again."

"Be fruitful and multiply," my father said.

"Oh, Bertram."

"No one to carry my name?" he asked.

She kept crying, but softly.

I heard his footsteps as he walked briskly into their bedroom, paced it needlessly, and came back.

"Bertram," my mother said. "We don't have to be like everyone else."

Now I wondered, if she'd had more children, whether she still would have managed the canning clubs, still would have had the time and desire to travel around the countryside, giving girls a way to see themselves apart from their homes, schools, and churches. I wondered, too, if she had honored my father's wishes and ever tried to have another child. And I wondered—I couldn't help it—if the reason I wasn't yet pregnant myself had something to do with the reason I'd been their only child.

The photos of Charlie came out fine. Some were a bit blurry, looking as if they'd been dipped in gray water, but Caroline put the best one into an old carved frame and showed it to everyone who paid a condolence call. It seemed to help her, having tangible proof that she had, indeed, been a mother.

The envelope that held the pictures my father had taken years before would be tangible proof that I had, indeed, been a daughter. But since the day Hank had handed it to me along with the batch of the roadster photographs, I had resisted the urge to open it. As long as I didn't, it was soothing to think that at some point, if I needed to, I might see my parents again.

George had quickly gotten over his peevishness about the time I'd spent with Caroline, but with the trial of Doc Allen now just months away, he seemed somewhat more solemn than usual. One evening, he asked me if I wouldn't mind listening to him practice his opening statement. Would I mind? I'd never forgotten how my father used to talk to my mother about the work of the farm: the pricing, the output, the field hands, the pros and cons of buying a new plow or repairing the old one.

George and I settled in the parlor, with me on the wood-framed sofa and him pacing the wide squeaking floorboards, his body blocking out the setting sun and becoming a silhouette each time he passed in front of the window.

"Gentlemen of the jury," he began. "We have a law in this state, in this country, against murder. From the time we're old enough to reason, we're taught that no man has the right to take the law into his own hands and kill another man. And we know that Dr. Allen here—"

George stopped pacing. The sunlight washed in, deepening the color of his hair and darkening the shadows on his face. "Do you think 'Doctor' sounds too formal?" he asked.

"Well, people do call him Doc."

"Right then," George said. "Continuing." He waved his hands as if he needed to erase the air before going on. I smiled. "And we know that Doc Allen here did take the law into his own hands. He did kill Burch Gardenhire. That is not in dispute. But that is not the whole story. Because Doc Allen had just discovered that his wife, and therefore the sanctity of his home, had been violated. When that happened, his rational mind shut off, and his instinct took over. His instinct was to defend his home. And the unwritten law, which we all understand, gave him the right to do that."

"The right to kill someone?" I asked, an interruption that startled us both.

George said, "Yes."

"But he killed him."

"We know that, Annie, of course. That's a fact. But it's not murder, not legally. See, I can argue that he was so delirious with rage that he had no intention of killing anyone."

"How can you be so sure of that?" I asked.

"Because you think if Walton Allen was planning to kill Burch Gardenhire, his weapon of choice would have been an eggbeater?"

"Objection," I said in my best court jabber voice.

"Yes, Counselor? State your objection."

"The Bible says, 'Thou shalt not kill.' It does not say, 'Thou shalt not kill unless thou art in a rage and thou art using an eggbeater.'"

"Overruled," George said, but then he smiled.

"I'm so glad," he said, softening his lawyerly posture.

"Glad of what?"

"That only men are allowed on a jury. Doc Allen wouldn't stand a chance against you."

Women had won the vote in 1920 three years before, but we wouldn't be allowed on juries till decades later. We were considered so sensitive that we'd be either too traumatized or too sympathetic to be fair about what we heard. Maybe it's just hindsight, but I think that if I'd been on the jury that heard Doc Allen's case, I would have been neither traumatized nor sympathetic. I would have locked him away.

But as it turned out, the "unwritten law" defense didn't seem to bother a soul, including the presiding judge and even Mary Sue Allen, who had returned from a long stay with her sister to sit behind the defense table, her face showing neither blame nor remorse. As far as I knew, no one had suggested that she had been in any way responsible for what had happened.

Just as he'd rehearsed it in our parlor, George argued that, given the circumstances, the doctor could not be blamed for his actions. The prosecution argued, maybe a bit halfheartedly, that Allen's level of venom revealed the dark nature of a man who posed a lethal threat to the town. But the jury unanimously acquitted him the same day. On the sunny green lawn outside the courthouse, Mary Sue looked on as men gathered around her husband and slapped him on the back.

George's triumph was unquestioned. He had ensured the continued freedom of a man who had merely defended what was rightfully his, just as any husband was expected to do.

Mercy never ceased to remind me—unnecessarily—that any husband was also expected to become a father. She promised deep-held knowledge about how to make this happen.

She said she'd always heard that if a woman didn't want to get pregnant, she should slap her own backside three times if she was in the company of two or more pregnant women.

"So it follows," Mercy said, "all you need do is find two pregnant women and not slap anything."

I laughed. It was an early October day, and I'd gone next door for some mint tea to ease my monthly pains and my monthly disappointment. The "Puppies" were playing in the front yard while Mercy was readying a bucket of her special cleaning solution—not to wash down the kitchen counters or floor, but to wash down the children before she'd let them back in the house.

Friends from church, friends from the Aqua, friends from the neighborhood, all offered suggestions, whether I asked for them or not. I was told to put stones in my shoes. Throw pebbles over my roof. Wear a pregnant woman's coat. Sit in a pregnant woman's seat. Now that the trial was over, even George weighed in with a suggestion, but it had nothing to do with superstition. On a trip to Chattanooga for someone's estate business, he had stopped to visit the library and read some medical journals.

"They have treatments," he told me one afternoon as I was in the kitchen folding the laundry, which happened to include the rags I used each month.

"Who does? What kind of treatments?"

"There's a doctor up in New York City. He uses oxygen to test out whether there's anything blocking the way."

To be clear, I knew how babies were conceived. Even if Caroline and I and the other girls hadn't whispered about it in high school, I'd grown up on a farm, after all. I understood that there was a seed and an egg, and that they were supposed to meet and plant themselves to grow inside my womb.

I put the stack of clean linens in the carry basket at the foot of the stairs. George followed me back to the kitchen as I took a second batch of linens from the sink, wrung them out, and loaded them into a bigger basket. In the backyard, I grabbed a fistful of clothespins from my apron pocket, and I said, "Isaac prayed to the Lord for Rebekah because she was barren, and then she conceived."

"Yes. What's your point?"

"That maybe you should be praying for me in church instead of looking things up in libraries."

"Medicine's answered a lot of people's prayers," George said.

I hid behind the sheets I was clipping to the line. There was no

way I was going to let some strange city doctor work against whatever the Lord had planned for me.

Looking back, I don't know if things might have turned out better if I had stopped George right then and asked him whether, deep
down, he trusted what science could do for me more than he trusted
what the Lord could do. Did he pray only in church? Did he grasp
the wonders that God had made? Had he ever watched a morning
glory closing up at dusk? Did he understand that the church was our
home, our family, our refuge? I should have asked him all that. But
this is what I know now: If you are in love—whether with a person
or an idea or the Heavenly Father—you will usually see what you
want to see; you will hear what you want to hear. And, really
whether you want to or not, you'll feel what you can't help but feel.

"Smile at me with those eyes, Annie," George said to me, grin-
ning, late that night. "Why are you so wonderful?" he said. "Explain yourself!"

And that was all I wanted to see in the shadows or hear in the
stillness.

One morning the following month, I woke up later than usual with
a light head and a queasy stomach. George was already dressed and
just about to leave for work.

"Rip van Winkle!" he said.

"Why didn't you roust me? What'll you do for breakfast?"

"Cheese and bread," he said. "I'm fixed."

He put his large, warm hand against my forehead.

"Do you feel all right?"

I nodded, distracted, as he kissed me lightly on the lips and
grabbed his hat.

After he left, I lay in bed for a long while, still not fully awake,
lazily reaching under my nightgown to let my hand move across my
flat, smooth stomach. I could hear, through the slightly open window, the sound of a tree being chopped down, and the laughs and
taunts of Mercy's children. I was dreamy and still, equally wanting

and not wanting the queasy sensation to go away. It was unpleasant, but in a way that was completely unfamiliar, which made the feeling more mysterious than upsetting.

"Did not!" one of Mercy's children shouted in the yard.

"Did too!"

I sat up, noticing a strange taste in my mouth. In the bathroom, I brushed my teeth, rinsed with water, and then, finding that insufficient, reached for the heavy glass bottle of Listerine.

Even after that, the taste remained: odd and something like metal, just as unfamiliar as the feeling in my stomach.

Looking at myself in the bathroom mirror, I saw my image blur as my eyes filled with tears. Grabbing hold of the sink, I lowered myself to the wood floor and sat, hugging my knees, crying. It had taken more than a year, but it had happened. I knew it had. I knew that I was pregnant.

"Thank you, thank you," I whispered. "Thank you."

There were superstitions that went with *being* pregnant too. Now that I was expecting, I was supposed to worry about the moon, which could take a bite out of my baby's lip if I didn't wear a key around my neck. I wasn't supposed to rub my belly, or my baby would be spoiled. I wasn't supposed to get a haircut, or my baby could be blind. And though there was no chance of this in the state of Tennessee, at least three women told me I wasn't supposed to go near an ocean, or the evil spirits that lurked underwater could reach up and steal my baby's soul.

I tried to adopt George's rejection of all such superstitions, but one day I came home from the market to find a tiny dead field mouse curled up on its side, just at the foot of the kitchen table. It was so small that at first I thought it was a dried leaf that had blown in from the backyard. But it was not a leaf, and though I had never been at all squeamish about anything on dry land, I recoiled in dread.

I was also told frequently not to buy anything for the baby or even for the baby's room. George insisted we ignore this advice. The only things in the room now were an unused, unmade guest bed, a small three-legged stool between the low windows, and two pine crates filled with coils of wire, tubes, dials, and all sorts of spare parts for George's amateur radio hobby. *Pretend radio* was what I called it, because he'd not yet gotten around to unpacking those boxes. But since college he'd belonged to one of the clubs for amateur radio "hams"—men who used their spare time and money to rig up their own radios and make contact with people they'd never meet. Once a month, George received his copy of *QST,* a magazine filled with cryptic lists, tables, and diagrams.

It was intriguing, but not so intriguing that I didn't tease him. From time to time, I'd read out some random passage from a randomly chosen article: " '9EK used a 50-watt tube which drew 100 milliamperes from a 500-volt battery of Burgess B dry cells.' "

"What a great story!" I'd say. "What happens next?"

Now, as he passed me on his way to the attic, one of the crates of spare parts in his arms, I asked, "Are you sure all that's for a radio? You're sure you're not planning to build a thresher up there? Or an airplane?"

George laughed.

"You'll see," he said. "Someday, when I put this rig together, we'll be able to talk to people all over the state. Maybe across the country if I can get a strong enough signal."

I smiled, but I couldn't imagine what would be so exciting about getting in touch with some stranger across the country, or even ten miles away. In the early winter of 1924, I was sure that George, our baby-to-be, and however many other children we might someday have would make the world the perfect size for me.

After George had brought the crates up to the attic, he went to Main Street and returned with a can of white paint, several brushes, a few old sheets, and the insistence that I leave the house so the paint fumes wouldn't harm the baby.

"Never heard that one," Mercy said as we sat on her porch, drinking lemonade.

"It's not a superstition, Mercy," I said. "I'm pretty sure it's a medical fact."

The next Saturday, George took me to John Morgan's store on Market Street, and I felt a genuine thrill when we picked out a rocking chair, a standing lamp, and a small pine dresser.

At home, I asked him to try the chair in a bunch of different spots until finally he sat in it and pulled me onto his lap.

"You've got to be really careful now," he said.

"I will, George."

"And Doc Marsden?"

"He's the best in town."

"You know, my mother died when I was born, and—" he began.

"I know, George," I said. "That was nearly thirty years ago. I'm sure it's safer now."

He shook off his serious expression.

"What is your plea?" he asked. "Boy or girl?"

"You know I don't know."

"Boy or girl?" he asked again. "Deviled Egg or Sugar Plum?"

It was almost Christmas, and in Mercy's kitchen I helped her knead dough for the cookies her children would be making later that day.

"Why in heaven's name would you want to risk buying anything for the baby yet?" she asked.

"It was George," I said.

"What does George know about being with child?"

"George doesn't go in for superstitions. You know that."

In Mercy's dining room, a Christmas tree was skirted by presents wrapped and labeled with each of her children's names. Three boys and a girl. I wanted at least one of each. If the doctor's calculations were right, my baby would be born in August. The heat would be unbearable, and I wouldn't mind it a bit.

"You listening?" Mercy asked.

"Sorry."

"I heard one more," Mercy said. She swept her arms out to the sides, as if she were at a pulpit. "Avoid seeing bears, camels, and monkeys."

I laughed.

"Where am I going to see a bear, a camel, or a monkey in Dayton, Tennessee?"

This of course was a question that God would answer in the fullness of time.

8

Walton Allen hadn't been around much in the half a year since George had gotten him off the hook for Burch Gardenhire's murder. The doctor's practice had been dwindling even before the night of the crime, and afterwards—however much everyone seemed to forgive his manly frenzy—no one was exactly lining up to sit in his exam room. That didn't seem to bother him. Nothing seemed to bother him. He drank constantly. Corn liquor, which had helped fuel the killing in the first place, now kept him in a state of constant stupefaction.

The gossip was that there were two weeks straight when Doc Allen drank no water, no lemonade, no coffee, no tea. He got so boozed up that one afternoon, right on Market Street, he walked directly into the side of a horse, fell, and was promptly sprayed with pee. This trio of actions, followed by his sputtering confusion and rage, seemed so hilarious that the few people who'd seen it, and many who hadn't, tried to outdo each other in reenacting the great slapstick sequence.

Everybody stopped laughing on a Sunday in early April when,

loaded as usual, Walton was at the wheel of his beat-up Ford, on the way home from a family drive. His son, W.P. Jr., was nine years old then, a remarkably sunny boy despite the whispers that always trailed his parents. A few miles out of town, near the Broyles Farm, Walton abruptly pulled the car over to the side of the road, yanked up the brake, drew a pistol from his pocket, turned toward the back seat, and blew his son's brains out.

Mary Sue leapt over the car's door and started to run.

Walton scrambled out after her. He fired two shots at his wife. Both missed. Then he put the gun against his own temple and blasted off the top of his head.

Sunday was the Lord's day, but George had stopped by his office after church to pick up some papers. He was just on his way back out when he heard shouting from the street and saw people rushing toward him, each more eager than the next to tell him what the man he'd kept out of jail had just done to himself and to his son. Later, Willie Quinn, who'd been in that crowd, would tell me that George merely asked where it had happened, said nothing else, and slipped away through the hubbub. I had gone to visit Loula Hodge, whose rheumatism was acting up, so I wasn't even home when George got into the roadster and drove away.

All day, the gossip hoofed its usual course around Dayton, stopping, inevitably, at our front door. But there was no word from George, so I knew nothing more than the neighbors did.

I made his favorite supper that evening: a chicken pot pie with a crust I rolled so thin you could almost read a newspaper through it. At seven o'clock, I set it on the table as if it were bait. Hours passed. At around nine, seeing that George's car was still not back, Mercy came over to sit with me.

"I'm sure he's just found some whiskey somewhere, Lamb," she said.

"You know George doesn't drink."

"Well, there are other ways to blow off steam," Mercy said, and then, eyeing the pot pie, she asked, "You didn't eat? You've got to eat for that baby, remember."

I shook my head. "I can't," I said.

"Mind if I tuck in?"

"Help yourself."

Mercy picked up a fork and dug into the pot pie with gusto.

"Delicious," she said, and then, after her next bite, "Did I teach you to make this?"

That made me laugh.

"No," I said. "Eva Jenkins did, at the Aqua."

"Best pot pie I ever had. What's the secret?"

"I don't know," I said. "I guess I make it a lot. It's George's favorite."

I could feel my nose turning red. If I'd been alone, I would have been crying.

"Men," Mercy said between bites. "You've got to understand, Lamb. Men don't like their wives to see them when they're feeling those weary dismals."

I watched as Mercy left through the kitchen door, tugging and straightening her skirt around her ample backside. In the night windows of the kitchen door, I saw my own image broken up in the panes.

Dear Lord, I prayed, *bring him back to me.*

I fell asleep on the parlor sofa and woke with an ache in my left shoulder that seemed to travel up that side of my neck to beat inside my left temple. I couldn't fathom why George hadn't called. He had to know I'd be waiting by the phone: that fancy new telephone that he'd insisted we have.

I tried a warm compress and then a teaspoon of sal volatile in water, but my headache was stubborn. Despite it, I set about cleaning. On my knees, following instructions I'd read in *Housewifery,* and ignoring any of George's previous warnings about paint fumes and pregnancy, I used turpentine to strip the kitchen floor of its grease and dirt, then wax and old rags to polish it. In the parlor, with love and faith, I dusted every book, then mixed George's volumes, by author, in with my own, something I'd been meaning to do since he'd first put his on the shelves. When my worry turned to anger, I used sandpaper to scrub even the bottoms of the pots and pans, trying to make them look as shiny as they had when the folks at the Aqua Hotel had given us new cookware as a wedding present.

Using a sea sponge to clean the grout between the bathroom tiles, I stopped to stare at that one tile whose cracks seemed to form the letter *G*. I thought of all those years when I'd been alone, marooned between the safety of my parents' farm and the safety of George's embrace. I thought of those years with a shudder. From the first time George had said "I've got you," I had felt protected, and now my whole being seemed clad again in paper-thin skin. I traced my finger along the initial as though inscribing it anew. *G. George.*

By evening, my headache had eased, but now my chest felt tight. I knew I should make myself eat something, but I simply didn't feel capable of movement. The phone didn't ring. I was running out of things to clean.

I lost the baby the next day. I would never know if the turpentine had anything to do with it. I decided I didn't want to know. I was only four months pregnant, but I was in labor for nearly three hours. I had grown up hearing that all pain had a purpose, though it was often known only to God. Standing beside the table where I lay in Dr. Marsden's office, Mercy reminded me that the pain of childbirth was one pain without mystery—Eve's punishment for eating from Eden's forbidden tree. Squirming from side to side, I did not want to think about Eve or about Eden. I thought about the baby and the family I'd believed I was meant to have, and I wept in pain and despair.

When it was over, Mercy and Caroline brought me home, tucked me into bed, gave me soup and cornbread, and insisted I have at least one sip of a very dark red wine that Mercy had brought in a small medicine bottle. When I hesitated, Mercy took a swig to show me there would be no harm. But Caroline was pregnant again—just a month behind me, in fact, so she declined.

Head swimming, I instinctively moved my hand to my stomach, where I was used to seeking the reassurance of a hard, smooth bump. My stomach was the same size it had been that morning, but there was no tautness to it. I was emptied out.

"Poor Lamb," Mercy said. "You're worn slap out. Close your eyes now."

I must have slept for a while. I was still groggy when she came back.

She handed me a card that her children had made. There were colorful smudges all over it.

"Those Puppies, they got into a huge ruckus about who was going to draw the biggest flower," Mercy said. "Two of them ended up walloping the other two."

Good, I thought, and only later would I feel ashamed of my bitterness.

"You'll see," Mercy said. "You'll be pregnant again in no time."

I nodded, but I wondered how many times my mother had heard the same words.

George called the next morning. I wanted to tell him right away about the baby, but I made myself ask first where he was.

"I'm all right, Flossie," he said sadly.

"But *where* are you?"

He didn't answer.

"George?" I said. "Where are you?"

"Kentucky," he finally said.

"Why?"

"I don't know."

"When are you coming home?"

"I don't know," he said again.

"George—" I began, intending my next words to be about the baby, but I started to cry before I could say anything.

"Don't cry, Little Fish," he said.

"But, George—"

"I'll be all right," he said and hung up.

I held the phone, pointlessly, to my ear. The absence of sound, like the absence of the baby, deepened.

Two days later, he had still not come home, and while I blamed myself for not having told him right away what had happened, I blamed him too—for not sensing it somehow.

On the third day, longing for solace, I sat at the kitchen table and finally opened the envelope that held the pictures my father had taken, the ones that had been in his Brownie when I'd first used it to photograph George and the Ford.

The first picture was obviously a mistake, because my father had taken two exposures over a single frame, and neither image was clear. Next, there were three photographs of our farm. A horse named Bob that I'd ridden when he was a colt. Some strawberry bushes, not yet in fruit. The Tennessee mountains, looking no different from blankets of burly fabric. The fifth photograph was of my mother and me standing on the porch, her arm around me. I had no memory of posing for this picture, but as I looked at the image now, I could almost feel the softness of her arm, and I remembered how, at every age, at every size, I had felt sheltered by that arm in exactly the same way. In the picture, my mother was wearing a kerchief around her head. I still had my braids. Her eyes were open. Mine were closed.

The last two images were of my parents, each standing in the same spot in the front yard, clearly having just traded places. I had forgotten the way my father's eyes grew larger when he smiled; the smile said, "All right, Bethany, have it your way"—as if he was merely humoring her. The very last shot was of my mother. She was looking directly into the camera, directly through time. At that moment, it seemed completely unjust that I was no longer either a daughter or a mother.

In the parlor, I turned on the radio, listening to news from Nashville, then Chattanooga, then jazz from who knew where. I kept the music on all that day. Eddie Cantor singing "No, No, Nora." Some choir-like group singing "Sleep." A band playing the Charleston. At least twice "Yes, We Have No Bananas." And then, as if that song was not enough to tweak my heart, I heard Irving Kaufman warble:

> *I wish there was a wireless to heaven*
> *And I could speak to Mama ev'ry day*
> *I would let her know,*
> *By the radio,*
> *I'm so lonesome since she went away.*

Reverend Byrd had become well known around Rhea County as a soft-spoken but strong pastor, someone who seemed to occupy a perfect place between the earth- and glory-bound. On the earthbound side of things, he had marshaled the boys from Sunday School to fix up our church, restoring the floors, the walls, the tall, narrow church doors, and even the thin arched windows that had been dusty and dark but sparkled anew with their yellow and white stained glass. "Never trifle away time" was one of the rules for pastors in the Methodist-Episcopal Church, and the pastor had quoted it to us often. When the church repair was done, he'd built a modest clapboard parsonage beside it for his young family, with only the Sunday School boys to help.

On the Sunday of the week I lost the baby, Reverend Byrd invited me into that small, neat house after church. It was a lovely little home, exactly the kind I'd dreamed of having—not the bustle of Mercy's kitchen, but this pleasant, simple setting where even the children were tidy and polite. Reverend Byrd had dark eyes that seemed to deepen into tunnels whenever he asked a question. Some people found that unnerving, but I had always been reassured by it. He listened intently while I told him about George's disappearance, his too-brief phone call, and then, figuring he'd probably already heard the news from someone in town, I told him about the baby, too.

"I don't understand anything," I said. "I don't understand why I lost the baby. I don't understand why George hasn't come home."

Reverend Byrd smiled and touched my hand. "You know how if a bobcat gets injured in a fight, it'll squeeze itself into a corner to seek for comfort?"

"I don't want George finding comfort anywhere but home," I said.

He finally came back early the next morning, closing the front door quietly behind him, as if he didn't want to disturb me, an almost laughable notion. His usually bright step was wobbly and slow. He hadn't shaved, and with thick stubble unevenly scribbled across his chin and cheeks, he looked less like himself than like the vagrants and drunken farmhands he'd often defended in court.

I had sworn to myself that I'd tell him about the baby the minute he walked through the door. But when I saw his face, I knew my news should wait just a little bit longer—until he seemed more settled in himself.

He looked as if he'd left his soul out on the road somewhere.

"What can I get you?" I asked him.

If he was grateful for my lack of reproach, that didn't show. His face was expressionless, drawn, almost old. But then he looked at me—really looked at me—and his eyes widened when they met mine.

"What is it, Flossie?" he asked, but before I could answer, he said, "My Lord, you must have been so fretful—so worried about me. I'm so, so sorry. I just had to be away from this town to pull myself together. What Walton did—Well. But in any case—" He slid one hand down to my belly. "In any case, I shouldn't have left the two of you alone."

I lifted his hand away.

"What?" he asked.

"It's just me now," I said. "The baby's gone."

I don't think I'd ever seen the expression on anyone's face change so quickly. Weariness and apology were replaced in an instant by panic and concern.

"Annie," he said. "What happened?"

"I don't know," I said. "I just started bleeding."

"My Lord."

He put his arms around me and kissed my forehead, my cheek, my neck. I sobbed. Then he led me to the parlor sofa.

"Are you all right?" he asked.

"Better now that you're here," I said.

"No. But I mean your body. Your health. Your—your body."

"I'm fine."

"But when I think about what could have happened—"

"It did happen," I said.

"No, Flossie. I mean *you*."

Then I remembered about his mother.

"George, *I'm* fine," I said firmly. "Doc Marsden said I'm fine. We have plenty more chances."

"Chances," he repeated, already looking doubtful and distant again. His whole body seemed to sink, and exhaustion overtook him. "More chances mean more risks," he said.

"More chances mean more chances," I said. "Let's get you some coffee."

He followed me into the kitchen.

I turned the crank on the coffee grinder and scooped the grounds into the pot.

"Toast?" I asked him.

He shook his head no.

"Eggs?" I asked him.

"No, thank you, Flossie," he said quietly.

He walked off into the backyard.

I didn't follow him. I merely waited for the coffee to brew, leaning against the kitchen table with both hands, head down, praying.

Dear Lord, bring him back to me.

9

I don't know how word reached Mary Sue Allen so quickly that George had returned, but within an hour she was pounding on our front door. Dark hair flying and unkempt, she pushed past me into the parlor. She was walking off-kilter, just as George had been.

"Where is your husband?" she asked, and before I could answer, she repeated the question with a cruel new emphasis. "Where is *your* husband? They're still finding parts of mine's brains on the road near the Broyles Farm."

She didn't wait for an answer. She barged on into the kitchen. George was sitting at the table now, a pencil in his hand, a blank piece of paper in front of him, a blank expression on his face. He stood up as if another person were making his body move, and he extended his long, graceful hand. She slapped it away.

"No!" she shouted.

"Mary Sue Allen," George said in a voice that seemed barely to escape his throat. "I am so sorry for your loss."

Mary Sue's mouth twisted, tightened.

"Losses," George added.

"He was nine years old!" she cried.

"I know it," George said.

"Nine years old! And he'd still have a whole life if you hadn't let Walton go free."

George looked helpless.

"Mary Sue!" I said. "It was the *jury* that let him go free."

She turned from George to me and back to George, who said nothing. She clenched and unclenched her fists.

"*Everyone* wanted Walton to go free," I added. "Remember how everyone couldn't wait to put up his bail?"

She gasped, and then wailed. "I don't have anyone left to love!" Then she spun back to look at me, seething. "And don't you or anyone else dare tell me that I should love the Lord, or that the Lord loves me."

"Let me get you a cup of tea," I said; it was all I could think of saying.

She stared back at me, disbelieving. "Why would you think I'd ever take anything from this house?"

She turned to leave, but I followed her to the front door, where she stopped, her face warped by pain and rage.

"Oh, Mary Sue—" I began.

"*You* wouldn't understand," she said viciously. "*You've* never even had a child."

She slammed the door behind her.

Shaken, I went back to the kitchen. George was sitting at the table again, the piece of paper still in front of him, still as empty as his eyes.

"She was upset," he said woodenly.

I didn't know how to answer him. Either he hadn't heard Mary Sue's parting words, or he'd heard them but failed to understand how brutal they had been.

I stood in the kitchen doorway, just looking at him.

"What is it?" he said as I leaned on the kitchen counter. "What? Please don't try to tell me that it wasn't my fault."

He wasn't thinking about me any more than I was thinking about Walton Allen. But even without the murder and suicide, even without the depths to which they had thrown George, I knew that losing the baby would always mean more to me than it would to him. I still don't think any man can truly understand the sense of power and mystery that pregnancy imparts, how being pregnant feels as if you're walking around with a story inside you, how having a miscarriage, no matter if you're ever pregnant again, means that that particular story will never be told—yet, somehow, never forgotten.

He stood up, his posture perfect, the way it usually was when he was dressed for court. But it was hard to see that calm, sturdy man through his weariness and my despair.

"Mary Sue was right. That child would be alive if Walton Allen had gone to jail," he said.

"He'd also be alive if Mary Sue hadn't fooled around with Burch Gardenhire. Or if she'd left Walton for good after the murder, and taken the child with her," I said.

George looked briefly startled, possibly by the idea that Mary Sue could have chosen to leave, possibly by the mere fact that I had suggested a wife might have choices.

But we nursed each other through the day, deep in our losses. I made us a dinner that neither one of us could eat.

"Was anyone with you?" he finally asked.

"Caroline and Mercy. They were really kind, and Mercy said all the right things, but she already has her four children, and Caroline's still got hers on the way."

"It's all right," George said. "We don't have to be like everyone else."

It was, word for word, what my mother had said to my father so many years before. I don't think it comforted me any more than it had comforted him.

George's and my eyes met for the briefest moment, but I saw nothing there except the twin reflections of my own searching look.

· · ·

For that whole first week after coming home, George didn't leave the house.

At the market, at Robinson's, even at the cobbler shop, people stopped me to ask about him. They knew he had left town after the shootings, and they knew he had come back. They knew he hadn't been to church, and they knew Mary Sue was blaming him for winning her husband's freedom, even though they couldn't deny that they'd all cheered George—and Walton—in the hours and days after the trial.

George barely ate or spoke. He didn't go to the office. I went to church and went about my chores, damping down the need to ask him for anything. Washing on Monday. Baking on Tuesday. Dusting and cleaning downstairs on Wednesday. He was rarely in the same room with me for more than a few minutes. On Thursday I noticed that he had found the time to rearrange the parlor shelves, separating his books out, putting them back the way they'd been before I'd alphabetized them with mine.

"You don't want even our books to be together?" I asked.

"I have a system" was all he said.

We didn't talk about the shootings. We didn't talk about the baby. We didn't talk.

Friday night, while he was sleeping, I slid out of bed and, for the first time since the miscarriage, opened the door to the spare room. I sat in the rocking chair that George had insisted we buy. I looked at the small pine dresser, with its three unfilled drawers; the fresh but blank white walls; the bare floor; the unmade bed. The room was as empty of life as I was. I wrapped my arms tight around my knees, allowing my tears to fall on them. Eyes squeezed shut, I wondered if I would have another chance at motherhood. I felt alone in my body in a way that I never had.

"Annie," George said from the doorway. "I never wanted to see your heart broken."

I wiped my eyes on my nightgown sleeve.

"We just need to start again," I said.

But if he understood that I meant to start our family, that didn't show.

This was the beginning of an entirely new marriage, one in which loss, the most isolating, insistent, of human emotions, would start to fill every empty space inside and around us.

On Monday morning, George left the house for the first time, even before I'd gotten dressed. As soon as I had, I ran across to Mercy's house to tell her.

"All right now," she said, as if she'd known a dozen such situations. "You have to ease him back in slow."

"I will. I am," I told her.

"Just be patient with him," Mercy said, swatting a fly with a wet dish towel and brushing it to the floor, satisfied.

"You always tell me that."

"Always true. Also, I hear Mary Sue's moving back to be with her sister up in Corbin. Maybe that'll ease George's mind a tad bit."

Back home, I started supper—fried chicken, sweet potatoes, and collards—and George walked in even before the water had boiled. He wasn't dressed in office clothes, and he wasn't carrying his satchel. He was wearing denims and an old linen shirt, and he was carrying a strawberry crate filled with tools, cables, sheets of metal, and stiff boards that stuck up above the sides.

"What's all that?" I asked him.

"I need to build a cabinet to hold all the parts."

"The parts for what?"

"For my radio."

"Your *pretend* radio?"

He didn't smile.

"You'll see," he said. "My Morse is probably rusty, but I've still got my licenses."

"So," I said as gently as possible. "You didn't go to work today?"

"Next week," he said.

"That okay with the Baxters?"

George nodded in a way that made me feel sure he hadn't spoken to them at all.

"It's fine," he said. "I'll go in next week. Meantime, I've got all the things in the attic and this stuff for starters, and I've ordered a bunch of some new tubes they're making in Michigan. Joe Early said he'd help me build a workbench upstairs."

"A workbench? In the baby's room?"

"Someday, when it's a real baby's room, I'll move the rig somewhere else. The attic gets too hot."

I had to look away from him.

"But see," he said, putting the box on the front hall table. "Seems there's something in here for you too."

George lifted some newspaper pages from a corner of the box and withdrew a gray kitten with white paws and enormous yellow-green eyes.

"A kitten?" I asked.

"She's for you," George said. "Joe Early's outdoor cat had a litter a few weeks back. I chose the sweetest one for the sweetest wife."

George handed me the kitten, took his box, climbed the stairs, and disappeared.

Growing up on a farm, I'd had tender feelings for a lot of animals—our colt especially. But the closest I'd come to having a pet was the fruit bat that flew into the house one day and that my mother, seeing how scared it made me, insisted was also named Annabel.

Now I looked at the gray kitten warily. What was I supposed to do with her? Was I supposed to love her? Did George think, for even one blind moment, that she could take the place of the baby we'd lost?

Tentatively, I lifted the kitten to rub against my cheek, but she stretched out an awkward white paw and pushed my face away.

George didn't go back to his office the next week. He didn't go back until three weeks later, and when he did, he wasn't wearing his seersucker jacket or his straw hat. He had his sleeves rolled up and no tie on, and he left the house looking as nervous as a child on his first day of school. A new routine began. He went in late and came home early. He took on only the most mundane cases—wills, contracts, house closings, and so forth—the very things that he'd hoped to leave behind by becoming a trial lawyer. Sometimes he'd give me a peck on the lips. But there was no more affection from him than that. I believed that having a baby would shake him out of his haze. But how was that going to happen if this distance kept on between us?

"Maybe you should talk to Reverend Byrd," I said one evening.

"I'm fine," George said, taking my hand in the least convincing way possible.

"George—"

"Have I got you or not?" he asked, his eyes searching for mine, the tether dangling before me.

I sighed. "Of course you've got me, George."

"Then please just let me be."

It had taken only a few weeks for George to transform the baby's room into a radio shack. Part of an old barn door was laid across two sawhorses as a workbench. On and beside it were shelves George had built from strawberry crates, and in these I could see boxes of glass tubes, spools of wire, copper fittings, and Mason jars filled with screws, bolts, and brackets. He had thrown a sheet over the mattress and covered it with a grid of other unidentifiable objects, as well as a dozen dark smudges that, from my angle, looked indelible.

In the center of the workbench were two pieces of wood, each about as thick as a breadboard, and on these were various glass and metal parts connected by tidy skeins of thin black wires.

He forced a smile. "Hi there, Flossie," he said.

He bent over the table, methodically winding a wire around a short spindle. When he finished, he lifted his hands away as if he had just managed to balance an egg on its end.

"What's that for?" I asked him.

"Wait," he said.

He took hold of a heavy black metal handle and, with some effort, lifted it to switch on the power. As the glass tubes on the receiver started to glow, he bent over them.

"What are you doing?" I asked.

George shook his head and sniffed. "Checking for smoke," he said.

"What? Why?"

"You always check for smoke."

"I sort of wish you hadn't told me that, George."

Now, static, sounding like the kitten scratching at the screen door, came into the room, insistent, mysterious, and undeniably intriguing. George turned a large metal dial until the static stopped. He leaned in toward a microphone and said, "CQ CQ CQ. This is 4DG calling, 4DG, Dayton, Tennessee. Over."

There was silence, and George repeated what he'd said several times.

I wondered if I'd put the butter and milk in the icebox.

Finally, another voice came through. "4DG this is 2WA 2WA 2WA. Over."

Would there be enough time to make a proper supper, or should I just boil some water and make macaroni and cheese?

George said, "2WA this is 4DG. Thanks for the call, old man. Name here is George, location is Dayton, Tennessee, about forty miles northeast of Chattanooga. Your signal is very strong. Antenna is an end-fed wire up twenty feet. Name again George. Over."

"4DG from 2WA. Roger, George. Good signal here in Plattsburgh, New York. Some fading but very strong. Name Cal. Over."

"Thanks, Cal, 73 to you and good luck! Please QSL George Craig, Walnut Street, Dayton, Tennessee. This is station 4DG signing off. Clear."

George moved the heavy switch back down, satisfied.

"New York!" he said happily. "You can't usually reach New York since there's so much traffic in the daytime."

"Well, that's great, George," I said sarcastically. It irked me that some imagined stranger in a state he'd never been to could make him happier than I could.

The kitten, whom I had still neither named nor started to love, came tumbling into the room at that moment, pouncing on a dangling cord, then pouncing again when George tried to pull it out of her grasp. When he did, she reached for George's shoelace instead, and when he bent to take that away, she scratched his hand. Seeing the pink welts rise there, I felt a guilty satisfaction.

"Spitfire," I said.

"What?"

"Spitfire. Her name is Spitfire."

I picked Spitfire up and walked out of the room.

Late in the summer, I said, "Come to church with me, George."

"Not today."

"You've said that every Sunday."

We were in the bedroom—a rare moment together—and I was just fastening the buttons on my flowered cotton frock.

"Let me ask you this," he said, as if I were a witness and he was cross-examining me. But this was not our friendly court jabber. "Why do people pray?"

I stopped, hiding my frustration by turning away to brush my hair.

"Did you pray that your father would live?" he asked.

"Of course."

"Did you pray that your mother would live?"

"Yes, George."

"Did you pray for the baby? Have you *ever* gotten what you've prayed for?"

"God is not Santa Claus," I said, repeating the words I had learned in Sunday School and that my mother had often said as well. "And anyway," I added, walking past him to the head of the stairs. "I prayed that I would meet you."

I had understood from the start that, while George was not exactly a heathen, he was at best a quiet Christian. I had assumed my faith and the faith of the people in town would bring him closer to God. I had imagined that I held a beautiful bowl—for some reason I pictured it as many-colored, like Joseph's coat—and this bowl was filled to overflowing with faith. George held a bowl, too, but it needed filling, and I had eagerly imagined pouring some of what I had into his.

I should have known that the Allen killings had ripped that bowl from his hands and dashed it to the ground, and that if he was filling it again at all, it was with something other than faith.

"Count it all joy, George," I said before I walked down the stairs.

"How's that?"

" 'My brethren, count it all joy.' That's what James says to the twelve tribes in the Bible. There's a purpose for everything. Even the awful things."

"I'm supposed to count it all joy that I got Walton Allen free?"

"George, if Caroline could keep her faith when Charlie passed away, and if I could keep my faith when I lost my parents—and when we lost the baby—"

"Yeah," he said, "I really don't know how the hell you did that."

I stared at him, stunned by his words. They were the most brutal I'd ever heard him utter—to me or to anyone else.

I walked to church alone and late. I sat in one of the back pews, exchanging waves with Caroline and Willie. A few friends from the

Aqua turned to see that I'd come. They were good friends, I re-membered, and Reverend Byrd was the church embodied: strong, solid, and full of light.

Half-listening to him, I noticed a young man sitting just to the right and one aisle up from me. I didn't recognize him. He was dressed tidily, like most of our usual congregants, wearing a clean white shirt and a pale blue bow tie. As far as I could tell, he was half asleep.

I looked behind to see if Mr. Bailey had noticed, and just as I turned, the old man launched one of his famous pencil stubs, which hit the stranger on his left shoulder, then fell to the wood floor with several telltale raps. A few congregants chuckled knowingly. The young man sat up straight, brushed his shoulder, and looked around to see the source. As he did, he caught my eye, and I smiled at him, sympathetic, remembering how I'd warned George that he might one day become just such a target. The young man shrugged, smil-ing, then stood up to sing as Reverend Byrd instructed:

> O for the peace that floweth as a river,
> Making life's desert places bloom and smile;
> O for the faith to grasp heaven's bright forever
> Amid the shadows of earth's little while.

On the church steps, standing in the shadow of the portico, we waited in line to shake the pastor's hand.

"Are you new to town?" I asked the young man.

He nodded. "Came down from Paducah. Just got hired to coach the football team and sub for the science teachers."

He touched his left shoulder, where Mr. Bailey's pencil had left a small mark. "Is this how all newcomers are greeted here?"

"Just the ones who fall asleep in church. Even if they were born here."

"I'll have to remember that," he said with a smile. There were freckles on his nose and cheeks. Behind his tortoiseshell glasses, his eyes were mild and blue.

"I'm Annabel Craig," I said, shaking his hand.

"The lawyer's wife," the man said.

"Oh, you've heard about that."

"I reckon everyone has," he said.

I tried to hide my embarrassment.

"And you are—?" I asked.

"My apologies," he said. "My name's John Scopes."

Part Two

1

It was just about a year later when John Scopes walked out of Robinson's Drugstore, answered a few of my questions, and went back to his tennis game. On my way home that afternoon—past Loula Hodge's camellia bush and the children playing tag on Chestnut Street—it occurred to me how eager I once would have been to tell George what I'd just seen and heard. But by now, it had been four dismal, confusing seasons since Doc Allen had killed his son and himself; since George had lost his confidence; since I had lost our baby; since I had met John Scopes. By now, George had thoroughly retreated, making even the most basic participation—in daily chores, in regular meals, in listening together to a radio program—seem like a special favor. Every once in a while, he would remember to thank me for something, and at Christmas he gave me a nifty new camera, much smaller than my father's Brownie. But I had to wonder if that was less a way of acknowledging my hobby than of making sure he'd have the freedom to pursue his.

I didn't have much to go on when it came to what I could expect—from my life or life in general. I struggled to stay patient. His temper was often short, his manner sometimes downright rude.

He'd stopped coming to church entirely. He'd stopped making love with me. I didn't know whether he'd stopped finding me appealing or he'd stopped wanting a family, but he spent as much time as he could in the spare bedroom, the room once meant for our baby but now reconstructed as his radio shack. He closed the door when he worked in there and closed it when he left. When he went to the law office, he was still avoiding all cases where violence had been wrought or where it might later occur—say, on some dusty road with a loaded gun and a little boy of nine.

If there was any urgency or ambition still driving George, it was now pretty much limited to the endless tinkering and distraction of his ham radio rig. There was no meal, conversation, or chore that couldn't be cut off abruptly by the squeals and garbled sounds that came from the extra room. In the mornings, when we'd just awakened, George's first act was to slip next door and turn on the rig. Even when we were in the same room, it was hard to feel alone with him. He might be dressing for work, and still I'd know that he was straining to hear if some voice was breaking through the static. At any moment, people I'd never met, from places I didn't know, could enter our home through the air. At such times I wondered if there was anything that could make me seem as important to him as the system he was assembling. It sometimes seemed he was building himself a boat that could take him to other places.

The only boat I had ever wanted was the one in the old folk song:

> The water is wide, I can't cross o'er
> And neither have I wings to fly
> Build me a boat that can carry two
> And both shall row, my love and I.

Back from Robinson's, I didn't bother to call up to George. In the kitchen, I tucked my new photos into the cupboard, washed my hands, and put the cast-iron pot on the stove. I peeled potatoes, chopped onions and carrots, and shelled peas. I struck a match and lit the stove, put some lard in the pot, and began to brown the cubes of lamb I'd bought at the butcher's the day before.

Once, when I was a child, a puppy had gotten stuck behind a fence near our farmhouse, and after everyone else had failed, I had managed to coax it out until it huddled in my arms and then, like a baby, wriggled around and put its head up on my shoulder. Instinctively, I'd always known that you had to be gentle with a frightened, needful thing. But no amount of coaxing had helped to bring George back to me. He was wedded to the hobby I'd come to hate as much as I hated my own loneliness. I had never imagined that either emotion could fill so much space in my marital home. For all the advice I'd been given—by Mercy, by Caroline, by Caroline's mother, even by the major—it hadn't yet occurred to me that the vessel of love, like the vessel of faith, was not unbreakable.

While I cooked, Spitfire, ever vigilant, watched me from her favorite perch on the windowsill behind the sink, her eyes half lidded, her tail alternately flicking and wrapping around her like a belt. As the stew started to simmer, I sat on a kitchen chair and let her jump onto my lap. I kneaded the slight dimples behind her ears.

At five o'clock, I finally climbed the stairs and knocked on the spare bedroom door.

"In a minute," George said.

I went to our bedroom to wait. These days, George's minutes tended to be variable in length. I lay on our bed. With Mercy as my tutor, I had sewn lace curtains and tied them loosely with wide sashes, so when a breeze came in, they billowed and looked like bouquets of white flowers. I had dressed up a lampshade with orange and white ball tassels. I had crocheted a throw for the foot of our bed. Nothing had helped to draw George to this room.

After fifteen minutes, I forced myself to get up and knock on the door again. This time, George opened it. He smelled of pipe smoke and, faintly, of sweat. He had always been slim, but he was so skinny now that his khaki pants were held up, barely, by thin, twisted suspenders. His shirt was past due for a laundering, his face past due for a shave. And yet he was smiling at me.

"You'll never believe what I heard," he said.

Behind him, the static from the receiver made it hard for me to believe he'd heard anything at all. But he told me he'd been tuning around in search of a clear signal when he heard someone mention Dayton.

"At first I thought they had to be talking about Dayton, Ohio," he said, "because whoever talks about Dayton, Tennessee? But then I turned on the Westinghouse downstairs and there was something about Robinson's and something about a trial."

"I know," I said, cutting him off.

"You know? How do *you* know?"

It smarted, the way he stressed the word *you*.

"Because I just saw it happen. I was right there in the drugstore when Frank Robinson and George Rapp and a bunch of the others asked John Scopes if he'd let himself be arrested for breaking the anti-evolution law."

With his brow furrowed, George turned off his rig. The silence was sublime.

"John Scopes?" he asked me. "The baseball coach?"

"Football," I said. "But he taught some science review classes, so they say he must have used the textbook that has evolution in it."

George looked back and forth between the rig and me, apparently torn about where he should turn his attention, perhaps where he could get the better information. Finally, he faced me and smiled.

"Something smells good," he said.

"What?"

"Is there supper?" he asked.

"You're hungry?"

Over these many months, I had cooked him beefsteaks and stuffed potatoes, pork stew and lamb chops. I had made the thick tomato sauces that he had once liked with everything from scrambled eggs to nut loaves. Of course, I'd baked him all manner of strawberry desserts. But he had usually left these things untouched, occasionally taking something furtively while I was out doing errands.

George nodded and reached up for my hand. "Let's go downstairs," he said.

It wasn't until later that evening—after he had eaten supper and filled his pipe and for once not retreated to his radio shack—that he mentioned John Scopes again.

"Do you know him?" he asked me.

"A little."

"How?"

"Well, for one thing, church of course—"

I said it as if meeting John was one of the many wonderful things George had missed by spending his Sunday mornings at home.

"And for another?"

"And I took his picture with the football team for the yearbook."

"Big-talking fellow?"

"No, actually. Kind of shy."

George relit his pipe as if rekindling his ambition, drawing on it eagerly, his eyes and the tobacco in the bowl both brightening.

"And he's going to stand up in court to say he broke the law against teaching evolution?" George asked.

"That's what they said."

I started to clear the supper dishes.

George put the pipe he'd just lighted onto one of the plates I'd not cleared.

"Mind if I go out for a bit?" he asked then.

"Would I mind?"

"Yes."

I laughed.

"What's funny?"

What was funny was his asking if I minded anything.

"Of course I don't mind, George."

He bolted upstairs, a move I was accustomed to only when the noise of his rig was calling. Before I had swept the last crumbs from the table, he'd returned. His hair was neatly parted, and he was wearing a fresh shirt.

"Where are you going?" I asked him.

"I'm going to find John Scopes."

If you grow up on a farm—or, I guess, anywhere there's open space—you know that there are twilights on opposite sides of midnight, and if you could see a color photograph of that pink and gray haze, you wouldn't be able to tell if the sun had just set or was just about to rise.

That was how I now felt about George.

Perhaps if I stayed completely still, I'd be able to figure out what was ending and what was likely to begin.

I was asleep when George came home that night, and he was already in the kitchen when I went downstairs in the morning.

"When did you get home?" I asked.

"Late."

"What happened?"

"Well, it took me a while to find him. Mary Early told me John Scopes was staying at the boardinghouse, and I thought she meant Guffey's. Turns out it was Bailey's."

"Toast?" I asked gently, not wanting to break whatever spell had been cast to give my husband a normal appetite.

He nodded.

I cut a thick slice of fresh bread and pushed it into the toaster.

"Juice?"

Another nod.

I took the pitcher from the refrigerator and filled a glass for him.

"So, John was at Bailey's?" I asked casually.

"He was," George said.

"And did you talk him out of it?"

The toast popped up. George stood to put on his jacket.

"Talk him out of it? Why would I talk him out of it?" he asked. He bent over the table to butter his toast.

"Because they just twisted his arm," I said. "Rapp and the rest, they just want him to say he taught it so the town can get some notice."

With his buttered toast in one hand and his glass in the other, George paused in a solemn but silly pose, looking like the scales of justice.

"John wasn't even that sure he'd covered evolution," I went on. "I bet he didn't, really."

George's smile was a mixture of zeal and condescension—a facial expression, incidentally, that would soon spread throughout Dayton, among people who held opposite opinions with equal certainty.

"Oh, Annie," he said, as if speaking to a child. "You don't understand."

He downed his juice in one gulp and started toward the front door, his toast still in his hand.

"What don't I understand?"

"I don't want to prosecute him, Annie. And I don't want to talk him out of it. I want to defend him."

"Because he didn't really do it," I said.

That smile again, and just as he stepped outside: "No. Because he did."

2

Natural disasters can change a town overnight. Back in the spring of 1917, a flood had hit Dayton, even covering Market and Main Streets. The Tennessee River had risen for days, with pumping stations submerged by backwater, and residents forced to float through town in small boats and on homemade rafts. But not even that act of God could compare to the changes wrought to Dayton by the coming trial of John Thomas Scopes. From the moment the ACLU took him on as their test case, there was no other subject—no joy, calamity, birth, or death—that took precedence over the promised drama and hoped-for business the trial would bring. Even though John had not yet been formally indicted, even though the next grand jury session wasn't supposed to be held until August, Dayton in May had already begun a strenuous course of primping.

On my way to the market, I saw men scaling the side of the hardware store with yards of cable, wound up like skeins of wool, wrapped over their shoulders. At the barbershop two doors down, a young towheaded boy was using a soapy sea sponge to wash years of dust and dirt from the barber pole, the suds from the sponge dripping down to darken the pavement. The red stripes on the pole turned from cranberry to ruby, the blue from black to sapphire.

Outside the Aqua Hotel, Fred Whittle was wiping the perspiration from his brow with an already damp handkerchief. If I hadn't known him better, I'd have thought he looked not just anxious but fearful. His jacket was rumpled, too, surprising for a man whose crisp clothes had long been an emblem of the hotel's Southern grace.

"I need you, Mrs. Craig," he said to me with uncharacteristic urgency.

"Excuse me?"

"I need you at the Aqua. I need all the help I can get."

"Fred, you do know I don't work for you anymore?" I asked. "That I've got my own household to run?"

"'Course I know, that, Sugar," he said. "But I also know you've got no little ones to keep you fixed. Not yet, anyhow. Plus, from what I'm hearing, your husband might get so busy with John Scopes that he won't care a fig if there's a little dust on the floorboards and a cold supper in the icebox."

Though it always stung to be reminded that we didn't have a child, it was refreshing to hear George mentioned with respect instead of concern or pity.

"When do you need me?" I asked.

"Could have used you yesterday."

I agreed. Truth was, if something big was going to happen in our town, I didn't want to be stuck on Walnut Street when it did.

At home, I was delighted and somewhat amazed to find George, John, Rapp, and two other lawyers sitting at our kitchen table. George had a nickel-size spot of shaving cream just below his left ear. He was wearing a fresh denim shirt. Even more surprising was the fact that all the men were drinking coffee—coffee George must have brewed and poured for them himself.

"Annie!" he said joyfully, as if I was the one who'd been absent for months.

Reaching up over his shoulder, he took my hand. "You know everyone here?" he asked. His voice was warm and cheerful, the way it used to be on Saturday afternoons when we'd asked friends and neighbors in. Like them, these fellows made a pleasant, chatty group. On the table, one of my parents' earthenware plates was filled with cigarette butts, burnt tobacco, and used pipe cleaners that looked like long, muddy caterpillars. There were unwashed dishes in the sink, too, hardly a welcome sight. But it meant that George had eaten, and for a moment—a lovely, misguided moment—it seemed that everything would be fine again.

Things were usually quiet at the Aqua in springtime, but when I showed up the next day, the place was an active hive. I stepped through the empty doorframe, which one of the handymen had stripped of its dusty screen in order to replace it. At the front desk, Fred stood in a state of nervous paralysis, a desk fan gently lifting and dropping the tip of his short pale blue tie.

"Where do you need me?" I asked him.

"Dining room. Kitchen," he said. He already looked spent.

I walked on through the lobby, the smells of fresh paint and fresh biscuits equally pleasant. For at least five minutes, I stood in the wide entrance to the busy banquet hall, receiving reticent smiles from Curtis and Lester, two of the waiters I'd been friendly with years before. Almost all the waiters at the Aqua were Black—and if a patron didn't like that, Fred Whittle always said, that patron was welcome to try to find a place with white waiters who served food this good. The waiters wore identical skinny blue ties and long-sleeved white shirts with futilely starched collars. They seemed able to spot an empty biscuit basket from anywhere in the vast room, and some of their sons and cousins kept the Victrola wound up.

The waiters were also—and necessarily—abidingly deferential. In a town of eighteen hundred residents, only about one in ten was Black. Most of them were the grandchildren of slaves, and even though a lot of white men in East Tennessee had fought with the

Union, churches and schools were still segregated, and everyone knew that many people in East Tennessee—possibly even some of the Aqua's patrons—were among the many millions who belonged to the Ku Klux Klan.

In the little world of the kitchen, though, we had all been equal in the eyes of Eva Jenkins, whose skin had been the color of hickory wood, except for some black splotches on her hands and forearms, the scars of countless grease fires and spattered oil. Every once in a while, when tensions rose in the kitchen, she would turn over a milk crate noisily, step up on it, wave a wooden spoon, and declare:

" 'But I say unto you, love your enemies, bless them that curse you, do good to them that hate you!' "

Eva had died of heart failure in 1921, the year before I met George.

"You devil!" she had always said whenever I tried to surprise her by sneaking up behind her.

Like the major, she had given me hope and faith and some sense of safety. She had loved me, and I had loved her, and stepping into the kitchen now, I felt her absence. Zippy was gone, too—one of her suitors apparently having proved real.

One thing that hadn't changed was the never-dwindling stack of dishes to wash, the inevitable result of the Aqua's signature serving style. For seventy-five cents, every meal included a main course surrounded by exactly nine miniature bowls, each one holding two or three spoonfuls of a different side dish: mashed potatoes, fresh peas, collards, radishes, noodle salad. Bowls piled up unrelentingly on the kitchen counters.

Sliding in today beside a young scullery maid whose forehead was shiny with sweat and whose fuzzy blond braids were coming undone, I introduced myself and was nearly knocked over by the girl's grateful hug. Gretchen Hubbert, it turned out, had been washing dishes alone since breakfast. Eva Jenkins's replacement—a steely, gray-eyed broomstick of a woman named Mabel Finstock—apparently wasn't the kind of boss to notice or to care.

"Fred told me you used to work back here," Mabel said.

"I sure did."

"And then you left to marry the fellow who defended that murderer."

"Well, yes," I said. "He's defended a lot of other people too," I added.

"Then I heard he left town," she continued.

"He came back," I said, trying not to sound as protective as I felt.

I shuddered to think how much gossip had been spouted in this room alone. At church, Reverend Byrd had quoted various proverbs about slander to keep the chatter to a minimum. Here, Eva (in her day) would have silenced them all. But George, I thought, if George was really going to leave his radio shack behind, then he just might shut all the whisperers up for good.

After a three-hour shift, my hands were raw, and my knuckles looked as if they'd been dabbed with red paint. The kitchen still had a tub of Sana-Balm near the back door. Outside, rubbing it into my hands, I looked up at a pasty, overcast sky and saw black birds flying by in the shape of a garden spade, digging into the gray, inscrutable clouds.

3

Messages posted on the big board in the drugstore window usually announced things like town council meetings, new movies at the Gem, or changes to practice schedules for the Rhea Central sports teams. But on the morning of Wednesday, May 13, only one week after John Scopes had said he'd be willing to stand trial, there was a clipping from the Knoxville newspaper that beat anything anyone in town had ever seen:

WILLIAM JENNINGS BRYAN
To Take Scopes Case
DEFENDS BUTLER ACT
HEADED FOR DAYTON, TN

Newspapers flew around town that day as if they had actual wings. In 1925, William Jennings Bryan was one of the two or three most famous people in America. In politics, he had stood up for farmers, laborers, merchants, and miners. He'd earned bunches of nicknames, including "the Great Commoner"—though my father used to say Bryan wanted to be great a lot more than he wanted to be common. The major, as well as most of the other men at my church, had voted for him all three times he'd run for president. The fact that he'd never won hadn't lessened their loyalty to him. All around the South, huge crowds still gathered at tent meetings and lecture halls to hear him speak. People trusted him for the ways he claimed to be like them: simple (although he was anything but); down-to-earth (although his ego soared); common (although he had built a small fortune in Florida real estate). But I knew, at least vaguely, that he had stood for fairer taxes, votes for women, and bans on both liquor and unchecked power.

What I hadn't known, until the spring of 1925, was that he'd said the Bible was the only book anyone ever needed to read. Or that he'd been fierce in his warning that the teaching of evolution was going to poison children and thereby threaten civilization. Later I would learn that it was exactly this message that had moved John Washington Butler, a farmer and state representative, to draft the anti-evolution law that John Scopes would stand trial for breaking.

Suddenly, Dayton's excitement turned into frenzy. Every resident, from carpenter to hardware store clerk, from dressmaker to farmer, had even more plans to make and more work to do than the initial announcement of the trial had inspired. Long gone was Dayton's typically slow, humid pace of early spring. Even Mercy, who was usually too busy with her children, her household, or whatever was happening on Walnut Street to express any opinion beyond it, was beside herself at the news.

"William Jennings Bryan!" she said. It was a sterling day, with a rare dry breeze coming through her open kitchen door. Her kids were playing in the yard, and she was making shortbread cookies, twisting an empty jam jar to cut out the circles. She was so riled up, though, that she was using none of her usual care in keeping the circles close together. Comically, I kept gathering the spare dough, and Mercy kept adding more flour to it and rolling it out again.

"When I was just a little slip," she said, "my mama took me to a Chautauqua meeting in Kentucky, and I saw that great man myself. 'Course, there was no such thing as a microphone then, but

Lord stir me dead, you could hear his voice all the way up in the back seats."

Naturally, I had heard Bryan on the radio many times myself, and it was true that the rise and fall of his voice seemed to lift and lower me with it.

"Remember anything he said?" I asked Mercy.

"Not really, if I'm honest. I just recollect he was so tall, and he had the shape of a Golden Boy soft pear, and his voice was so strong, and my mama had her hand on her heart—"

Mercy laid her own flour-covered hand against her chest, leaving a dusting of white fingerprints.

"Lord help the poor man who goes up against the Great Commoner to defend the likes of John Scopes," Mercy said, and I was, if not exactly embarrassed, then at least unprepared to tell my closest neighbor how that "poor man" might turn out to be my husband.

The scene at the Aqua was near chaos. I understood the urgency, but not yet the magnitude, of what was happening—that for the rest of my life, whenever I said I'd been born in Dayton, Tennessee, people would ask me if I'd ever met John Scopes or seen William Jennings Bryan in the flesh. For now, with George and the other lawyers occupied and scuttling from one office to another, I was just trying to help Fred Whittle. On Thursday, I was tidying the hotel's front lobby, dusting the etched-glass light shades, when a disheveled, gray-haired man with a yellowing shirt collar stepped through the still-empty doorframe. His trousers nearly covered his shoes, his lapels seemed strangely large and lopsided, and his face looked like a walnut shell. But he bowed slightly as he took off his hat, and in a gravelly, genteel voice, he introduced himself as Professor John Randolph Neal and asked if I knew where he could find John Scopes.

"I expect everyone's trying to get ahold of him these days," the professor added.

I offered him one of the lobby armchairs and, in the dining room, found Ezra Weems, the nine-year-old son of one of the waiters. Ezra, seemingly hypnotized by the record currently spinning on the Victrola, reluctantly agreed to go find John.

It didn't take long. I fetched the old man a plate of biscuits and some sweet tea with shaved ice, and he was still sipping it when Ezra reappeared, tugging on John's hand as he pulled him through the doorframe.

"Ezra here told me you wanted to meet me," John said to the professor.

"Yes, and I do apologize greatly that we sent this young one to convey you here," Professor Neal said. He stood and handed Ezra a nickel that looked as if it had been in his jacket pocket for half a century. Flicking biscuit crumbs from his wide lapels, he extended his hand to John.

"My name is John Randolph Neal," he said, and then, sounding as if he'd rehearsed the sentence, he declared: "I object to any force that would try to limit the human mind in its search for truth."

John nodded, apparently unsure of what kind of response was expected of him.

"Boy," Neal continued, "I'm interested in your case and, whether you want me to or not, I will be available to you night and day to handle your defense."

I froze, dusting cloth in hand, too confused to pretend I was doing anything besides eavesdropping. Much as I was unsure about the idea of my own husband opposing a national hero, I'd been loving George's revival and his departure from the radio shack. If John Scopes accepted John Neal's offer, then what would that mean for George?

I stalled, needlessly dusting already dust-free side tables, until John suggested that he and Neal talk things over next door at Robinson's. I had to fight the impulse to follow them.

I reached home in time to make supper, wondering all the while whether George had completely deluded himself about representing John.

But George came home full of fire. Whatever the truth of the matter, he told me that he had never imagined he would head up the defense. Of course not. But he would be on the team. And everyone he'd talked to that day agreed that Neal was a great choice to lead them. He was a dusty, crusty lawyer who had taught for decades at the University of Tennessee. Naturally, George said, no one would be able to match Bryan for fame and eloquence. But Neal was a Southerner—a Tennessean to boot—and his folksy accent and shambling manner might engage a hometown jury in a way no city slicker could.

After supper, George didn't go upstairs to turn on his rig. The house was quiet enough that I could hear the crickets outside and have a sense of what our home had been like before Walton Allen had killed himself and his son. George just sat for more than an hour at the kitchen table, covering lined legal pads with notes and coffee cup rings. When I started upstairs, he followed me.

"Smile at me with those eyes, Annie," he said in bed when, to my utter amazement, he slipped a hand under my cotton nightgown, stretching his long fingers across the valley that lay between my hip bones. "How'd you get so wonderful? Explain yourself."

It had been months since he had reached for me that way. When I'd lost the baby, Mercy and Caroline had promised me I'd be pregnant again in no time. Neither they nor I would have guessed that George's sadness and sense of defeat would mean that in the coming year my chances for that happening would be so few. Tonight, however, George was ardent enough that even I wasn't thinking about the child we might conceive. I was thinking only about him. His eyes, in the semidarkness, were tethered to mine once again. From the top of the bureau, Spitfire looked on, unmoved. But I slid toward and beneath George, clamped my legs around him, and folded my hands firmly over his shoulders.

"You've got me," he said.

I remembered what it had been like to float in his arms that first day at Oak Tree Pond; to see our reflections in the store windows in Chattanooga; to have him catch me when we'd skated in winter. All of this came back to me, and even after we had stopped moving together and he had fallen asleep, I put my arms around him from behind, as if he were a pillow. I didn't want to let go.

When I got up the next morning, it was as if the whole last year had been someone else's story. George was standing at the foot of the bed, his fine brown hair neatly combed, his seersucker jacket hanging loosely around his still-too-thin frame. But the corners of his eyes wrinkled into stars as he looked at me. He swept his boater from the closet shelf, twirled it around his forefinger, leaned down to kiss me on the lips, and said, "You know what? You are the squirrel's eyebrows, and I'm going to see you later."

Before the next day was over, John Neal had been officially taken on by the ACLU to defend John Scopes and had signed up George, several clerks, and another attorney and sometime judge named, strangely enough, John Godsey. But talk continued, even among this mostly homegrown group, about whether they could find someone else as well, someone weighty enough to rival Bryan in celebrity.

Drunk on the publicity he'd been promising since that first day in Robinson's, George Rappleyea suggested the British science fiction writer H. G. Wells. Others got excited too, ignoring the facts that H. G. Wells was in London, not a lawyer, and, when asked, expressed absolutely no interest in the drama about to take place in some tiny East Tennessee town. But just days later, word went around that another celebrated figure, Clarence Darrow, had volunteered to defend John Scopes. The headlines were dramatic:

LINES DRAWN FOR EPIC BATTLE

and

IS DARROW AN INFIDEL OR NOT?

and

THEY'LL ROAST MR. DARROW AS A SIDE ORDER

"Darrah," as he was called in Dayton (Bryan was "Brine"), was sixty-eight that summer and known even in Dayton, though mostly with suspicion. Like Bryan, Darrow was famous for championing the little man: union members, farmers, and cobblers. I had heard him called a fighter for lost causes, and just the year before, he had gotten life instead of death sentences for two young murderers who'd confessed to killing a teenage boy just for the thrill of it. Darrow believed everyone deserved a defense. He didn't believe in capital punishment. He didn't believe the rich should have it better than the poor. But, more important than any of that to the people of Dayton, he didn't believe in God.

"Clarence Darrow!" George said, in exactly the same way Mercy had intoned the name of Bryan. George would have been overjoyed just to meet the man. But with the possibility of actually working beside him, George all but galloped out of the house on his way to prepare with Professor Neal and the rest of the defense team.

He came back while I was preparing supper and draped his jacket over the back of his usual kitchen chair. He was smiling, and he kissed me. Perhaps feeling good about himself was all it took to make him feel good about me.

I had already made a tomato and bacon pie, and now I had water boiling for some green beans. As George sat, I stood at the table, snapping the ends off the beans—a simple but satisfying task. George picked one of the beans from the bowl and tried to copy me, but he broke it in the middle, and it ended up mangled. I laughed.

"You've got to really snap it," I said. "Short and quick."

He picked up another. "I'll pretend it's Bryan," he said and briskly snapped off one end, then the other.

"What's William Jennings Bryan ever done to you?" I asked.

"It's not what he's done to me. It's what he's done to all the people who think he's some kind of prophet. You know what he says about science? What he actually says?"

I shook my head.

George grinned. "He says science is religion's enemy."

"Why is that funny?" I asked.

"Now, don't get your back up."

"I'm not."

"It's funny because think of where we'd be without science. Think of where *he'd* be. How would that man get from Florida to Tennessee? On foot? By mule?"

I said nothing, just gathered up the ends of the beans.

"And how would the Great Commoner get to read about himself in the newspaper without his glasses?" George continued. "How would that newspaper get printed, come to think of it? You think the Bible tells you how to build a car or make spectacles or design a printing press?"

He sounded so smug. My heart felt cramped.

"Mercy says she and Tim would choose Sunday School over regular school for their children any day," I said.

George laughed, using a furry beige pipe cleaner to scrub out the stem and shank of his pipe.

"Only ignorant people want to stay ignorant," he said.

It was such a nasty thing to say, and what was worse, he said it so casually. It made me feel sick to my stomach.

"What?" George asked in response to my silence. He was filling his pipe with tobacco now. He was happier than I'd seen him in months.

"Do you think I'm an ignorant person?" I asked.

He was startled. "Just not properly educated," he said. "Not your fault. It's how you were raised."

"So, you do. You think I'm ignorant."

"Flossie, I went to college. Then I read law. You didn't get those chances. Not for book learning."

"You know, George," I said. "I read books."

"I know you do."

"And I also pray every single day."

"I know that too," he said, still full of good cheer. He stood to take a matchstick from the box above the stove, lit it with a stroke on the cast-iron kettle, and put it to the bowl of his pipe. Then, sighing, he sat down across from me. "No one wants to stop you from praying. But if William Jennings Bryan is coming to Dayton to prosecute the man I'm helping to defend, then if you're with me, you'll pray for me."

Maybe it was growing up in the long shadow of the Civil War, but that division—between the Union and the Confederacy—had often seemed to make all other divisions equally stark. There were girls and there were boys. White people and Black. City folk and country. Believers and atheists. Even Methodists and Baptists. You had to be one or the other of each. And it was rare to find anyone who fell outside or between the tribes—or even wanted to know what the other side thought or felt.

For anyone who hasn't tried—truly tried—to understand an opposite point of view, there's rarely a chance of succeeding if you attempt to do it alone. Years later, when a magazine first sent me overseas on a photo assignment, I would come to understand that foreign ideas are like foreign countries, with languages, habits, and conventions of their own. If you want to cross the border and you're brave enough to try it, you're going to need a guide, preferably someone who was once an outsider too. What do you do, in the new country, once you manage to get comfortable? Is there a moment when you have to strain to use your old language? At what point do you start speaking the new language in your dreams?

I was still a far distance from the border of a new country that night in May. In all honesty, I didn't understand what John Scopes's defense would be or could be. I knew from Walton Allen's trial that even if a person had clearly broken a law, he could be found not guilty for other reasons. In the case of Walton Allen, the other reason had been the "unwritten law," the right of a husband to defend his wife. In the case of Scopes, there was no unwritten law, at least none that I knew.

"Please stop a minute," I said to George the next morning as he pulled a coffee cup from the shelf. "No coffee until you explain this to me."

"Explain what?" he said.

"Explain how you can defend John Scopes when he's *admitting* he broke the law."

Slightly annoyed, maybe just impatient, George reached for the coffee pot and filled his cup.

"What does the First Amendment to the Constitution say?" he asked.

I rummaged wildly through my brain.

"Freedom of speech," I said.

"Right. And what else?"

I knew how to can tomatoes, how to write in script, how to roast a chicken, how to take a photograph, how to feed a fire, how to be a friend, and how to pray. I knew dozens of Bible verses by heart and the words to hundreds of hymns. I'd read more than a hundred books. But I couldn't, for the life of me, remember any more of what the First Amendment said. I shook my head.

"Also, freedom to assemble," George went on. "Freedom to petition. But in this case what's most important is the very first freedom."

"And what's that?"

George looked at me from a great moral height and sipped his coffee contentedly. "It's called the Establishment Clause," he said. " 'Congress,' " he recited, " 'shall make no law respecting an establishment of religion, or prohibiting the free exercise thereof.' "

I asked him what that had to do with evolution.

"Simple," he said. "We're not allowed to have a national religion in this country. It's what makes us special. The government can't say everyone should be Methodist. Or Baptist. Or even Christian at all. And the government can't *keep* people from being any of those things, either. And the government pays for the public schools."

I thought about that. "So, the Butler Act isn't really an evolution law," I said. "It's more like a public teaching law."

George nodded, perhaps a little too surprised that I had absorbed what was, after all, a fairly straightforward argument.

"A government school—a public school," he said, "can't teach children to be Christians any more than it can teach them to be Jews."

In the days and weeks that followed, I would come to understand that this argument—that the Butler Act was unconstitutional— would be just the first of several defense strategies. The next, assuming the judge rejected that argument, would be to call expert witnesses who could explain not only the science behind evolution but also the difference between knowing something scientifically and believing something spiritually.

In short order, Dayton's chief commissioner appointed four men to comprise a "Committee on Reservations." Its sole purpose was to handle the latest wave of requests for lodgings during the trial. There were only three hotels in town, and they were bound to be filled up quickly, so a call went out for volunteers to house the visitors. When I asked George if he thought we should offer up our extra bedroom, I really didn't expect he'd want to, but he said, "The more the merrier!"

"Really?"

"Why not?"

"Well, we'd have to clear your rig out," I said, "and clean the room."

"Of course."

"Should I start?"

"Be my guest," George said gaily, as if the door that had been shutting me out, in every way, had never been closed. I called Fred Whittle and tried to calm his nerves as I told him I wouldn't be able to help at the Aqua for a few days.

For the last year, I had been granted only the briefest glimpses of our spare bedroom, but I knew that getting it in shape would not be just one morning's task. Now, for the first time since George had turned it into his radio shack, I stood alone in it, trying to make sense of the mess. Beside his receiver and transmitter lay a tangle of unattached wires, metal cylinders, and some gadgets that looked like mousetraps. The strawberry-crate shelves, which had seemed so carefully organized before, were jumbled now. Metal and plastic boxes of diminishing sizes were stacked atop one another like miniature but tottering Towers of Babel.

The George I had married—the George who did certain things at certain times, who folded his undershirts before he put them in the laundry basket—had hidden all this chaos beneath a veneer of calm and behind a closed door. It was hard to know where to start, but I began by sorting—gathering spare wires and cables of different colors, then notepads, then metal parts. What stopped me cold was the section of the table strewn with postcards, each one stamped with large red or blue numbers or letters. 1QPD. 4SD. 9AXR. I'd always thought George had insisted on getting our mail because the bills were his responsibility. Now I wondered if he'd just been intentionally concealing these cards. Clearly, each message had come from some contact he'd made at such-and-such a date and time, in such-and-such a place. Certainly I recognized some of the words: *transmitter, receiver, plate*. But what was a *QSS*? What about *QRH*? What was the meaning of *Hw abt a card om*?

There were dozens—maybe a hundred—of these cards, each a bit different in design, and as I picked them up, I saw the places they'd come from: Chattanooga and Memphis, yes, but also Skillman, New Jersey; Carlisle, Massachusetts; Hastings-on-Hudson, New York. He had made contacts, if not friends, with dozens of strangers who'd been connected not in any real place but in crackling, magical air. For the most part, there were no names on these cards, no news of families or work or weather—unless weather had interfered with reception. The men who'd sent them were no more real than the players on baseball cards, but these cards were written proof of a life George had led without me. This, not our marriage or the law or the church, is what had given him pleasure, or at least comfort. I stacked them up neatly and tied them with a string, but I wished that I could burn the whole lot.

At seven o'clock that evening, George came home carrying papers and books bundled tight by a leather strap. He took me by both hands and then twirled me, singing, "Yes, we need no more lawyers. We got Clarence Darrow today!" He spun me into a backwards hug, his arms reaching around my waist. Even as the phone rang and he picked up the receiver, he nuzzled the back of my neck and pulled me to him. I giggled. This was doubly delightful because it was clear that whoever he was talking to was someone he'd actually seen that day, not spoken to in code, however many hundreds of miles away. "I know," he was saying. "I thought if Rapp drank one more Coca-Cola, we'd have seen him sprout wings and fly right out of Robinson's."

Now I turned to stand up against George and rest my head on his shoulder. His answers grew shorter and his hold on me more intimate. "Yes," he said. "Surely." "I can do that." "No." "Ten o'clock?" "I'll be there."

He hung up and took me upstairs and kissed me so deeply that I remembered how a kiss could draw together bodies, sensations, emotions, and thoughts all at once. A great kiss was like a magnet, like that giant red-and-black horseshoe-shaped thing that I remembered from seventh-grade science, when Mrs. Fox had swept it all over the classroom, picking up tacks and needles and eraser tops. In this magnet kiss, in addition to desire, was my conviction that George had truly come back.

4

The next morning felt as fresh as the night before. I took a long shower, using up more hot water than I usually did, but embracing my sense that all things could be renewed. Usually, I washed my hair with the shampoo I made from boiled soap flakes. But last Christmas, Caroline had given me a bottle of Glorilox, and this morning I indulged myself by using it, lathering my hair so richly that I could almost sculpt it. Then, in a fresh gingham shirtdress, my shiny hair twisted into a tight bun, I was ready to face the spare room again.

With the door to that room opened, the morning light on the landing was rich. Stepping in, I was delighted to find that George must have come in while I was asleep. At least half his table was cleared now, the strawberry crates turned right-side up and filled with the least identifiable and, I assumed, most delicate objects. I got back to work on the piles of things I'd left the day before. Spitfire had just jumped up on a crate and seemed ready for a nap when I heard the front door open and the ponyish steps of a child on the stairs. I ducked out to the landing to find Caleb, Mercy's second-oldest boy, just clearing the top steps.

"What's wrong?" I asked.

Caleb placed his fists on his hips, exactly the way his mother often did, but he was so skinny that his hands slid right down his sides.

"Caleb, tell me," I said.

He tried again with his fists.

"Mama says you gotta come right away."

"Right away?" I asked. "Is Mama all right?"

"She just says I gotta bring you."

Worried, I followed him down the stairs and out to the front yard. Mercy was standing, austere and unmoving, on her side of the fence. The morning sun was dappling her face through the maple leaves, but there was nothing soft about her expression. She reached into the deep front pocket of her apron and withdrew a newspaper, already smudged from use.

I knew what it was going to say before Mercy uttered a word. I had been dreading it. The story in the *Chattanooga News* listed the names of all the lawyers on both sides.

Mercy was merciless.

"How could he? How could you let him?"

"Let him? Since when has George been under my control?"

"A wife has the power," Mercy said.

What about 'Wives submit yourselves'?" I asked.

"To a Christian," she said. "Not to a heathen."

"Mercy, George is not a heathen."

"An unbeliever. An infidel."

She was giving voice to my worst fears about what would happen if George went up against Bryan: not only that George would be trying to undermine the great man, but also that the town would never forgive him for it. Mercy didn't see it in the logical way that George had explained it to me. She hadn't been reminded, or informed, about the First Amendment and the way it was meant to keep the government from establishing a national religion. Nor had she been swept up in a magnet kiss and what followed it. She didn't love George. She didn't want and need to keep loving him.

"He's just starting to come back to himself," I said.

Mercy would not be mollified.

"Does he not believe in God? Is this why I haven't seen him at church? Are you married to an atheist? Don't you worry about his soul?"

"Of course I do."

"He won't be admitted to heaven," she said. She looked fearful and injured. "Don't you pray for him?" she whispered.

"Of course I do," I said again, which was true. But if I'd been really honest, I'd have admitted that I'd prayed more often for him to return to me than to God.

Mercy gestured to her kids in the yard.

"Do you want my Puppies going to school to learn that God didn't create Adam? Do you want them growing up without God?"

I did not want Mercy's children growing up without God. No one and nothing but God could have sustained me after my parents' deaths, the bleak years at the boardinghouse, the losses of Eva, the baby, and, for much of the last year, George. But I did not think God would desert Mercy's children—even if my husband helped make it possible for them to learn about evolution.

I decided to visit the major. It had been at least a month since I'd seen him, but today the visit would be as much for me as for him. It was one thing to be scolded by Mercy for what George planned to do. I had known her only a few years. But the major was a link to the past—in a way, even to my parents, because he had known them in our church. Despite myself, I think I was hoping that he would see George in a kinder way than Mercy did.

It had rained heavily all morning, and it was still drizzling when I arrived. I wiped my boots on an already muddy doormat, kicked the door in the right spot, and stepped inside. The major was sitting in his usual place, in a peeling red kitchen chair at a sloping, pock-marked table. He was eighty-eight years old now. His face was so deeply creased and wrinkled that his features seemed to be sinking. But he stood up as he always had, his arms spread wide so I could squeeze his hands.

"Harder," he said today after I'd done my part. "Are you getting weaker? You surely can't think I am."

I smiled and squeezed again.

"You hear that W. J. Bryan is coming to this very town?" he asked.

"That's what they're saying," I said. "Might even stay at the Aqua."

"I sure would like to shake that man's hand."

"I think everybody would," I said.

"Voted for him three times," the major said. "Saw him twice, too, at camp meetings. Hard to believe he was never president. But no telling. Maybe he did more good this way."

"I've only ever heard him on the radio," I said. "But his voice does cast a spell."

It wasn't close to sunset, but rain and clouds were darkening the sky. I switched on the overhead light, but it barely threw a shadow. The major settled back in his red chair. Soon Ruth, his son's widow, would be coming to bring him his supper.

"I've known you since you were a girl, Annabel. What's wrong? Your eyes are looking stormy. Better sit down," he said, and I did.

"You sick?" he asked me.

"No."

"George sick?"

"No."

"You want something to eat?" he asked me. "Mrs. Krendall, she brought me a cobbler. It's in the icebox."

I shook my head no.

I had heard that Catholics were encouraged to confess their sins to priests, who could grant them forgiveness. The major wasn't a priest, and I hadn't exactly sinned, but I wanted to know what he thought about George's deeds and my doubts. So I told him how

Mercy had said taking John's side would keep George out of heaven. I told him about how happy I was to think that George was climbing through the gray fog he'd been in, but how I'd hoped that when he came out of it, it would be into God's light, not a different kind of darkness.

Before I could ask what the major thought, he was shaking his head emphatically.

"No," he said. "No, no, no!"

He placed his knuckles on the table, shakily bracing himself as he stood up. Then he walked out of the room.

"Are you all right?"

"Hold your horses, I say."

He had gone into his parlor to get something from the cabinet where he kept his war mementos. After a minute, he returned, placing a hinged double picture frame on the table. He was wheezing slightly, and he coughed. I looked at him expectantly, and he opened the frame like a butterfly's wings. Two photographs, ancient and dark, looked out at me from beneath slightly curved ovals of glass. Two seemingly identical young men in uniform.

"Which one is you?" I asked softly.

He pointed a skinny, shaking finger at the image on the left, the young soldier in the lighter uniform, a bold look on his unscarred face.

"I didn't know you had a twin," I said. "Did he get—"

"Killed in the war?" the major said. "No. We both lived. Me barely." He grinned a little, lightly touching the scar on his face. Then he closed the frame. "But Duncan, he fought for the Yankees. Then he went his way. Lost his way, more like. Moved up to New Jersey."

"You say *New Jersey* like you're saying *Sodom*."

"Not much difference, as I hear tell."

"Oh, Major—"

"You listen," he said. "You don't know a thing. When I was a youth, men and women wore homespun cotton clothes that were long enough to hide our knees, and the men didn't wear paper collars, and the boys didn't sport red ties, and the women didn't paint their cheeks. Everyone knew their place. And people were decent. Parents would walk five miles so their children could hear a preacher."

He was talking so fast now—was so upset—that I knew I couldn't argue with any part of what he was saying.

"There's more money spent on one schoolhouse now than on all the schools fifty years ago, but the new learning's not doing anyone any good. You throw this evolution into those classrooms, you can kiss the Good Lord goodbye. The boys are close enough to being monkeys now anyway."

"But, Major—" I began, though I wasn't sure if there was anything I could say.

"No, you listen to me, child," he said. I'd never seen him so fierce.

"Why are you so stubborn?" I asked.

"Why do you think? So's I can stay alive."

"But—"

"You let your husband take to combat with what Mr. Bryan says, and don't you plan on coming to my door again."

"But—"

"Not ever, I say. I'd tell you don't even talk to me in church, but maybe you won't be coming there anymore."

"That's not true," I said. "That'll never be true."

"I didn't fight in that war just to see what I hold dear be swept away."

I was heartbroken. I could feel my nose turning red, my throat starting to burn. He would not let me meet his eye, and so, after what felt like a long battle of silence, I left.

I managed not to cry until I was two blocks away, and then I walked over to sit on the steps of the high school, abandoned as I now felt.

What had the major fought for anyway? "The South" was all he had ever said, as if the South was one pure splendid idea. I'm not sure if that's what I thought it was in the summer of 1925. The

South was a place that grew perfect strawberries and green tomatoes and white pumpkins and fat dogwood trees. It grew glorious
church choirs and generous neighbors and grace. But the South I
think of now was also a place where people strained for salvation,
and lost things they loved, deplored Catholics and Jews, and got
hanged for having dark skin. The South grew bullies who would
use anything at hand—threats of damnation, mocking songs, blue
blazes of brimstone—to build a wall against the future because of
what it might destroy.

I tried to remember biology class. What had Mr. Cavendish told
us about evolution? Had he told us that God didn't make man?
Wouldn't that have bothered me? I remembered him talking about
cells and plants. I remembered something about an experiment
with peas. Biology class was the year my parents died. I barely remembered that year at all.

I stayed on the school steps until I was fairly sure no one would
be able to tell I'd been crying, and then I walked back in the direction of home. On Market Street, I joined a small group of people
who had stopped to listen to a young, bearded singer who was
playing a guitar next to a boy with a fiddle. The singer's name was
Carlos McAfee. The song he was singing would sell eighty thousand records before the year was out.

> *Then to Dayton came a man*
> *With his new ideas so grand*
> *And he said, "We came from monkeys long ago."*

> *But in teaching his belief*
> *Mr. Scopes found only grief*
> *For they would not let their old religion go.*

> *You may find a new belief*
> *It will only bring you grief*
> *For a house that's built on sand is sure to fall.*

And wherever you may turn
There's a lesson you will learn—
That the old religion's better after all.

If the major had heard the song, he would have sung along, and if I'd heard it even a month before, I would have sung it too. Instead, I just listened and then made my way home.

5

The third week of May, Flip Guffey from the Committee on Reservations called to tell us that the person we'd be putting up was a reporter from the *Chattanooga News*. I was wary, but George seemed delighted. Perhaps the coming of the press was reminding him how much he'd once enjoyed his own prominence. Perhaps he hoped not only to regain it but to surpass it.

"A reporter," he said. "That should be interesting."

"You think he'll want to interview you?" I asked, and George just shrugged and looked down, but I could tell he was quietly pleased at the thought.

The reporter called the very next day, and it turned out that he was a she. Her name was Lottie Nelson, and she told me that, even if she could get a hotel room once the trial started, she'd rather stay with regular folks than with gawkers from out of town.

"I like to get a real sense of a place," she said. "Are you and Mr. Craig truly willing? I surely don't want to put you out."

Her voice was soft, even gentle, the voice of a demure Southern lady, the kind of reporter who would usually want to know only things like who was visiting whom, where they had come from, and what kinds of cake had been served with the tea. Soon I would learn that Lottie was no society columnist. Maybe it was people's assumptions about what a lady reporter usually did that had spurred her, repeatedly, to pursue other sorts of stories. She had once snuck onto a train to get a personal interview with President Harding. Just the year before, in Knoxville, she had talked Babe Ruth into letting her take batting practice with his barnstorming team. Plenty of male reporters wouldn't have had the gumption to do that.

When it came to John Scopes's trial, she was the first reporter—man or woman—to ask for and be granted a press pass. That slip of paper would guarantee her a reserved seat in what would come to be a mercilessly overcrowded courtroom. For now, though, she was on the telephone, speaking in her gentle, unassuming voice, and we agreed that she could come a few weeks before the trial began and stay till it was over, however long that would be.

In the days that followed, I managed to get the rest of George's things in the extra bedroom cleared out, and then I scrubbed the floor, the tops of the baseboards, and the windowsills. I washed the curtains, too, lingering in the backyard after I'd hung them on the line, hoping to smooth things with Mercy, frustrated that she was nowhere in sight.

In town, I bought two new pillows, a fresh set of hand towels, and a yellow-and-blue checked tablecloth for covering George's workbench. From the closet, I retrieved the lovely pink lamp that Reverend Dowling had given me so long ago, and I placed it back on the mantel. I put rose petals in the dresser drawers and spread a fresh lace cloth across the top. I had not forgotten the beauty and elegance of the Chattanooga hotel room where George and I had spent our honeymoon, and though I knew I couldn't come close to re-creating its opulence, I could at least attempt the sparkle and charm of the Aqua.

George seemed briefly disappointed to learn that the Chattanooga paper wasn't sending a man; he worried that meant they weren't taking the trial seriously. But his work at the law office and at our kitchen table overwhelmed his doubts. He was heady with the assignment he'd drawn from Professor Neal—namely to find as many scientific experts as he could who would be willing to come to Dayton to testify about evolution. Whenever he came back from the office, he was carrying letters—actual letters, not ham radio cards—from universities all over the country.

Meanwhile, Dayton was growing loonier by the day. There was no subtlety at all in the way the older folks were shaming any residents who hadn't already deadheaded their peonies, repainted their fences, washed their front windows, or otherwise acknowledged that the biggest event of their lives was about to take place. Tensions and voices rose around town. And then came the morning of May 20.

Main and Market Streets weren't yet the crazy quilt that they would become. Still, there was more than the usual noise, more than the usual number of people, and as George and I got there—he on his way to the office, I on my way to the Aqua—we saw Billy Kingsman slam out of the barbershop, lather still clinging ridiculously to his chin. Not ten seconds later, Dennis Marsh followed, waving a pistol and shouting, "I ain't no goddamn monkey!"

You could be arrested in Dayton for public profanity alone. But that was the least of it. Standing directly between two halted horse-drawn wagons, Dennis fired one shot clear across the street, causing both horses to buck. Billy turned with his own pistol drawn, fired back, hitting nothing, and then dodged out of sight. Dennis seemed to catch his breath, look around to see who was watching him, and then went loping after Billy.

The rest of the action on the street froze.

"What was that?" George said.

"Doesn't make any sense," I told him. "They've been friends since grade school. Billy was best man at Dennis's wedding."

With one exception, the reporters who soon wrote in colorful detail about the fight they had heard about second- or third-hand didn't think to ask if or for how long the two men had known each other. Instead, they all wrote about how pretrial tensions were climbing in Dayton, and they repeated and embellished the "inside story" of how Billy and Dennis had been sitting side by side in the shop's two barber chairs when Billy said he reckoned Dennis's arms could use a good shave, too, lest people confuse him with a monkey.

"Enraged by Mr. Kingsman's casual jibe," one reporter wrote, "Mr. Marsh shouted an epithet and ran after Mr. Kingsman, shooting a pistol and narrowly missing his sworn enemy."

The only reporter who guessed that the whole scene was a stunt was Lottie Nelson—and she wasn't even in Dayton yet.

"Mr. Marsh," she wrote after calling around from Chattanooga, "was shooting a gun loaded only with blanks."

I would soon learn that Lottie Nelson had many talents, but perhaps her greatest was her ability, even her need, to scratch like a foxhound at whatever the prevailing wisdom was.

Her article pointed out that there had been rumors that leaders in Chattanooga were planning to put up their own test case, claiming with some logic that the city was better equipped than Dayton to handle the thousands of visitors an evolution trial was bound to attract. The incident in Dayton, Lottie wrote, had followed a town meeting in which some residents speculated that action might be needed in order to cement Dayton as the inevitable location for the trial.

"From the very start, the meeting seethed with passion and outrage," Lottie wrote, "and afterwards, some of the original drugstore conspirators contrived a publicity stunt by which two old friends enacted an argument starting in a barbershop—with the men in a literal lather of shaving cream—and ending with the firing of blank bullets."

But the scheme, as silly as it had been, was successful: A special grand jury was quickly convened a few days after the barbershop incident, John was officially indicted, and the trial was scheduled to start on July 10. The frenzy intensified. Lottie Nelson called to fix a date for her arrival. Fred Whittle decided that the Aqua's façade needed a fresh coat of paint, and though I tried to talk him into using white, or perhaps a pale shade of aqua, he insisted that only a screaming shade of bright yellow would be sufficiently vibrant to match the occasion.

For George's part, anticipating Clarence Darrow was all-consuming. Darrow. *Darrah*. George talked about him constantly, quoting from past trial summations and newspaper articles, making sure I understood just how many unlikely courtroom victories the great man had won. Talking about Darrow, George reminded me of Reverend Byrd speaking about the Holy Spirit, whose many gifts might include special knowledge and wisdom. Whatever else George did or did not believe, he appeared to worship Darrow with faith abiding.

On the morning of June 6, it wasn't George's faith but his hopes that were shaken. I woke to the sound of him in the parlor, slamming down the phone and cursing. By the time I had washed up, thrown on a frock, and run downstairs, he was sitting awkwardly on the sofa, and when he looked up, I could see that his eyes were glassy.

"George? What's wrong?"

He put his head in his hands.

Spitfire, who I guessed must have been startled by the sudden noise, had taken refuge under a chair.

"He's gone," George said. "John's gone, and Professor Neal with him."

"What are you talking about? Gone where?"

"Gone to New York City," he said.

"Why?"

"The ACLU. They're not sure that they want Darrow after all."

"I thought it was the ACLU that started the case," I said. "I thought Darrow had volunteered."

"They did. And he did. But I just hung up with Rapp. He said

John and Professor Neal left yesterday afternoon, that a whole
bunch of lawyers in New York are meeting to talk over strategy."

"But Darrow's such a big cheese," I said.

"They're thinking maybe too big," George said miserably.
"Everyone thinks he's this famous atheist. Actually, he's agnostic.
Doesn't believe one way or another. But they think that's splitting
hairs for a Dayton jury."

"An agnostic in Dayton," I said with a grin.

"This isn't funny, Annie. It's a catastrophe."

"Well," I said, searching around for some source of comfort, "if
they don't want him, won't that mean you'll get more to do?"

He shook his head impatiently, almost violently.

"That's not the point," he said brusquely. "The point is, if it
isn't Clarence Darrow, I don't get to work with Clarence Darrow."

He put his head back in his hands.

"Isn't the point to keep the government out of religion and religion out of the classrooms?" I asked.

He didn't answer, and I was out of pertinent questions. "Do you
want me to make you some coffee?" I asked instead.

I touched him lightly on the shoulder.

"Annie," he said softly. "I don't know what to do."

I was startled, almost worried, by this change of tone. I took a
breath, then sighed, and as gently as I could, I said, "It's never
wrong to pray."

"Pray to God to send me an agnostic?" he asked with a faint
smile.

"George," I said. "Pray for guidance."

It had been months since George had come to church, but the
next morning, he was dressed and ready before I was.

"Are you working today?" I asked him.

"Church," he said, as if I'd forgotten that it was Sunday.

Sitting beside him on the worn wood pew, I felt sure that if
George was praying, it wasn't for the chance of guidance but for
the chance of glory. And despite everything that the coming trial
had already done to revive my husband, I no longer knew if it

would do the same for our marriage. I wanted the George I had married, and I wasn't sure if he was coming back.

The past—the recent past of George and his ham radio and his year of absence—pulled at me, the way the water at the pond could tug at my toes. For the next few days, all sorts of news came from New York. Darrow was out. Darrow was in. The ACLU lawyers didn't want a contest between the Bible and evolution, or the "Duel to the Death" that some people were calling a would-be meeting of Bryan and Darrow. What the ACLU wanted was a test case that would allow them to defend not evolution but the First Amendment–given right to teach it.

But finally, on Tuesday afternoon, George learned that God, or at least the ACLU, would be sending Darrow to represent John after all. Additionally, Darrow would be joined in the effort by a man named Dudley Field Malone. Malone, though considerably less famous than Darrow, was nearly as unlikely a fit for our town, Lottie told me on the phone. Not only was he an international divorce lawyer, but he was himself twice divorced and, worse, a lapsed Catholic. If he'd spent any time in a small Southern town, it had to have been because he'd gotten lost on his way to somewhere else. But whatever concerns the ACLU or anyone else had, in the end it was up to John Scopes himself to choose who would lead his own defense, and he wanted John Neal, Clarence Darrow, and Dudley Field Malone. Where that left George wasn't yet clear, but when I passed him on Elm Street that afternoon, he seemed elated. His hero was coming after all.

6

Lottie Nelson arrived at our house on June 25, a month after John's indictment and, as promised, two weeks before the trial was to begin. George opened the door for her eagerly. She stood there for a moment, a small mustard-colored straw suitcase in one hand and a large black typewriter case in the other. Her face, like her voice, was soft and sweet, but the rest of her body was all sharp angles and restless determination. She was a skinny brunette with shiny hair, fully bobbed, just like the city women I'd seen in so many magazines. She had perfectly even lips and a nearly flat chest. She was wearing a peach-colored skirt and a matching short jacket, almost like a man's jacket, and she took a step into the house a few seconds before George invited her in.

"So nice of you to have me," she said.

We introduced ourselves. I asked if she wanted something to eat or drink, and George asked if he could carry her things upstairs.

"I'm fine," she said to both of us. "But I'd like to wash up from the trip, if you don't mind."

I took the stairs first, followed by Lottie and then George. Even though she didn't say a word, I could already sense her curiosity, and I was suddenly conscious of every picture on the wall, every scuff mark on the stairs. In the bedroom, I saw on her face what I'd felt on the stairs. She seemed positively rabid for information, and as politely as she could, she was surveying the room, seeking out details. I hadn't noticed at first how small and dark her eyes were. Inside that soft, round face, they were like two tiny camera lenses, and I got the sense that they would capture every single thing they saw.

She hoisted her typewriter case onto George's workbench and her suitcase onto the foot of the bed. The first things she withdrew from it were a stack of blank paper and a bunch of pencils of all colors and lengths, oddly tied by a ribbon, like a bouquet.

"Would you like me to bring you a vase for those?" I asked.

She laughed. "They're my souvenirs," she said. "It's childish, I know, but I always try to take a pencil from every place I visit."

"That's lovely," I said.

"I'll tell you what's lovely," she said. "This room is lovely."

I probably blushed a little. I was so pleased.

"The dresser's empty and clean," I said. "You can put your things right in there."

"Oh, dear," she said. "That means there must be some crowded drawers somewhere else, doesn't it?"

George, by now impatient with the pleasantries, said, "I'll leave you ladies to it," and hustled down the stairs.

"Jumpy," Lottie said, smiling, with a nod in his direction.

"He just wants to get back to work," I said. "You know, he's on the defense team."

I was expecting her to be impressed, or at least intrigued, but she nodded. "I know," she said. Then she looked around. "This room must have belonged to someone else."

In retrospect, that wasn't such a remarkable guess, but in that moment it seemed to suggest that she had unusual insight.

"Well, my husband's been using it as a ham radio shack," I said. "But otherwise?"

"It almost belonged to someone else," I said.

There was just a second or two while she took this in. "I don't have children either," she said.

That was just a taste of the way Lottie could gather up a person's secrets by casually trading away her own.

I left her to unpack the rest of her things and went downstairs to pour some of the sweet tea I'd been chilling since morning.

When she walked into the kitchen just ten minutes later, she was holding what looked like a brand-new composition book. A maroon fountain pen with a gold-colored clip was fixed to its side. It didn't take me long to figure out that Lottie would sooner go somewhere without shoes than without this notebook.

George and I were sitting at the table, but Lottie remained standing as she drank her tea in just a few gulps. "Delicious," she said, putting the glass down firmly. "Ready?" she asked me.

"Ready for what?" George said.

"Annabel's going to show me around," Lottie said.

"I am?"

"If you don't mind," she added.

"Well—" I began, looking at George.

"You want to do this?" he asked me.

I nodded.

"Well, make sure you're back before dark," he said.

Lottie's eyes flashed from mine to George's and back.

"What happens after dark?" she asked.

"After dark, women don't walk around here unescorted," George said.

Lottie chuckled. Her lips closed in a smile that seemed to be holding in a larger laugh. I smiled too. In the depths of his radio days, George had never noticed how often I'd actually been out after dark—sometimes to Caroline's house, sometimes to Mercy's, once or twice to a picture show—anything to get away from the relentless scratching and chattering of his rig.

Outside, Lottie asked, "Do you usually need his permission to stay out after dark?"

I laughed. "Have you spent much time in a small town?"

She smiled but then stood still for a moment, apparently trying to figure out which way to walk. She tilted her face upward, like a dog searching for a scent.

"This way," I said and steered her toward the Aqua.

The minute we stepped inside, she pulled the maroon fountain pen from her notebook with a little click, scribbled DAYTON on the cover, and folded it back. I was just about to introduce her to Fred Whittle when she tapped my elbow gently, her eyes already fixed on a trio of workmen.

"Do you know them?" she whispered.

I didn't.

"'Scuse me a second," she said and promptly ditched me.

I started to follow her, but Fred pulled at my arm.

"What is it?" I asked, impatient. I was trying to keep my eye on Lottie.

Before Fred could answer me, George and Ova Rappleyea came rushing in from Main Street, Rapp looking every bit as frantic as usual. As far as I could tell, he had remained in a state of high excitement ever since he'd first talked John into being the defendant. His wife, Ova, known as Precious, was a Dayton girl, and she had the exact opposite demeanor. Precious had been a nurse before marrying Rapp, and the story was that they'd met in a hospital after he'd been bitten by a snake. These days, they made a formidable couple. He had big, dramatic ideas, and she was patient and efficient.

"We need your help," Precious told me, standing with Rapp and Fred in Reception.

"I think I'm leased out to Fred," I said.

"You're still leased out to me," he said, "but I'm subleasing you to Precious."

Even before the trial date was set, the Rapps had been restoring the Mansion, a huge Victorian house about five miles from the Aqua that had been empty for years and that people swore was haunted. In its day—a day in the nineteenth century—it had been known as one of the largest and most gracious houses in all East Tennessee, but now its faded yellow paint and peeling brown trim made it look like a very large, very rusted tin toy.

Nevertheless, the Rapps had decided it would be the perfect place to shelter the visiting members of the defense team and whatever witnesses they were planning to call. To make the Mansion a place where anyone—especially anyone coming from out of town—could be comfortable was an ambitious task, and to do it in such a limited slip of time seemed almost ridiculous. But Precious had a plan, and she wanted to show me how it was progressing and to see how I could pitch in.

I looked over to the lounge area to explain all this to Lottie, but I saw that she was now deep in conversation with one of the three workmen. She was sitting across from him in the same chair where I'd settled a much more tentative Professor Neal when he'd first come to Dayton—and she was leaning forward intently, her back a straight diagonal, her notebook open on her lap. Other than the fact that she had apparently made herself perfectly at ease without any help from me, I was struck by the way she seemed able to take notes without looking down at what she was writing. Rather, she kept her keen eyes fixed on the man's face. I asked Precious to wait a minute.

"It looks like I'm needed a little ways out of town," I told Lottie. "You can come with me, and you'll get a sense of the place."

"I'm getting a pretty good sense of the place right now, from this gentleman," she said, and she introduced me to the man who, it turned out, had come all the way down from Bell County to do maintenance work on the Aqua's boiler.

I felt responsible for Lottie and, at the same time, maybe a little annoyed by how quickly she'd made herself comfortable.

"You want to stay here alone?" I asked her, slightly baffled.

"Would George not approve?" she asked with a wink. "Let's just meet here later," she said.

"I shouldn't be longer than an hour," I said.

She nodded and turned back to the man.

"So. What are they saying up in Kentucky about all this fuss?" she was asking as Precious and I walked out the door.

When Precious and I got to the Mansion, we found two painters on each side of the house and at least three men up on the roof. The old gravel driveway was packed with cars and trucks, many of them still loaded, while the front porch, drooping like an old apron, was covered with chairs, lamps, kitchen appliances, and unopened crates.

Inside, even the old music and billiards rooms had been fitted out with beds, and I found Caroline gathering crisply pressed curtains onto shiny curtain rods. Her new baby—a now-nine-month-old son—was fixed to her hip with the sling she'd used for Charlie; when she saw me, she gave me the awkward, sorry look she always offered when she had the baby with her. It didn't bother me today; I was already so intrigued by Lottie that all I wanted was to get back to her.

"So, Precious snagged you too," Caroline said.

Precious was two steps behind me.

"Precious did," Precious said, but for now we just toured the many rooms, making lists of what was needed. Then, much to my relief, we rode back to town so I could fetch Lottie and be home in time to make supper. At the Aqua, though, an unflappable Lottie insisted on a quick walk down Market Street before we headed home. I'd never thought of myself as someone who moved slowly, but then I'd never had the experience of trying to keep up with Lottie Nelson. Lottie had long, skinny legs that weren't much wider than my arms. For some reason, they didn't bend much, so it always looked as if she was walking on stilts. And boy, did she cover ground.

I was relieved that George wasn't home yet. Lottie followed me into the kitchen. I was expecting her to offer to peel vegetables or help me chop, but instead, she sat at the table, crossed those long legs, took her hat off, and opened her notebook.

"You're not going to write things about me, are you?" I asked.

She chuckled. "No, not yet."

"Not yet!"

"Oh, don't you worry," she said. "I just want to ask you where I can find a bunch of these folks."

She had a list. In no time, she'd figured out that she wanted to meet Reverend Byrd, Doc Robinson, and of course John Scopes. She wanted to see the Mansion, the drugstore, the schoolhouse, and the courthouse. She wanted to meet the judge who would be trying the case before he'd be too busy. And she wanted to go to our church this Sunday, and to as many of the other ten churches in town as she could.

"What do you do when you're not being his wife?" Lottie asked me. We were sitting at the shore of Oak Tree Pond. It was a sultry Saturday, two days after her arrival. I'd promised her a glimpse of what young people did on weekends when they weren't at church, but there was almost no one at the pond today. Even the young people had gotten tied up in making preparations, it seemed.

"I'm always his wife," I told Lottie.

We had taken off our shoes and white stockings, and we were sitting side by side in the grass, just as I had with that gap-toothed farm girl on the day of the Tomato War—a day when I'd still been a farm girl too.

"Well, I know you're his wife," she said. "But I heard from Caroline Quinn that you take pictures too. Is that right? You're a photographer?"

I noticed that the skin around her ankles was almost translucent, her veins so clear that it looked as if she had been standing in a bucket of blueberries.

"How did you meet Caroline Quinn?" I asked.

Lottie smiled. "I'm not sure you've really figured out what I do yet," she said.

"No, I know. You snoop," I said.

"I snoop and I write and then I snoop some more."

Three huge dragonflies danced around our heads; she ducked and I didn't, which gave me a modest sense of pride.

"Is Caroline right?" Lottie pressed on. "Are you a photographer?"

"What makes a person a photographer?" I asked. "I take pictures."

"What kind of camera do you have?"

"A Vest Pocket Kodak," I said proudly. "George gave it to me for Christmas."

"Does it hold a lot of film?"

"No," I said. "But you can fit it in your handbag."

"Or," she said, smiling, "I'm guessing, in your vest pocket."

"It's got a leather case," I said.

"Are you any good?"

I thought up the humble answers first: "I reckon," "I guess so," and "I don't know." But I was already under Lottie's spell.

"I'm really good," I said, trying on her confidence as if I were trying on her hat.

She looked delighted.

"I know the *News* is sending the usual cartoonist," she said, "but maybe they'll be able to print some photographs too."

It was rare in those days to see anything but portrait photographs in a newspaper. Drawings and cartoons were usually used to describe big events.

"Has any other paper hired you yet?" she asked.

I managed to hold back my laugh. I had, naturally, planned to take as many pictures as I could. I especially wanted to photograph Mr. Bryan. I imagined keeping one picture for myself, but if I could take only one, then I would bring it to the major, whose forgiveness I continued to crave. But the thought that a newspaper would actually pay me to take photographs was completely exotic.

"No" was all I said. "Not yet."

"Well, then, I'm going to hire you," she said, and next, as if it was part of the same thought: "Let's swim."

She stood up suddenly. Barefoot and barelegged in the grass, she looked even more like a girl than she had when she'd first stretched out beside me. In the two o'clock sunlight, as she stood directly in front of me, I noticed a scar on the outside of her right shin, or rather a spoon-shaped cluster of scars, some pink, some purple, one almost silver—around what looked like a deep gouge.

"What happened there?" I asked her.

"Where? Oh! Hah! Most people don't see my legs bare. Come to think of it, I'm not sure I can remember the last time."

"It looks like a bite."

"Yup. A possum," she said. "You'd think after a dozen years it would have faded more than this."

"Where were you and that possum a dozen years ago?" I asked.

"At college. I was trying out for the school newspaper, and I was showing off. I spent the night in some woods that were supposed to be haunted, and I stepped on the poor thing."

"You went to college?" I asked.

"Sweet Briar," Lottie said proudly.

A couple of girls I'd gone to high school with had gone to college, but they'd both gotten married, and neither had come back.

"Let's swim," Lottie said again.

"In what?" I asked.

"In the pond, of course."

She had her hands on her slim hips, and she surveyed the water as if even it could reveal something meaningful or memorable about Dayton.

"I mean, *wearing* what?"

She shrugged. "No one'll see if we go in quick."

She was, even as she said this, unbuttoning her beige linen skirt and white cotton blouse to reveal a full slip. A boy on the other side of the pond shouted to a friend, but Lottie plunged in before his friend could get a look too.

While the boys' voices carried across the lake, Lottie floated on her back, her slip catching a pocket of air and billowing up around her.

"Come on in!" she said to me. "What are you waiting for?"

I wasn't going to bother to tell her what Mercy or George or even my own conscience would think of me peeling off my clothes in broad daylight. I didn't need to.

"I don't know how to swim," I said, and she made me swear, on an invisible stack of Bibles, that I was telling the truth.

As she emerged from the pond, her slip clinging to her flat frame, she quickly covered her top with her blouse but left the bottom part of the slip to dry in the sun.

"How could you never have learned to swim?" she asked, settling beside me again. "Aren't you a country girl?"

"I almost drowned right here in this pond when I was a little girl."

"We're going to have to do something about teaching you to swim," she said, pulling up her stockings, which darkened in the places where her legs were still wet.

"Actually," I answered, "we're not."

"You scared?" she asked me—a taunt, a dare.

"Yes, I am," I said.

"Why?" she asked.

"Do people need a reason to be scared?" I asked.

"Usually," she said. "In my experience."

She put on her shoes, tying the laces tight.

"What scares you?" I asked her.

She smoothed down her hair and picked up her bag. "Missing the story," she said.

7

The story could not and would not be missed. People started writing and talking about "The Monkey Trial." Implied in those three words was not just the question of man's origins but also the idea that the citizens of Dayton, Tennessee, were making fools of ourselves. However, with dizzying speed—either deciding to ignore the insult or not understanding that it was one—the people of my town came up with ways to cash in on it. After all, making money had always been the plan.

MONKEY BUSINESS IN FULL SWING
Dayton Plans to Cash In on Evolution Trial
BY LOTTIE NELSON

Dayton, TN (Special) Whatever else has been or will be written about this small East Tennessee town, no one can argue with the sheer breadth of its audacious entrepreneurial spirit. Monkeys are the source of endless inspiration. At John Morgan's Furniture Store, furry monkey dolls are lined up for sale and have already proven popular with the town's young girls, who fling the toys' long soft tails around their necks like feather boas. "Simian Sodas" can be sipped at

Robinson's Drugstore. Malcolm Murray, president of the Dayton Bank and Trust, found a souvenir shop way up north that was willing to manufacture medallions and watch fobs with the profile of a monkey's face where a president's should be. In the high school lunchroom, a group of diligent local women have been gathering daily to paint watercolor postcards of monkeys and gorillas—also for sale at Robinson's, along with pins saying, "Your old man's a monkey." Jim Darwin (no relation, it turns out, to the Darwin whose *Origin of Species* is in certain respects to blame for the whole evolution controversy) decided to take full advantage of his name, hanging an eye-catching sign above his dry goods store that says, "Darwin is Right" and then, beneath a finger pointing to the storefront, "Inside."

Sincere though he remains in his desire to see the Tennessee statute against teaching evolution upheld, Vernon Wentworth, 63, has all but given up hope that the trial will cast Dayton in a positive light. "Jesus said, 'Ye cannot serve God and Mammon.'" But for the most part, Daytonians seem perfectly capable of serving both.

A week before the trial's opening day, town ordinances sealed off Main and Market Streets from automobiles and horses. A patch of flat ground four miles from town was cleared as an airplane landing strip. A platform was built outside the courthouse, a makeshift plywood promise of the speeches that were to come. More than two hundred reporters prowled. Some had crossed the country. A few had crossed the ocean. I now understood why Lottie had wanted to get a jump on all of them. While they were just getting their bearings, she had already had long conversations with John and Rapp and Robinson. She'd even met the judge and gotten cozy enough with him to suggest he have the courtroom repainted, and then she had written about that, too:

DAYTON IS SET FOR TRIAL
Town Prepares to Host Thousands
BY LOTTIE NELSON

Dayton, TN (Special) Judge John T. Raulston will call the circuit court to order at 9 a.m. Friday morning for the start of what is expected to be one of the most important trials in United States history. And in this usually quiet mountain town, no detail has been too small to address in preparation for the anticipated onslaught of visitors.

Daytonians have talked about little else for the last two months. Generosity, and perhaps a bit of opportunism, are running so high that residents are offering up their parlors and extra bedrooms to visitors, this reporter included. Meanwhile, food stands are popping up within shouting distance of the Rhea County Courthouse, while tourist camps, an airplane landing strip, and emergency medical services are also being made available.

The interior of the courthouse has undergone its own transformation, thanks to the initiative of Judge Raulston and several prominent lawyers in town. The walls of the second-floor courtroom, where the trial will be held with room for 700, have gotten a fresh coat of paint, a subtle cream color much more pleasing to the eye than the previous dirty gray. The judge has even been provided with a new, long-coveted chair for his stand.

The Dayton Hotel—smaller but bolder than the better-known Aqua—has put a stuffed gorilla in its lobby. Sam Wilkins of the Dayton police department made a sign saying "Monkeyville Police" and put it on the back of the P.D.'s own motorcycle. And outside the drugstore, lest the origin of the trial be as open for debate as the origin of man, Doc Robinson has nailed up a sign the width of both windows that says, "WHERE IT STARTED."

Events that in normal times would have filled whole weeks with anticipation now happened multiple times a day. Western Union and the telephone company strung miles of wires and cables. One of the Chicago newspapers sent three tall metal microphones from WGN to broadcast the news nationally, something that had never been attempted—not just in Dayton, but anywhere in the country. WGN stood for World's Greatest Newspaper, and everything seemed either a greatest or a first.

But early on the morning of July 2, I woke to discover George's side of the bed empty, and I had a sense of foreboding when I didn't see him in the kitchen, dining room, or parlor. It felt like a repeat of the morning he'd discovered that John and Professor Neal had gone to see the ACLU in New York. But so far as George's behavior went, it was worse.

I found him in the backyard. He was holding a copy of *QST*, his radio magazine, and he was walking carefully, heel to toe, using his feet as a ruler to measure the distance from one side of the yard to the other.

"George?"

"Shh."

I waited until he stopped moving.

"Forty-five feet," he said to himself and took a flat carpenter's pencil from behind his ear to write the number on the cover of the magazine.

Then he moved to the far end of the yard, preparing to pace out the distance to the front.

"What are you measuring for?" I asked.

"A radio tower," he said.

He turned to a page of the magazine and showed me a large advertisement. In bold black letters, it said:

Now You Can Build Your Own Tower!

Above the words was a drawing of a tall needle-shaped metal scaffolding, with wavy lines pointing to a house and a barn below. In the background of the drawing there were other small houses and a church steeple.

His damn radio, I heard myself think. Without warning, I felt the betrayal of a hundred distracted mealtimes, lonely afternoons, loveless nights.

"Why would you want to build a tower?" I asked him as calmly as I could.

He stared at me. "To get a stronger signal."

"Did Darrow drop out?" I asked.

George shook his head.

"Did John?"

"No."

He told me that one of the New York lawyers had asked a judge to move the case from Dayton to federal court.

"Now? Why?"

"Mainly," he began quietly, and then shouted the rest: "because he thinks we're damn hicks!"

I followed him into the house, and we sat in the parlor, the room where so many difficult things had happened. This was where I had waited sleeplessly for him to call or return after his flight from the shootings. It was where I had told him about my miscarriage and realized how much less it would mean to him than to me. But it was also the room where we'd welcomed neighbors and listened to the radio and where I'd first had the thrill of seeing him pacing and practicing a jury speech. *A lawyer.* What does your husband do? *My husband is a lawyer.*

I could hear Lottie upstairs, opening the door to the spare bedroom, then closing the one to the bathroom. I knew we didn't have much time to sort things out, and I didn't want her to see George so rattled.

"Tell me," I said gently.

George wasn't shouting now. "The lawyer's telling the judge that even if the Butler Act is a Tennessee law, it doesn't need to be tried in a Tennessee courtroom, because the question of whether it's constitutional is a federal question."

"And if the judge agrees—"

Lottie was at the top of the stairs now.

"If the judge agrees, then the jig is up," she said.

She arrived—full of mischief or guile—at the foot of the stairs. Naturally, she had her notepad at her side. At her hip, actually. It crossed my mind that she should have a holster for it.

A tense few days followed. It was the weekend of July 4, and normally that would have meant a parade down Market Street with the school band, and flags and bunting everywhere. But the decorations were already up for the trial, and nothing was going to compete with the READ YOUR BIBLE and REPENT, YE SINNERS signs, not even for an afternoon, and not even for Independence Day. Nobody seemed in the mood to celebrate anything anyway. The specter of Dayton being sidestepped for a federal court was making everyone miserable.

I brought Lottie with me to the Mansion, which none of the new reporters seemed yet to have discovered. The preparations were continuing furiously, and a few of the women looked sideways at Lottie. After all, she was carrying no bedding or food, no provisions of any kind. She had brought only her notebook and a pencil from Dayton's butcher shop that I assumed would one day be gathered into her bouquet of mementos. For now, she toured the Mansion's three floors, taking notes, while I helped Precious line dresser drawers with brown paper and rose petals.

Rapp himself showed up around three. His electric-socket hair seemed even wilder than usual, and his face looked not just pale but pasty. Precious was beside him in less than a minute.

"You know anything yet, Hon?" she asked him.

Lottie brandished her pencil. But Rapp just shook his head, uncharacteristically speechless.

"You want us to keep going?" Precious asked him. "We've got a heap of food being carried over from the Aqua tomorrow. Mightn't be too late to cancel."

Rapp shook his head again, looking like the host of a garden party who'd just heard thunderclaps. I did feel awful for him. He had done everything he could to make this trial happen—from handing John a soda at Robinson's that first day in May to staging the crazy street fight so that Dayton could be "put on the map." What would he do—what would any of us do—if this thing that had already brought so much change didn't actually happen? Would we change back? Could we? Would I want us to?

I'd never know. The lawyer's request to move the case was another false alarm. A federal judge in Cookeville denied the motion. Professor Neal came to the house with John and George and said if liquor were legal, he would have bought a bottle of Old

Forester. Lottie wrote that down, and I grabbed her pencil and crossed out what she'd written. She hesitated, then closed her notebook.

"Oh, fine," she said. "I guess there'll be plenty more quotes to come."

8

In the South in 1925, at least in the South I knew, women made the small decisions and men made the big ones. The small decisions often had the biggest consequences, like how a family handled hardship, or how far a dollar could be stretched, or what a child was taught to believe. But the big decisions made more noise. The men—wearing their bow ties and short sleeves and proud expressions—owned the businesses, ran the churches, and led the town meetings. The women, encircled by their apron strings and their children's arms, were usually less apt to swagger, at least beyond the confines of our own backyards. So I was more than a bit tickled to see these same brash men getting jumpy as the day for meeting William Jennings Bryan drew near. Bryan himself had been described as someone who knew how to strut sitting down.

He finally arrived three days before the trial was set to start. Our piddly Dayton depot was swarmed by nearly a thousand people, shouting, jumping, and waving their hats and fluttering their handkerchiefs. People were wearing their Sunday best, though in many cases, their Sunday best was older than they were. Mercy had dressed up for the occasion, however, sporting a new hat with a floppy flower and trying to corral her children, as one by one they broke loose from her, jumping and leaping with glee, even though they had no idea why they were excited.

Sam, the youngest, came running over when he saw me. I held his hands, as I'd always done, and let him climb his bare feet up my legs so he could do a flip-over. As he landed proudly, I saw that Mercy was watching and smiling, but she stopped and looked away as soon as I caught her eye. She wasn't ready to let me enjoy any enjoyment I'd helped to create. But I walked over to where she was standing, steering Lottie beside me.

"Mercy, this is Lottie Nelson. She's been staying with us."

Mercy said a tight, polite hello.

"I think I've seen you in the backyard," Lottie said. "You're the house to the left of Annabel's, is that right?"

Mercy nodded, looking wary.

"Lottie's a reporter for the *Chattanooga News*," I said.

I knew Mercy was too much of a gossip not to want to find out whatever she could about Lottie. Lottie! A lady reporter from Chattanooga! I could just imagine Mercy pulling up a kitchen chair for Lottie, plying her with sugar cookies and lemonade. As different as they were in so many ways, they were equally wedded to the habit of seeking and trading information.

"Is that right?" Mercy said now, but it wasn't a question. Just like Sam's flip-over, Lottie's background wasn't going to be enough to get me off the hook.

Meanwhile, there was a tussle near the tracks as the train huffed in. After a few expectant minutes, Bryan stepped onto the platform, and men vied for the chance to carry his bags: a briefcase, a worn leather satchel, and a suitcase made of alligator skin. He was wearing a tan, broad-brimmed hat, the kind I'd seen in pictures of men going on safari.

"Maybe he really thinks he's going to see wild animals here," Lottie said.

Stepping into the crowd, he took off the hat, revealing an almost entirely bald head already crowned with perspiration. He was sixty-five years old but still tall and imposing and, just as Mercy had described him, shaped like a pear. He had a jaw that seemed hinged like the Tin Man's, and his thick eyebrows rose into sharp peaks. He was wearing a dark bow tie, a dark suit, and a smile that suggested he'd just come home after many burdensome years away. Barefoot boys in coveralls and caps ran back and forth from him, not knowing how to act. The lawyers who would be working with him tried to look all business, but they seemed not much less flustered than the boys. As Bryan stepped forward, I noticed that his suit was wrinkled, and his pockets seemed to be bulging.

"What's he keep in there?" Lottie asked, jotting down the question and clearly not expecting me to have the answer.

"Greetings, good people. Greetings," he kept shouting above the crowd.

Lottie and I had been standing right on the platform, and I'd thought it would give me the perfect vantage point for taking photographs. But Bryan moved through the crowd much more quickly than I'd expected, a fast swimmer followed by a wide, frothy wake.

Frederick Richard Rogers was the pharmacist at Robinson's, and so it was somehow fitting, in an all-things-come-full-circle way, that he'd earned the honor of putting up the Bryans during the trial. The Rogerses' house, on South Market, was bright and white, shaded by magnolia trees and rimmed by patches of sunflowers. From its worn brick steps, Bryan gave a speech before his bags were even carried inside. He gave a second one after he'd drunk a strawberry ice-cream soda at Robinson's, and a third at the Aqua banquet that was held in his honor that evening. From what I saw even that first day, it seemed he was living in the midst of one continual speech, his inner thoughts flowing directly to and from his lips, interrupted only by his needs for food, sleep, and the reassurance of laughter and amens. I was spellbound.

Bryan's appetite for food was the stuff of legend. (Lottie found out that the reason his pockets bulged was that he kept radishes in them and munched on them whenever he got peckish.) At the banquet, he ate, indiscriminately, every dish that was put before him, followed by three helpings of strawberry shortcake and what seemed like a gallon of coffee. Then he pushed back his chair, dabbed the corners of his mouth with a blue gingham napkin, and rose to speak.

"My friends," he began, and all the talk at the other tables stopped, and all the kitchen staff came in to stand along the sides of the room to listen to Bryan express his gratitude for the hearty meal and the hospitality, and then he began:

"A boy is born in a Christian family. As soon as he is able to join words together into sentences, his mother teaches him the Lord's Prayer, and each day he lays his petition before the Heavenly Father: 'Give us this day our daily bread,' 'lead us not into temptation,' 'deliver us from evil,' 'forgive us our trespasses.'

"He goes to Sunday School," Bryan continued, "and learns how precious our lives are in the sight of God, how even a sparrow cannot fall to the ground without His notice. All his faith is built upon the Book that informs him that he is made in the image of God, that Christ came to reveal God to man and to be man's savior.

"Then he goes to college and a learned professor leads him through a book six hundred pages thick, about all the ways he resembles the beasts about him, and that everything found in a human brain is found in miniature in a brute brain. This is what the boy learns when he goes to college! That the development of man's moral sense can be explained on a brute basis without any act of, or aid from, God!"

Bryan seemed to grow taller as he reached his conclusion, his voice full of preacherly hope and grief. "If evolution wins, Christianity goes! Think of man! Of man! Made in the image of his Maker, when the morning stars first sang together!"

George was the only person I knew who didn't seem moved or at least impressed by Bryan's energy and eloquence.

"He's a showman," he said dismissively as we were getting ready for bed, and I was trying to recall and recount all I'd seen and heard. "He's given his speeches a thousand times. He's like a carnival barker."

I didn't answer. I was exhausted from the day's work and excitement, and I didn't want to tell George what I felt.

What I felt was uplifted. I couldn't understand how anyone could *not* have been inspired by Bryan's words. Everything about him seemed like a loving, worried parent saying, "I'm here for you. I've got things to teach you. Come back to me." And that was what I longed to do.

I wasn't there when Clarence Darrow arrived by private car the next day. I was still sprucing things up at the Mansion, which was where Rapp had decided Darrow himself should stay. George, whose only contact with Darrow till now had been by mail, was on hand to greet him, though, and so were John and Professor Neal. I knew this because George told me, of course, but also from the photograph that was printed in several of the next day's papers. ("Why didn't you get that picture?" Lottie would later scold me.)

In the photograph, Darrow was wearing a white string necktie against a white shirt, and a straw boater with a wide band. Professor Neal, rumpled as always, appeared to be standing on the cuffs of his own pant legs. Darrow was shaking John's hand. And George was right next to Darrow, a newspaper tucked under his arm, his straw hat in his hand, and a look of sublime anticipation on his face. The rest of the people in the picture—the people in the crowd—were looking somewhat less enthralled but hardly unhappy. If they'd been expecting some manifestation of the Devil, they were apparently disappointed by Clarence Darrow's appearance.

When I first saw him in person, that night while I was helping fill water glasses for his welcome banquet at the Aqua, I thought he had one of the kindest faces I'd ever seen. He actually looked a bit like my father, or at least like the photograph of him I'd rescued from the old Brownie. Darrow was tall, shambling, and balding, with what was left of his hair parted wispily to one side. His head was enormous. But no matter how grand or combative his convictions might have been, they didn't show on his face. It's not that he looked uncertain. He just didn't look angry or pompous. He looked like someone—a doctor, maybe—who might quietly listen to all your symptoms and wait for you to finish, even if he knew right away what was ailing you.

The calmness of his expression appeared in exact contrast to the look on Fred Whittle's face. Somehow, Fred's demeanor had changed from stunned paralysis to anxious overreaction. Orders tumbled from his lips more quickly than they could possibly be understood, let alone carried out.

"Somebody's gotta give that man some whiskey," Mabel Finstock said in the kitchen, retying her kerchief and tucking in her silver-white stray hairs.

I hadn't known she could be funny.

"He does seem a little overwrought," I said.

"Overwrought!" she said. "If you strapped him to four wheels, he'd beat anyone in a soapbox derby."

"Why weren't you at the banquet?" I teased Lottie later that night, trying to answer her scolding with some of my own.

For once we weren't sitting in the kitchen but on the steps in the backyard, where she'd lit a cigarette, and I'd willed myself not to find it shocking.

"I wanted to meet some of the supporting characters in the play," she said, exhaling contentedly.

I asked her who.

"Well, I met John Scopes's father, for one. He came down from Paducah today. He was hauling three huge grain sacks filled with mail."

"Right, I'd heard John was from Kentucky," I said.

"And would have been there now if he hadn't stayed in town that week after school closed."

"How's that?"

Lottie grinned like a person who's just had the most delicious bite of pie. Prolonging the suspense, she took another drag on her cigarette.

"Seems he met some blond girl, and she told him there was going to be a box social at her church. The only reason he was even *in* Dayton the day that Rapp got ahold of him was for the chance she'd invite him."

"So, if he hadn't met that girl—"

Lottie laughed. "Well, for one thing, you and I wouldn't be sitting here."

Nor would the whole history of Dayton's summer take place the way it did, or the thousand arguments that went with it, or, perhaps the shape of the rest of my life. But for now I laughed too.

She had met other visitors, she told me, clearly satisfied: Wilbur Glenn Voliva, an evangelist who hoped to testify that the earth was flat; John Butler, the Tennessee legislator who'd written the law being tested; and Reverend W. H. Moses, who represented the largest Black Baptist organization in the country. She had managed a lengthy interview with T. T. Martin, the evangelist who had written the book *Hell and the High Schools* and who, Lottie told me, said that Germans who gave children poisoned candy during the war were angels compared to the Tennessee teachers who taught evolution.

But the person Lottie was most anxious to meet was the Baltimore writer H. L. Mencken. He had already made himself notorious in town. Airplanes landing each evening on the little strip past town had been bringing the latest papers—so we already knew he'd been writing about the people of Dayton as "rubes" and "rednecks" and "Homo Neandertalensis" (a term I didn't understand but knew was no compliment). He had already written about John as "the infidel Scopes"—not because Mencken himself believed John was an infidel, but because he was making fun of the way he thought my people saw him. I wasn't sure I was that eager to meet Mencken myself, but I had to laugh when Lottie talked about him. Here was yet one more celebrated man who had a nickname that sounded as if it had been given to him as a royal title. I knew that Bryan was the Great Commoner and Darrow was the Champion of Lost Causes; Mencken, it turned out, was known as the Sage of Baltimore.

It occurred to me that Mercy had Bryan; George had Darrow; and Lottie had Mencken. They were each starstruck, each thrilled to be seeing an idol—maybe even seeing a more perfect version of themselves. I envied all of them the comfort and clarity that went with having a hero. To be honest, if I'd had to choose one on that day, I still would have chosen Bryan. But George had already started to sow some doubts in me about him, and in any case the only person whose wisdom I trusted utterly had died when I was sixteen.

Lottie literally tripped over her feet when she first saw Mencken. We were standing in front of the Aqua, and on those stick-straight legs of hers, she dashed right up to him as he crossed the street.

"Sir," she said. "I'm a huge fan of yours."

He wasn't a tall man, but he managed to look down at her; without hesitation, he said, "You're not that huge."

"Lottie Nelson," she said, composing herself and extending her hand. "*Chattanooga News.*"

He smiled. He didn't need to introduce himself. He was boyish looking—if a man in his fifties could be considered boyish. His straight brown hair was parted down the center, but it darted off into cowlicks and flopped across his forehead. Like Lottie's, his eyes were restless, and now that he'd crossed the street, they settled on me.

"Who's this?" he asked rudely.

"I'm Annabel Craig," I said.

"Local?"

"Born right here," I said.

"Good for you. You'll be my guide."

"I found her first," Lottie said. "She's my guide."

It was an instant thrill, feeling important to a famous writer, even if I already guessed that all he really wanted was to prove that my townsfolk were fools.

Mencken turned to shake hands with a few other people, and as he did, Lottie tugged on my sleeve.

"Where's your camera?" she whispered.

"In my purse. But I need film," I said.

"You should have it with you! You should *always* have film with you!" she scolded. "This is just like when Darrow got here. A dozen other people will photograph H. L. Mencken in Dayton today. Don't you want *your* picture to be the one the newspapers print?"

To my surprise, I did. Truth was, I wanted it very much. In retrospect, I think that was the first time I got a glimpse of how I would feel when I made a mark outside Dayton.

I popped into Robinson's and bought a half dozen boxes of film on credit. By the time I came out, Mencken had gone, but Lottie had already made a plan with him and had, audaciously, started to call him Henry.

Part Three

1

Since our very beginning, George had introduced me to modern things: the radio, the Model T, the idea of treatments to help me get pregnant, the rejection of superstitions when I finally was expecting. After Walton Allen, the burden of George's own sense of failure had kept us apart. Now the contest between Bryan and Darrow—or religion and science, as the papers kept calling it—had pushed him even further into that other, more modern, more secular, country. Lottie, on the other hand, seemed unfettered by personal feelings, at least about the argument between religion and science. She seemed to understand enough of both not to be beguiled by either. She never put down her notebook, never ceased to be an outsider, but every once in a while, she seemed to remember where I was standing and, with surprising patience, she reached for me across the border.

Friday morning, July 10, I woke to feel a tap on my toes and find Lottie hovering at the foot of our bed. George was still asleep, on his side, facing away from us. Beyond the windows, the sky was dark, and the birds hadn't started their morning song. I smelled the marvelous, earthy aroma of slightly burnt coffee.

"You made the coffee?" I whispered.

"Get up," she whispered back, and from the doorway she added needlessly: "Now."

Excited and instantly wide awake, I washed up, put on a dress, and grabbed my shoes. Downstairs, I found Lottie scooping four hard-boiled eggs from a pot. It was just before six o'clock.

"Eggs?" I said, buttoning up my shoes.

"Not for us. For George, when he wakes up."

I could hear the shower running.

"He's up," I said and pulled three coffee cups from the shelf.

"No time," she said. "We have to get there right away if we're going to get you a perch."

"But George is still in the shower," I said.

"And he'll find some eggs and a fresh pot of coffee waiting for him when he comes down. Got your camera? Got film? Good. We're going."

It was what I'd hoped for but hadn't had the nerve to ask for straight out. On the walk to the courthouse, I felt exactly the way I had fifteen years before, the morning when my mother woke me and let me come with her to the canning club. It was dawn. I was a novice. I was going on an adventure.

The sky was just beginning to brighten, and the Carolina wrens, hidden in the summer trees, were beginning their rapid two-note calls. The heat was already palpable. Men on Market Street hammered nails into the makeshift stands where in the days to come they would peddle lemonade, funnel cakes, blueberry muffins, cinnamon squares, hot dogs, souvenirs, pamphlets, and Bibles of every size.

It was still only a little past six. Jonah Caruthers and Horace Carter were manning the courthouse doors. Lottie showed them her press pass.

"You got one, too, Annabel?" Horace asked, laughing at me.

"She's my photographer," Lottie said.

Jonah looked doubtful, but I'd known Horace since before his voice changed.

"On the level?" he asked.

"Cross my heart," I said and showed him my camera. He shook his head a little, then shrugged and opened the doors for us.

The second-floor courtroom of the Rhea County Courthouse was said to be the largest in all of East Tennessee. I had been in it several times before. The first was when I was working at the Aqua. A hotel guest had made off with some silver candlesticks, and I'd been called as a witness. The second time was when I'd seen George defending Walton Allen. Today, I knew I would have to save my film, but the huge, empty space was a beautiful, pristine site, one I correctly guessed would be unrecognizable within a matter of days, if not hours. So as Lottie settled into a seat in the front of the three rows marked off for the press, I circled the courtroom, finding the light as it brightened the windows and touched the surfaces all around.

The regular jury seats had been moved aside to make way for the press and the extra chairs around the lawyers' tables. There were bright pink azaleas in a Mason jar on the judge's bench, palm-leaf fans—printed with the names of local businesses—on the jurors' seats, and brass spittoons near the lawyers' tables. The wood on the banisters, doorframes, chairs, and tables gleamed with fresh varnish. Most striking, though, were the windows. I'd never noticed how the top of each one was arched; a wood sash lay horizontally a foot beneath the peak; a bar rose vertically, bisecting the panes, and the effect was the creation of a perfect cross in every window. It was as if the architects of the courtroom had hoped that someday Christ would find his way in.

By seven, we could hear the crowd outside: a persistent clamor, highlighted by the occasional single voice, exhorting, but otherwise unclear. Several clerks came in carrying files and satchels, which they proceeded to spread out on the prosecution table. No one had yet come for the defense.

"We should have had coffee," I said to Lottie.

"Trust me," she said. "You won't need it."

A dozen men carrying microphones and cables came in next, and Lottie got to her feet.

"You will die in a bloody battle before you let anyone take my seat," she instructed, and I grinned in agreement.

Then she went to interview them as they set up their equipment.

I was fiddling with the strap on my camera when Mr. Mencken dropped a copy of an advertising pamphlet the town had put out called "Why Dayton?" onto my lap.

"Why indeed?" he asked wryly. He was wearing a suit and tie and taking in the sight of the courtroom as if it were the vista up at Walden's Ridge.

"That thing got enough film in it?" he asked me, pointing to my camera.

"As much as it can hold," I said.

The room filled in minutes. Even during the Allen trial, with all its luridness, the crowd hadn't been like this. By eight o'clock, every seat was filled, and just half an hour later, people were standing, some three deep, around the perimeter of the room. Aside from the reporters and lawyers, almost everyone was dressed in their every-day clothes: denim pants and coveralls and shirts with the sleeves rolled up. There were some women, too, wearing pale cotton frocks that had been washed and pressed but were wilting in the heat. Already the smell of bodies was so overpowering that it took deter-mination for me to concentrate on other things.

At eight-thirty, Judge John Tate Raulston strode in with his wife and two daughters, both of whom were wearing identical sailor dresses. Raulston was a district judge who lived west of Chattanooga and was himself a lay preacher. His manner was stub-bornly cheerful. Some weeks back, he had suggested building a temporary courthouse to accommodate the twenty thousand peo-ple he wrongly expected would want to attend the trial, and several times this week, he'd seemed just a little too eager for me and any-one else with a camera to photograph him and his family.

The chatter stopped when he appeared, just the way it did in church when Reverend Byrd arrived at the pulpit. And, just like Reverend Byrd, the judge was carrying a Bible. Next, Darrow appeared with Professor Neal, Rapp, John, and George behind him. I didn't know how George would react to my being there, but if he saw me, he didn't acknowledge it. I could tell that he was nervous. After setting down a stack of books, he looked first at the judge, who nodded a vague hello, then at the prosecution table, where the five members of Bryan's team were waiting for the great man to appear.

Finally, at exactly nine, William Jennings Bryan made his entrance, and everyone who was seated—even some of the reporters—rose to their feet and started to clap. I rose too. When Bryan and Darrow shook hands, the applause got even louder. But the enthusiasm was soon muffled by the rap of the judge's gavel and his first official words:

"The court will come to order. The Reverend Cartwright will open court with prayer."

In an instant, a room full of spectators and reporters became a congregation.

I had never seen Reverend Cartwright. I figured he'd been brought in from some neighboring town. His expression was so somber that it seemed almost threatening.

Mencken was two seats to the left of Lottie. "Prayer," I heard him scoff. His amusement was evident. Here we were at a trial that was essentially setting up a contest between the Lord and Charles Darwin, and the judge was having us plead to the first for guidance about the second. It seemed to me it was like asking the coach of a rival football team to be the referee.

"Oh, God, our divine Father," the reverend began, "we recognize Thee as the supreme ruler of the universe in whose hands are the lives and destinies of all men, and of all the world . . ."

At first I bowed my head, but before I could close my eyes, I saw that Lottie had begun to scribble furiously in her notebook, and after just a minute or two, I decided to save my prayers for later.

For the first time since one restless Sunday in childhood, I lifted my head despite the instruction to pray. That is when George's eyes met mine. His expression was a mixture of surprise and satisfaction, though I wasn't sure if he was satisfied with himself or with me. Darrow, like the other members of the defense team, stood unbowed. He seemed not entirely surprised to find an appeal to God being made, but he did appear increasingly astonished by the length of the prayer.

"O God, in the midst of all, help us to remember that Thou art on Thy throne and that Thou knowest the secrets of our hearts . . ."

The secrets of my own heart were at that moment too many and complicated to grasp.

Reverend Cartwright, eyes shut, went on for what Lottie later told me she timed at a full ten minutes. Even the most ardent of the faithful began to look up furtively.

The reverend thundered his conclusion—no doubt meaning to impress Bryan.

"Hear us in these prayers. God help us to be loyal to God and loyal to the truth and in the end of life's tremendous trouble, may we so have lived and so have wrought in this world, that we may be admitted into the grace of Thy kingdom and honor, and there, amongst the resplendent glories of a living God, offer praise to Thy glory and grace for ever more. Amen."

"Well, that should settle that," Lottie whispered to me.

Official business followed. The presentation of the indictment, the calling of the case, the formal introduction of the lawyers from out of town. There was a lot of talk about how long it would take to pick a jury, and whether the visiting attorneys should get a chance to rest before that happened. Permission was requested and granted, in consideration of the heat, for jackets to be removed. But eventually Tommy Jefferson Brewer, four years old, was hoisted onto the judge's bench to pull the jurors' names from a hat.

"You're a fine boy, Tommy."

"You shake that thing up good."

Judge Raulston tousled the boy's hair.

It took just a few hours to pull a jury together. All but one of them were regular churchgoers. Two said straight out that they didn't believe in evolution. Another admitted he couldn't read. Undaunted, friendly, sporting a surprising pair of lavender suspenders, Clarence Darrow waved them sociably into the juror chairs. Little did those men know that there would be so many side arguments that they would spend far more time outside the courtroom than in.

There was a short break after that, and George came toward me, looking furtive and speaking quietly.

"How'd you get in here?" he asked.

I smiled and raised my camera.

"I got her in," Lottie said.

"But she doesn't have a press pass."

"No one needs to know that, George," I said.

He looked back toward Darrow and the defense team.

"Well, I'm glad you're going to hear this all firsthand," he said. "We're going to make history."

He squeezed my shoulder and called me Shutterbug. Then he was beckoned back over by Darrow and turned proudly to join him. On the other side of the room, Bryan was indisputably a much bigger attraction. Even Judge Raulston found an excuse at one point to ease his way into the pack.

Two hours later, he adjourned court for the day and, as if he was a member of the Committee on Reservations itself, invited everyone to enjoy the weekend in our fair town.

People seemed eager to leave the sizzling courtroom, though there was a bottleneck around Bryan that made for a difficult exit. By the time I was back out on the street, I could see neither George nor Lottie. Even in the open air, the crowd was thick, with shoulders bumping against shoulders, children stumbling over their feet, and all around, the smells of hot dogs and funnel cakes, the sounds of urgent voices threatening damnation or promising redemption.

I was used to trying to translate the world of colors into black-and-white, but never had that seemed so fruitless, because never had the streets of Dayton been so vivid. Our usual palette of faded denim and pale calico had been turned into a mere canvas on top of which were extravagant dabs and strokes of color: deep red, pink, and purple flowers on women's hats, shiny royal blue sailor dresses, drawings of monkeys with large pink lips, freshly painted signs in hues that the Tennessee sun had not yet bleached.

WHERE WILL YOU SPEND ETERNITY? one of the banners asked. But my immediate focus was where I would spend the afternoon.

Starting east, toward home, I felt a tug on my upper arm and knew before I'd turned around that it was Lottie.

"Where are you going?" she asked.

"Home," I said.

"Why?" she asked, incredulous.

"To make dinner, for one thing. To catch my breath, for another. Aren't you tired?"

Already her smile made me wish I hadn't asked the question.

"Tired! This might turn out to be the best story I've ever covered in my life. It's got everything, don't you see? The lunatics and the famous men and the hot dogs and the hubbub?"

"I need to get home," I said. "I need to make dinner. Feed the cat. Make the bed I never got to make this morning."

She shook her head, but fondly.

"Take off your hat," she instructed.

I was wearing an old bonnet. Her tone made it clear that negotiation would be futile.

I removed my hat and tucked my hair behind my ears as Lottie took my camera.

"How does it work?" she asked me.

"Simple," I said. "Just point at whatever you want to capture, make sure you see it clearly, and pull that lever."

She looked inside the viewfinder. "Well," she said, "I know I want to capture you, but I'm not sure I see you clearly."

She smiled as she clicked the shutter.

2

Seeking an antidote to the fever that was roiling the town, I was determined to cook a real dinner that night—something hearty and homey, something that would remind George that we'd had a life before the trial and would have a life when it was done.

I didn't learn till after I'd fried the chicken and boiled the greens and potatoes that there had been a huge cookout on the courthouse lawn that evening. It got to be seven o'clock. It was eight. And then, as I'd done so often when George was at his worst, I ate alone. Next, I cleaned the pots and utensils I'd used. It was nine. I washed down the counters. I even took the kitchen mat out back and whacked it with the rug beater. Finally, just as I was laying it back on the floor, I heard George and Lottie coming in the front door together.

"Sassafras!" he called to me as he approached the kitchen. It was a new nickname, and of course it got me smiling.

"Sassafras?" Lottie asked.

"George likes to give me nicknames," I said.

Lottie smiled, tossing her bag and notebook on the counter.

George kissed the top of my head, then set down a large stack of papers beside Lottie's things.

They had both eaten, of course, and I felt foolish for having stayed at home. I poured us all lemonade, which we drank as we traded fragments of the day. George told us how the defense team had ribbed Dudley Field Malone for keeping his black jacket buttoned even as the sweat poured down his face and neck. I told George how I'd noticed the crosses in the windows. We talked about the endless prayer that opened the trial; the heat; the smell. George reminded us of the would-be juror who was excused when he said all he knew about evolution was that he didn't want to know about evolution. Lottie, saving the best for last, told us that at a dance up the road, a bunch of reporters had staked out the field next to the pavillion, and they'd persuaded a girl to ask John Scopes to walk her across. In the darkness, the reporters flashed on their headlights, and as the girl suddenly kissed John, a photographer snapped the shot.

George disapproved because he said it was just another example of people trivializing the case. Lottie disapproved because she said the setup put journalists in a bad light. And I disapproved because I felt so sorry for John, who, like me, had clearly wanted to have some semblance of a normal evening. But however different the reasons George, Lottie, and I had for disapproving, Friday night gave the three of us a moment of warmth and unity that I rightly suspected would not last.

Just about twenty-four hours later, George and I were back at the same kitchen table, only now he was busy taking notes on some textbook, barely looking up, even when I told him I was planning to go out with Lottie and another reporter.

"Too dark to take pictures, Shutterbug," he said, distracted.

"I know."

"So, what, then. You're going to be their guide? At night?"

"Going to try. I won't be long."

He just nodded and kept taking notes, and it wasn't until Lottie came in with H. L. Mencken right behind her that George looked up.

Mencken was actually shorter than George, but his energy over-powered the room.

George stood, flustered. "Pleasure," he managed to say as they shook hands.

"So, I gather you're one of those dangerous locals who first of-fered to defend the infidel?" Mencken asked.

George laughed, but I knew he was flattered that Mencken knew who he was.

"Glad to know that there's at least one man in Dayton ready to risk his eternal life," Mencken said.

"George isn't risking—" I began, but at the same moment, George laughed again and said, "Well, we can't all be saved."

Mencken's blue eyes widened with surprise.

"Pleasure to meet you too," he said, but then he added: "Good luck getting a word in edgewise with Clarence Darrow at your table."

He might have meant it in a casual way, but I hurried the two reporters out the kitchen door before I could see to what extent the comment had upset George.

Lottie had told Mencken that there were only three choices for what to do here on a Saturday night. They could go see the talkies at the Gem, they could go to a church dance, or they could go up the road to the banks of the stream where the Holy Rollers met.

No choice at all, Mencken had said. He'd come to see religion in action, he told her. So, we were off to find the Pentecostals, who would certainly provide the best chance of drama.

Like people everywhere, the people of Dayton worshipped in all kinds of ways. Growing up, I was naturally aware of that, but it didn't much matter. Church wasn't something you shopped for, like a pair of shoes or a new frock: You didn't go looking for the one that fit. I was a Methodist because my parents had been Methodists, and I assumed Baptists were Baptists because their parents had been Baptists.

In Dayton, as elsewhere, there was a North Methodist-Episcopal church and a South Methodist-Episcopal church—divided not by the town's geography but by our opposite allegiances during the Civil War. Still, no matter what our parents' and grandparents' views during the war had been, all Methodists believed in free will; believed in the Father, the Son, and the Holy Spirit; believed in the Bible as all that was necessary for salvation. That wasn't the same as believing it was literally true. But I'd never really thought about that. I'd never had to. You don't need to question the truths of a childhood until they are challenged—or contradicted. I grew up with light from candles, warmth from stoves, water hauled from wells in buckets. None of those things had any true meaning for me until they'd been replaced by light from electric lamps, warmth from steam heat, and water from a kitchen faucet.

Growing up, I knew nothing about Jews except that Christ had been one but had been crucified by a lot of others. I'm not sure I'd even heard the words *Buddhist* or *Hindu* then. I knew Catholics dressed things up with a lot of rituals that meant nothing to God and gave sermons in a dead language and prayed to dead people they called saints. I knew more about Baptists because they were the majority in Dayton. They were stricter about things than we were and tended to take the Bible literally. And Pentecostals—well, they were in an entirely different category altogether, generally looked down upon because they lived in the hills, worshipped out-side, and claimed the Holy Spirit could move them to speak in tongues and roll in ecstasy.

While the sky was still yellow and pink, I asked Lottie and Mencken to pose for me. Lottie obliged me for the first shot, but then she stepped away.

"You can keep that one for your scrapbook," she said. "I need one of Henry for the paper."

That portrait—of a slightly disheveled, middle-aged man whose blue eyes, even in black-and-white, looked dreamy and expressive— would be printed just two days later on the front page of the *Chattanooga News,* the official beginning of my newspaper career.

The other snapshot did indeed end up in my Dayton scrapbook. Even in the now-faded, admittedly blurry image, Lottie and Mencken look equally restless to move on to the night's adventure.

A bit reluctantly, I led them west, out of town and toward the back roads. It was still hot: Unlike any Southern gentlemen accompanying two ladies, Mencken took off his jacket without asking us if we minded.

In the waning day, with the night sky just beginning to envelop us, I could still see Mencken's blue eyes, which were gleaming with excitement and anticipatory contempt.

Richmond Creek lay like a shiny copper wire between two steep, dark embankments, and I led us to the side opposite the one where a gathering of the faithful was in full swing. If they'd been looking for us, they could have seen us, but I guessed we were just far enough away to blend into the landscape. As the sky grew dark, the moon teased us, ducking in and out of a cloudy sky. But there were also kerosene lanterns hanging from hackberry trees and, on the grass, a scattering of old teapots whose spouts held slowly burning cotton wicks. There were women as well as men, and there were babies being watched by young girls on blankets. It was hard, when the moon was hidden, to make out faces clearly. But the voices carried boldly across the creek.

"Hallelujah!"

"Praise the Lord!"

Even the branches of the trees seemed to be reaching up for God.

I'd never in my life seen a preacher who wasn't wearing at least a tie and a jacket, but this preacher was dressed in denim overalls, and he was walking back and forth across the edge of the creek, eliciting these cries with his questions.

"Can you feel the Holy Spirit? Do you want to be forgiven?"

Three or four more men emerged from the darkness, bringing more lanterns. Now, it was easier to see the people, and I searched for anyone I knew.

"These aren't my people," I whispered, as much to myself as to Lottie and Mencken.

Suddenly, a tall, broad woman, sweat sliding like tears down her flat, wide face, stepped forward, her arms reaching high above her head as she started to sing in a deep and surprisingly beautiful voice:

> *This night, O Lord, we bless Thee for Thy protecting*
> *care . . .*

A few other women began to dance and twirl, each to a separate inner rhythm.

I looked first to Lottie and then to Mencken, expecting to see them laughing or sneering, but both were busily scribbling notes. Lottie, even in the darkness, managed to write while only occasionally looking down at her pad.

Right at the edge of the creek, some men were lighting a bonfire.

Mencken reached around Lottie to tap me on the shoulder. "They still burn witches in Tennessee?"

I would have done anything to wipe the smile from his lips.

"Who will repent?" the preacher was asking. "Who will repent? Who will repent their sin?"

Next, a man and woman began to lead a young man—I assumed he was their son—down the embankment to a large rock about five yards from the creek. He was wearing a skinny bright red tie that, in the gloom, seemed to cast its own gaudy light.

A man wearing a red tie in 1925 Tennessee was every bit as outlandish and shocking as a woman wearing bloomers or smoking on the street.

"They gonna hang him by that tie?" Mencken asked.

They sat the young man on the rock and swarmed and danced around him, praying and shouting and throwing their arms across him. He was soon buried beneath this pile of people.

"Imagine the smell," Mencken said and lit a cigar.

All my life, I had heard about people talking in tongues. "The gift of tongues," it was called, and it was supposed to be a sign that a person had been entered by the Holy Spirit. I had never heard this kind of speech myself, and at first it was hard to separate from the rest of the voices, which piled on top of one another just as the bodies had piled on top of the young man. But soon I saw two women peel away from the group, drop to their knees, and start to make sounds without words or music or sense, but with a rhythm— almost like the calls of the cattle auctioneer my father had once taken me along to see. That man had spoken so quickly that I hadn't believed he was saying words at all.

"It's all a big act, right?" Mencken asked me.

"What?"

"You really think they believe this?"

"Yes."

"Just a lot of show," Eva Jenkins had said to me once—though I knew some of her kin worshipped as Pentecostals too. And yet by the candlelight, I could just make out real tears—of joy, confusion, gratitude—coursing down the faces that were yearning for salvation.

"Thank you," some of them whispered, some of them shouted. I believed what they were feeling was real. I also felt embarrassed. I wanted to yell at them to stop. But they kept twirling and rolling on the hillside, and soon they formed a circle around the young man, and, in faster and faster rhythm, they started clapping. Then the preacher stepped forward, face to face with the young man, who was now staring miserably at the ground. The preacher shouted, "Look at me, son!" With one hand, he took him by the shoulder, and with the other pushed against his forehead, hard, shouting, "In the name of Jesus Christ, devil depart!"

The young man fell back onto the muddy ground, and the crowd shouted "Hosanna!"

Meanwhile, the bonfire started to sputter and flare, and the smell of burning bark, dead wood, and old paper came floating across the creek bed. It was already a steamy evening, but the people by the fire seemed not to care about the added heat. The preacher and the young man's parents were leading him farther down the embankment, though I wasn't sure if they were leading him to the water or the fire. His shirt collar was open now, and his red tie was clenched in one hand.

"Help this sinner!" a woman cried.

Looking more sick than scared or sorrowful, the young man was forced to kneel on the ground before the bonfire.

"Burn it!" the preacher shouted.

Without ceremony or hesitation—almost as if he'd done it before—the young man threw his tie into the fire. It landed dead center, in a tight red ball, at first tamping down the flames. But as everyone watched, spellbound, the flames started to shoot up around it, and in the heat, the tie slowly opened and uncurled, just like a red garter snake.

"The devil!" one of the women shrieked.

"It is the serpent!"

Either because their work was done or because they feared the evil of the burning tie, the crowd began to scatter.

Lottie and Mencken and I watched as the tie gradually burned up and left a smoldering black strip among the simmering red embers.

Mencken puffed contentedly on his cigar. "Well, ladies," he said. "I give you the progress of humanity in the twentieth-century South."

His column the next day would describe what we'd seen as "a barbaric grotesquerie." He would use even more insulting words in the coming days. He would call us yokels, hillbillies, morons, and ignoramuses. He would make the world laugh at Dayton, and scorn us, as if every single resident of Dayton was filled with the zealous chaos of that night. For the moment, though, he seemed more thoughtful than contemptuous.

The walk back to town was sober and muggy. I could feel the back of my dress clinging to me. Mencken asked why the town was so keen on reviving its blast furnace when surely the weather itself could produce iron ore.

After that, no one said anything. It's possible that Lottie and Mencken were already rehearsing what they would write. For my part, I couldn't wait to get home and say good night to Lottie. I wanted to see George so much—the old George, the one who had once been my source of safety. I found him already in bed, reading by his bedside lamp.

Seeing me so distraught, he reached for me, surprisingly attentive. "Are you okay, Flossie?" he asked. "Come here. Tell me about it."

But we didn't talk. George's arms, on either side of mine, supporting his weight through his elbows, were like two strong columns of a structure that enclosed me. With Lottie next door, we were very quiet and purposefully slow, the need for discretion making every movement more exquisite. The muscles in his arms flexed as he moved above me, reminding me of the physical strength he had shown the day we met—when he'd lifted me from the bank of Oak Tree Pond and into the water.

He shuddered, holding back his cry, and then I kissed the top of his shoulder.

"George," I said as I edged out from underneath him.

"Shutterbug," he said.

No matter that he was on the team that was arguing against Bryan, against religion in science class. I had loved the sight of him in the courtroom the day before, bending toward the other lawyers defending John. He'd seemed every bit their equal, and I loved the strength of him now.

He smiled, satisfied, and he fell asleep in minutes.

I was not so lucky. I barely slept. It was hot, but no hotter than usual. George wasn't snoring, as he sometimes did. And I was so tired. But Lottie was typing, and there was a pressure I kept feeling, as if what was inside my body could simply not be at peace with what was outside. Maybe a storm was coming, I thought. I couldn't get comfortable. The scenes of the prayer meeting replayed themselves in my mind—not only the Pentecostals dancing but the way Lottie and Mencken had looked at them; the way Mencken had asked me if it all was an act; and, more than anything else, the sight of the red tie turning black in the smoldering embers of the night.

3

In the morning, I woke before either Lottie or George, got dressed for church, and went downstairs to put up the coffee and feed Spitfire. Lottie was the last one down, for once seeming almost reticent. Perhaps whatever attempts George and I had made at being private had failed, and maybe marital love was one of the few things that took her aback. Or perhaps she was merely exhausted from the night and the heat and all the hours she'd put in trying to get a grip on our town.

"Who wants flapjacks before church?" I asked.

They both smiled by way of answer, and so I cracked the eggs and mixed in the flour and milk and watched, satisfied, as the tops of the flapjacks turned golden. I was tired, too, but fairly content. I didn't notice at first that George and Lottie were sitting at opposite ends of the kitchen table, each of them intently taking notes, as if locked in a furious competition about whose work would prove more important.

The relative peace was broken by Mercy, pounding on the back door.

I hadn't seen her since Bryan's arrival at the depot, and I knew she had intentionally been ducking both me and my infidel husband.

She was here now, though—large, red-faced, breathless.

"They're going to wreck your church!" she shouted.

At that, both Lottie and George not only stopped working but immediately stood.

"Who?"

"Why?"

As they asked the questions, I turned off the stove and ran to get my camera and hat. George pulled on his jacket. Lottie, notepad in hand, was, naturally, first out the door, and with Mercy panting to keep up, the four of us hustled down Walnut Street.

Reverend Byrd was the youngest minister in Dayton and, as far as I knew, the most popular. Endearing himself to participants of all generations, he routinely allowed the children in our congregation to kneel at the feet of Helen Ticknor, the organist, and use their little hands to pump the foot pedals while her fingers worked the keys. The pastor's voice, like his bearing, was friendly but firm, and even some of the strict Fundamentalists who attended Mercy's church occasionally asked about his sermons with just a hint of envy. Until this morning, the most controversial thing about Reverend Byrd had been his insistence that we call him "Pastor Howard," which in any case we never did.

But while William Jennings Bryan was set to make an appearance at Mercy's Baptist church, Reverend Byrd had announced that a New York minister named Charles Potter would be talking to ours—on the subject of evolution. By the time George, Lottie, and I reached the church, we found its doors closed and our pastor standing warily on the steps outside. About fifty members of our congregation and at least a dozen reporters were gathered around him. People were shouting question after question at him—so many questions that none could be heard clearly, let alone answered.

Lottie could barely conceal her excitement. Here was an actual

rift to report. This wasn't a put-up job like the barbershop fight or
the kiss that the newsmen had staged for John. This was clear evidence that in Dayton, Tennessee, our passions ran deep—maybe
dangerously deep. Like a chicken picking up feed, Lottie darted
from person to person on those quick, awkward legs.

"What's happened?" "What'd he say?" "What do you think's
gonna happen now?"

Eventually, amid the hubbub, a lone voice cried out, "Silence!"

It was startling, not just because it was louder than any of the
other voices, but because its source was a ravaged but raging Major
McClure. He was leaning on Ruth, his daughter-in-law, and he was
literally shaking his fist. Spittle was running down the left side of
his chin. My instinct was to be at his side with a soft cloth and a
gentle hand, but when I managed to meet his eye, he merely glared
back at me. He had always been stubborn as sunshine, and I knew
if I could ever win him back, it would not be while he was raging
like this.

Having gotten the crowd's attention, the major shouted again,
but this time to the pastor: "All y'all mark me, Howard Byrd! This
won't be our church no longer if you let that Yankee into our pulpit!"

He pointed to the church corkboard, and the people standing in
front of it stepped away, revealing a flyer the reverend had posted
about Dr. Potter's talk. With what looked like red crayon, someone
had drawn the angular face of a bearded, horned devil over the announcement.

George, as soon as he saw this, went striding up to the corkboard. He tugged down the devil's face. The nail that had held it
went flying. He crumpled the paper into a ball and threw it on the
grass.

"We'll wreck this church!" another man shouted, and I don't
think anyone knew if wrecking the church meant tearing it apart by
acts of violence or of desertion.

Still near the corkboard, George shook hands with a tall, thin, tidy older man. Though he was dressed in a regular pale Sunday suit, he looked uncomfortably out of place.

"That's Potter," Lottie said unnecessarily.

Mercy, on my other side, punched me, hard, on the arm.

"Look on your husband's new friend," she said with a sneer.

"Mercy," I said, "don't you even want to hear what the man has to say?"

"In my church," she huffed, "we don't want to hear about this evolution."

On purpose or not, she made the first two syllables of the last word sound like *evil*.

I knew she had to have been on her way to the south church to hear Bryan talk, but the Big Dog would have gone ahead with the Puppies and saved her a seat.

Holding me by the hand, she led me away from the crowd and to the back side of the church, to the grassy area where Caroline and I always hid the Easter eggs and where ivy climbed in wild green swirls against the straight lines of the red bricks. Mercy's eyes were soft now, and it was clear that her desire to help me had overcome her anger.

"When was the last time you took time to really think on God's word?" she asked.

I smiled back at her, so glad she still seemed to care, but I didn't know what to say. I bowed my head, sorry and confused at the same time.

"For His glory and honor," she said. "You're supposed to be a strong Godly wife and keep George on the straight and narrow."

"I don't think George has sinned," I said quietly. "And I know I haven't."

"We are all sinners," she said.

I could see her fighting her frustration.

"If you're listening to that man from New York," she said, "how can your ears be open to the word of God?"

Now it was my turn to fight frustration.

"How can you be so sure you don't want to hear something if you've never heard it before?" I asked.

"No fancy New Yorker need tell me what to believe," she said.

"He doesn't look all that fancy to me."

"You know what my meaning is," she said.

"What if he's just fixing to tell you what *he* believes?" I asked.

She looked at me as if I'd lost my mind. "Annabel Craig," she said almost scoldingly. "There's not a thing in the world I need to learn that doesn't come from my Bible."

Was she really that sure? I almost envied her lack of curiosity, her apparent lack of questions. But I suddenly remembered my father once telling me: "God is big enough for your questions." And even as I hugged Mercy, I thought: If God was truly all-knowing, and truly infinite, why wouldn't He be able to answer the questions of our finite minds? At the moment, my finite mind needed to know precisely what it was about evolution that made it too dangerous for children to learn about in school.

Mercy surprised me by pulling me closer and embracing me.

"You do what you will," she said. "I'm going to hear Mr. Bryan."

Out in front of the church, the crowd seemed to be getting menacingly closer to Reverend Byrd, who moved back to a higher step, thus managing to retreat and rise above the crowd at the same time.

Just then, his wife, Sylvia, emerged from inside the church with Clara, the Byrds' two-year-old, clutching her mother's dress. Sylvia cradled their infant in one arm, and Clara tugged harder, making Sylvia stumble.

I don't know how I expected a New York minister to act, but when he saw Sylvia thrown off balance, Dr. Potter steadied her with one hand, then leaned down to say something to Clara, who giggled and didn't object at all when he lifted her onto his shoulders.

So, I thought, this was the Devil.

I wished Mercy hadn't just left.

"Dr. Potter," George said. "Are you going to speak?"

"I will not speak in this church," Potter said firmly. "I have no wish to unsettle a single soul."

Despite the fact that Clara had just managed to untie his bow tie, his tone was certain and formal. "It would not be fair to Reverend Byrd to cause such dismay among his flock."

"Will you speak outside of the church?" George asked him.

Potter looked surprised. "If you can find me a way," he said, "of course I will."

"We'll set you right up on the courthouse lawn," George said. "Would that be all right with you, Reverend Byrd?"

The pastor nodded calmly.

Dr. Potter lifted Clara from his shoulders, gave her a warm smile, and returned her to Sylvia's side. Without looking back, George led Dr. Potter away, along with about half the crowd. The others, frustrated by the closed church doors, began to disperse. Lottie, apparently torn between reporting on the congregants who remained and those who'd gone to hear Potter, motioned me over.

"Go with Potter," she instructed me. "Take pictures. Take notes if you can."

She tore a few pages from her notebook and handed them to me as if passing a stick in a relay race.

"Find something to write with," she added unnecessarily.

As I turned to follow George and Dr. Potter, I saw Lottie lunging toward the corkboard to grab the balled-up flyer from the grass. No doubt she would want to locate and interview whoever had drawn the Devil's face. Perhaps she would even find the red crayon and add it to her bundle of pencil souvenirs.

More than fifty seats—some stools, some wooden folding chairs, some benches—had already been set up on the west courthouse lawn for other speakers to come, and when I got there, Dr. Potter

was standing on the platform, waiting for folks to settle. George
was in the front row, leaning forward, but I sat farther back with
Caroline and Willie Quinn instead. I saw only a few reporters in
the audience; Lottie had stayed with the outraged congregants, and
I figured Mencken and most of the others had gone to see Bryan at
Mercy's church.

Part of me just wanted to go home. I was tired of trying to figure
out who was right and who was wrong, tired of the confusion and
conflict, so very much the opposite of what a Sunday was supposed
to be. But I took pictures and I listened. Dr. Potter was speaking
excitedly about the strange animals Charles Darwin had discovered
on some islands in the Pacific. He talked about God not as a person, but as a force that had created the natural laws by using supernatural power. He talked about the ways in which man had changed
over hundreds of thousands of years, not just in his height or his
posture but in the size of his skull and brain. He talked about bone
fragments and the ways scientists dated them. Branches of science
whose names I'd never heard. Museums and universities financing
expeditions and research all over a world that at that moment felt
larger and more exciting than it ever had. The kingdom of heaven
was and always had been my solemn destination. But the kingdoms
on earth he described—the ones inhabited by different species gradually changing over so many millions of years—seemed too extraordinary to ignore.

Dr. Potter's voice seemed to grow quieter, even conspiratorial.
"I'll tell you," he said, "Mr. Bryan and his followers think we're
destined for damnation if our children learn that we're related to
the monkeys and the rest of the animal kingdom. Here's my best
answer to Mr. Bryan's ideas about monkeys. My answer would be
to take an X-ray photograph of Mr. Bryan's spine."

There were murmurs among the audience.

"If I did make that X-ray photograph," he went on, "do you
know what I'd find? I'd find a little bone at the base of his spine.
That bone is no different from a monkey's tailbone. We humans,
we've all got one. And we've all got four muscles around it, and

believe me, if Mr. Bryan still had a tail, he'd be using those muscles to wag it all day long."

George was the first and by far the loudest to laugh. Not many others joined him. To say humans had a vestige of a tailbone was one thing. To say William Jennings Bryan had one was another.

"We ain't no monkeys! We're God-made men! We ain't no monkeys! We're God-made men!"

That chant came from a group of men who were moving swiftly along Main Street as they shouted their protest for all to hear.

Willie Quinn had a pencil in his front shirt pocket, and I grabbed it to jot down what they had said, as well as what Potter had said about Bryan's tail.

Potter talked for nearly an hour. He was calm, straightforward, way less colorful and dramatic than Bryan, or even Reverend Byrd. A few people left, and I couldn't tell if they were objecting to what he was saying or simply were bored by it. He finished with a prayer for tolerance and understanding. Afterwards, a few folks went up to talk to him. George beamed. I needed to find Lottie—to tell her what had happened and to give her the roll of film I'd shot. When I returned to the church, though, she was gone, the churchyard was empty, and the doors were open again.

Inside, several dozen people—Major McClure and his daughter-in-law included—were seated in the pews. Most of them were the same folks who'd caused such a ruckus just a few hours before, but now that the church doors were open, they had returned and were sitting, quiet and content, presumably feeling they'd vanquished their enemy and were just waiting for Reverend Byrd to bless them. But he was nowhere in sight.

In the front pew, Sylvia, the pastor's wife, sat holding a red and white paper pinwheel that Clara slapped at gently in the steamy, still air.

After a while, Reverend Byrd appeared, and the congregation leaned forward eagerly. He had changed into his usual Sunday jacket and tie and was carrying a Bible, as he did at any service. He took his place at the pulpit, looking out across the nave—his dark eyes seeming to land on each one of us before he spoke.

"There won't be a service in this church this afternoon," he said quietly. His voice was steady and strong. "There won't be a service here this evening, or next Sunday. At least not one conducted by me."

Above the murmuring, the major said, "But, Reverend, now you didn't let that Dr. Potter speak, we've all come to hear you."

"I'm well aware," the pastor said. "But I will not, I cannot, preside over a congregation too narrow to hear the words of a learned man from New York."

"So, you're a believer in *Devil*-ution?" the major asked, outraged.

"Evolution," Reverend Byrd said pointedly, "is not a faith. It's not something to believe. It's something to know."

"I know my Bible," the major said.

Reverend Byrd took a moment, seeming to weigh the impact of what he was prepared to say.

"Like you, Major, I believe the Bible was divinely inspired," he said simply. "But I do not believe it was written in heaven, printed on India paper, sewed with silk, and bound with calfskin."

A roar of arguments and objections rose. I realized my palms were moist.

"People who say they know the Bible from cover to cover but don't act on it are the ones who cause the trouble," he said. "Better to concentrate on this world than spend too much time thinking about the next."

Finally, he spread out his arms, the way he usually did when inviting us to pray or to sing.

"Lord," he said, "I know you are always listening to the prayers of our hearts. If it is your will, please hear mine now. Teach the people of this town, and all those who've come to mock it—teach them how to listen to each other, as you listen to us. In the name of the Father, the Son, and the Holy Spirit."

"Amen," we all said.

The reverend lowered his arms. "Thank you," he said. "For three years, my family and I have enjoyed living in this town. It won't take us but a week to pack up and be on our way."

William Jennings Bryan had once written and often said, "It is better to trust in the Rock of Ages than to know the age of the rocks." It was admittedly a catchy play on words, but the Rock of Ages, as people knew it, was Christianity, and the opening lines of the hymn were

> Rock of Ages, cleft for me,
> Let me hide myself in thee.

I couldn't avoid these two questions: Why were we hiding? And from what?

That evening, George strode in the front door, utterly transported.

"Did you hear him, Annie? Did you hear what Dr. Potter said?"

"You know I did, George. You saw me there."

"And?" he asked me eagerly. I knew what he wanted. He wanted me to say that I understood evolution, that I saw the folly of my neighbors and my upbringing, that I had crossed the border to his side, his country.

He still didn't appreciate how painful and perilous that voyage might feel.

He took off his jacket and hung it on the back of his usual chair with his usual precision. He looked at me expectantly.

"And," I said. "And I heard what Reverend Byrd said too."

"Is he really quitting the church? Or was he just trying to make a point?"

"He's really quitting the church."

"Is there any pie?" George asked, loosening his tie.

I looked at him in disbelief.

"Did you hear me?" I asked. "Reverend Byrd. The man who

married us. He resigned from our church because your Dr. Potter came to stand in our pulpit and preach about evolution."

"He is not my Dr. Potter," George said, and, in his best lawyer voice—not friendly court jabber—he said, "Allow me to call your attention to the fact that it was *your* Reverend Byrd who invited him here in the first place. No pie?"

He walked over to the refrigerator and opened it, disgruntled.

"There's no pie, George," I said. "No cookies. No biscuits. No shortbread. I didn't have time to bake."

"Uh-huh."

He closed the refrigerator mournfully.

"I'm sure Mercy's got some sweets over at her place if you've got such a hankering."

George laughed. "There's no way Mercy Applegate is going to feed me pie. All I'll get from her is a lecture about damnation."

"Suit yourself," I said, but then I added a "Sweetheart," to try to mask my anger. He was so full of his success and certainty that he couldn't see how, beyond the rift everyone was talking about between science and religion, there was a different kind of rift growing between us as well. And, though I wasn't quite aware of it yet, I was probably even angrier at myself—for not knowing anymore exactly what I believed.

Within the week, I would learn from one of the scientists that the heart is the first organ in the human body to form. Maybe that is why it takes so much effort for the mind to overcome it when it needs to. The heart beats with love—and swells with hatred—before the mind has time to grow thoughts.

There was a girl in my grade school class named Melody, and though she moved out of town before we even reached the middle grades, I never forgot her. Melody annoyed our teacher, and eventually everyone else, by repeatedly asking questions that were deep and unwelcome. Why were there just four seasons when there were so many different kinds of weather? Why were there *even* four sea-

sons when Tennessee winters were so much like Tennessee au-
tumns? Why did some pencils need sharpening so much more often
than others? And, at least half a dozen times, how could we know
we all meant the same thing when we said the word *green*?

"We learn our colors," Mrs. Finn had said, "the way we learn
other things. We can all agree what a flower is. What a house is.
What a desk is."

I remember Mrs. Finn rapping briskly on her desk.

"But green," Melody had said. "What if my green is different
from your green?"

"Melody," the teacher had said with a sigh. "Look at the leaves
on that tree."

Just outside the window was a lone but leafy elm.

"Let's pretend you're just a baby," she'd said. "I tell you, 'Look,
Melody. Look at the pretty green leaves.' That's how you learn
what green is."

"But what if I see something different when you point to the
leaves? What if I see orange?"

I was coming to understand that my God was different from
William Jennings Bryan's, from Dr. Potter's, from Mercy's, perhaps
even from Reverend Byrd's. And if George still had a god at all,
they certainly hadn't spoken for a while. But now, hearing him
downstairs as he scrounged around for something that could take
the place of the pie I'd not provided, I wondered if my idea of love
was different from his too.

My idea of love revolved around the memory of two grownups
in a farmhouse kitchen, up at dawn but laughing; talking in soft
voices so as not to wake their daughter, a quiet, small world unto
themselves. My idea of love was two people beside each other, not
face to face, not even hand in hand, but rather both in profile, facing the same direction, like the two Lincoln heads on a double-
stamped penny I'd once found in loose change.

Was that what George thought love was? At the start, we'd had
so much desire, but maybe, even before his ham radio days, what
he'd felt for me had been something less like passion—or trust—

and something more like protectiveness, pride, amusement. I wondered if the reason he didn't yearn for children the way I did was that he thought of me as a child. If I was honest, I'd have to admit that I sometimes felt protection from him that I hadn't felt since I'd lost my parents.

When he finally came upstairs, I was under the coverlet, pretending to be asleep. But my heart was so knotted up that I wasn't sleepy at all. I watched secretly as George undressed, hanging his tie on a hook in the closet, smoothing and tugging it down between his hands, as if he were ringing a church bell. He put on fresh shorts and a fresh undershirt, and by his long-standing and illogical habit, he loosely folded the ones he'd been wearing, then tossed them into our hamper.

Standing at our dresser, he looked at himself in the mirror, seemingly satisfied, then casually rearranged my things the way he used to do before Walton Allen: my hairbrush, comb, hand mirror, and a bottle of perfume he'd given me once. He lined these things up precisely, as if there was going to be an inspection. Once more, it seemed everything had to be the way that George thought it ought to be. He got into bed and yanked some of my covers toward him, a tiny, silent act of selfishness that I doubted he would have indulged in if he'd known I was awake. We fell asleep neither side by side nor face to face. Rather, we were back to back, turned toward opposite walls.

4

I slept, but I didn't dream. Lottie was once again at my feet when I woke, this time looking frustrated that I wasn't already up and dressed. I realized I hadn't told her that I was going to miss the morning's court session. After more than a month of fussing and primping, the Mansion was finally going to welcome guests. Specifically, most of the expert witnesses—many of whom George himself had helped to find—would be arriving throughout the day.

He seemed pleased when, downstairs, I told him that I would be part of the welcoming committee for the scientists at the Mansion. Maybe he was hoping some of their wisdom would rub off on me. But Lottie pulled me aside, frowning.

"Why do you want to be there, playing housemaid, when you could be sitting next to me in the courtroom?"

"I promised Precious and Rapp," I said. "I—"

George broke in.

"Those are important people she's greeting," he said. "They're coming from cities all over the country."

"Well, snap their pictures while you're at the Mansion," Lottie said to me, "if you can manage, that is, to put down your feather duster long enough."

"Don't insult my wife," George said before I could respond.

"Well, that was gallant," Lottie said. Then she winked at me. "It's okay. Annabel knows what I mean."

Did I?

"I'm sorry," Lottie added vaguely, while at the same time she was checking her notebook, fluffing her hair, eager to go and discover how the new day's drama was going to unfold.

"I'll catch up with you later," I said. "After lunch, maybe."

"I won't be able to save you a seat."

"I know," I said. "I'll stand on the side."

With two long strides on her stick legs, Lottie reached the kitchen door.

"See you in court, Counselor," she said to George and waved gaily as she left.

As soon as he heard the door close, George straightened his tie and ran an Ace pocket comb through his hair.

"Look me over," he instructed me. "I want to look sharp."

"You do."

"No," he said. "Really look. Any threads? Any wrinkles? Any loose hairs?"

He was perfect. He looked exactly the way he had when I'd met him. Elegant in that country way. Determined. Handsome. Smart.

Just then Lottie popped back in.

"And don't just take pictures at the Mansion," she called from the hallway. "Take notes too."

At the Mansion, the men arrived steadily, some of them two by two, just like the animals on the ark. They carried small bags filled with their clothing and larger bags filled with their books and papers. They seemed perfectly polite, not at all my image of what men from New York, Chicago, and Boston would be like when they came to town. Actually, of all the visitors I'd met so far, it was Bryan—with his big voice and his big belly and his big crowds—who'd seemed the rudest, or at least the most out of place.

They introduced themselves by name and by specialty. Biology. Geology. Zoology. Anthropology. I led them to their rooms and fetched them lemonade and iced tea, biscuits and shortbread. Along with Precious, Caroline, and a few women from the Aqua, I opened windows, turned on electric fans, and asked what each man needed.

None of them seemed to need much. They had each passed by the circus of Main and Market Streets on their way from the depot; none of them expressed a need to go back.

There was only one request, and it came from a Professor Atkins, head of the biology department at some Massachusetts university. He asked me if I could find him a copy of the textbook that John Scopes was accused of having used to teach evolution.

I told him I'd try. Normally—and it was an irony that plenty of reporters had pointed out—Robinson's Drugstore was the place that sold new textbooks, but I knew that those shelves had already been picked clean by the reporters. And while I'd kept so many books from my years working at the Aqua, I'd long since passed my textbooks down to younger students, just as mine had been passed down to me.

"I'll be back as soon as I can," I told the professor, and I started down the stairs.

I didn't go to Robinson's. Instead, I turned right and headed to the high school. Even though school was not in session in July, that didn't mean the schoolhouse was closed. The athletic fields were always open, and then, too, there were those women still painting silly monkey cards in the lunchroom. I slipped in by one of the side entrances and climbed the stairs to Room 201, where I'd sat years before in science class, trying my best to concentrate.

A Civic Biology, by George William Hunter, had been published in 1914, and so eleven years of smudges, notes, and drippings of syrup and juice were features of the books that circulated in school. I found a dozen or so copies on the classroom shelf, and though I knew that Professor Atkins would be hoping I'd come back right away, I wanted first to see—to remind myself—what the pages about Darwin actually said, what the state of Tennessee and William Jennings Bryan and the major and Mercy and her church had declared not only unfit to be taught but dangerous to our souls.

The textbook was more than four hundred pages long, and I must have learned something from it in high school, because I did make straight A's in science. But the only thing I could recall from the book was a set of photographs showing a city street and a country road. The text had said something about the crowded city being unhealthy and that had made everyone—myself included— feel good that we didn't live in a crowded city. The rest of what I remembered about biology class was not the textbook but the teacher: the ancient Mr. Cavendish, who would stand at the slate blackboard writing terms and drawing diagrams that, like his body, always slanted down and to the right. Had he covered evolution? Where had been the day that the life I lived as a Christian had supposedly been put into peril?

I sat at one of the pockmarked wooden desks and opened the textbook. The photos I remembered were actually right there on the first page. There was the city street, cramped and chaotic, filled with wooden pushcarts and men wearing strange hats; and there was the country road, wide and leafy. "Compare the unfavorable artificial environment of a crowded city with the more favorable environment of the country," the caption read. I felt sure that the men now settling into the Mansion did not consider the cities' environment unfavorable.

I scanned the chapter headings for "Evolution," or "Darwin," but I didn't find either. There were chapters on plants and animals, forests and nutrition. I turned more pages, passing vaguely remembered drawings of seeds, instructions for experiments with beans. About halfway through the book, I found what I'd been looking for: a simple illustration called "The Evolutionary Tree." With its circles of different sizes, it looked like the branch of a crab apple tree just coming into fruit. Each circle was labeled with the number of species in an animal group. Insects: 360,000; birds: 13,000; mammals: 3,500. Unless you knew that man was a mammal, you wouldn't have known where to find him. But I didn't have time to study it all. The instructions under the drawing read, "Copy this diagram in your notebook. Explain it as well as you can." Alone in the classroom, I laughed.

The text only explained it this way: "Evolutionary theory is the belief that simple forms of life on the earth slowly and gradually gave rise to those more complex and that thus ultimately the most complex forms came into existence."

Man, according to the textbook, had descended in time from simpler forms of mammals and was the most complex. "Man," Hunter wrote, "is the thinking animal, and as such is master of the earth."

It would be years before I'd have reason to reexamine these pages and discover how Hunter, like so many others of the time, asserted that man, like dogs and tomatoes and wheat, could himself be improved by selective breeding. Or how Hunter claimed that human beings existed as five distinct races, of which the "civilized," educated, white race was the superior. I'd like to think it would have appalled me if I'd read about eugenics then. But I didn't have time to read more of anything. Tucking the book under my arm, I felt I was carrying history in my hand, and I hurried back to the Mansion.

The place had become quite jolly in my short absence. There had been a problem with the plumbing, and though there were workmen still tinkering with the toilets, none of these scholars seemed to mind.

I found Professor Atkins in the room where I'd left him. Only his books and papers had been unpacked.

"Do you need help with your clothes?" I asked him, just as I'd asked innumerable guests at the Aqua years before.

"Oh, no, no," he said, smiling. "Little need for those right now."

I handed him the textbook, and he took it eagerly.

"Pretty well used," he said.

"I reckon."

"Did you grow up in this town?" he asked.

"Yes, sir."

"Go to the high school here?"

"That's right."

"And was this the book you studied?"

"In biology, yes."

"Mind if I ask you something?"

"What's that?"

"What did this book tell you about Charles Darwin?"

I hesitated, tempted to tell him what I'd only just read, but I decided to tell him the truth.

"To be honest," I said, "I didn't remember a thing about Charles Darwin from this book until I looked at it in the classroom just now."

"Nothing?"

"Could be other students did. My parents died when I was in high school. My brain wasn't really holding on to much."

"Oh, I'm sorry," he said. "I hope you found comfort."

"From friends, yes," I said. "And from the Bible," I added pointedly, half expecting him to scoff.

"Well, that is its great gift, isn't it?" he said without hesitating. "The consolation."

"You read the Bible?" I asked before I realized just how rude I sounded.

"Young lady," he said, smiling. "I'm a trustee of my church."

"Atkins!" someone called up from downstairs just then. "We're having a lunch down here that you won't want to miss!"

I knew there would be no way of getting inside the courtroom for the afternoon session. But two large bell-shaped loudspeakers had been attached outside the windows on the east and west sides of the building, and there were at least two hundred people on the lawn, all trying to hear—through the carnival hubbub from Market and Main Streets—what was being said inside the courtroom.

There was a lot of back-and-forth between the lawyers, and I kept hoping to hear George's voice in the mix, but the lawyers were talking over each other, and finally we could hear Judge Raulston say, "I'd ask the jurors to step outside." After a moment, the front doors of the courthouse opened, and a puffed-up Horace Carter led twelve very sweaty, very grumpy men down the steps and around to the east side of the lawn. I followed. Some plank benches had been set aside for them, though Horace first had to shoo away some squatters. The jurors who were still wearing jackets removed them with great relief. They rolled up their sleeves, lit cigarettes and pipes, and exchanged silent, sympathetic looks. I wondered whether, if Lottie were out here, she would try to interview them. But I figured if they had been sent out of the courtroom, it was to keep them from being swayed, and I cringed to think what George would say or do if it turned out that I had somehow gotten in the way of the trial.

On the other hand, I didn't think there was any harm in taking a photograph or two. And so I did. The men were all obliging, though I knew only two or three of them. This wasn't the formal portrait for which they had posed on Friday, looking tidy and serious on the courthouse steps, with the glory-grabbing judge beside them. In this one, they weren't posed at all. Just a dozen men waiting on wooden benches in shirtsleeves, one of them tugging at his bow tie, another scratching his forearm. It is still one of my all-time favorite photographs.

One thing was perplexing, though. I couldn't figure out why the jurors were sitting where they seemed no more or less able than anyone else to hear the proceedings through the loudspeakers. Hadn't anybody thought of that? I wondered if I could get a message to George. Or if he would just as soon let the jurors hear what Clarence Darrow was saying now.

Darrow's voice came over the loudspeaker, not preachy, like

Bryan's, but firm. "The Bible is not one book," I heard him say. "The Bible is made up of sixty-six books written over a period of about a thousand years by many different authors." Just then a sound began to underscore Darrow's words. It was a hiss and popping, like the sound George's ham rig had made so often. "It is a book primarily of religion and morals," Darrow was saying. "It is not a book of science. Never was and was never meant to be."

Darrow's words became more difficult to make out. ". . . geology . . ." "mystery" . . . "thought the sun went around the earth . . ." The hissing grew louder, and I started to think the speakers were breaking down. But then it was clear what was happening: A swarm of bees was spilling out of a hive under the courthouse eaves. It was a huge, dark swarm, like a cloud of smoke pushing into a room from a closed chimney flue. The buzzing got louder, then faded as the bees broke off and started to spread out overhead. No one seemed to notice or care.

I could now hear Darrow more clearly. "There are in the first two chapters of Genesis alone two different versions of the origin of man. In the first, Adam is created after the animals and Eve along with him. In the second, man is created before the animals, and Eve is created from his rib. Can Your Honor therefore say what is given as *the* origin of man as shown in the Bible? Is there any human being who can tell us?"

The question seemed to alarm the bystanders and, at the same time, refocus their attention. For my part, I don't think I was the only person who wanted to go grab a Bible at that moment and reread Genesis. Even though I had read it a hundred times and knew most of it by heart, I don't think I had ever noticed the contradiction. I felt both amazed and ashamed.

Then I watched as a man with a neck nearly as wide as his head got stung by one of the remaining bees, which fell to the courthouse lawn, dead. The man never moved, just leaned forward farther to hear how this foreigner, Clarence Darrow, was scheming to take away the wisdom of the Bible: a threat strong enough to silence two hundred people and overpower a swarm of bees.

.   .   .

At home, Spitfire seemed to have been waiting for me on the stair-case landing, but as soon as I said her name, she bolted away, as always her own mistress. I put some scraps of meat into her dish, and only then did she deign to join me in the kitchen. I was just starting to write George a note when he came in, looking tired but excited.

"You should have heard him, Annie!" he said.

"Darrow?"

"He was brilliant. He was magnificent."

"I did hear him," I said and watched my husband's face cloud up.

"When? How? I thought you were at the Mansion. I didn't see you in court."

"I *was* at the Mansion this morning, but there are loudspeakers outside the courthouse, George," I said.

"Oh, right," he said. "I guess I'm not thinking about it from an outsider's point of view."

Was he intending to belittle me by calling me an outsider?

"Well, here's one thing *you'd* know if you were sitting outside," I said.

"What's that?"

"The jurors can hear everything."

"They can what?"

"They're sitting on benches not too far from one of the loud-speakers."

George's eyes narrowed, as if he was calculating figures.

"Did anyone else notice?" he asked.

I shrugged. "They were all right there," I said. "And George? I'm going to be back in court tomorrow. I'm not an outsider. I'm taking photographs."

I put the plate of sandwiches on the table.

"Busy Bee," he said, a nickname landing squarely between af-fection and mockery.

5

Sometime during the afternoon, the furniture on the first floor of the Mansion, scattershot to begin with, had been rearranged into a rough oval. The double doors to the dining room had been flung wide open, and long tables, including some that were just boards set up on sawhorses, were now laden with cold meats, loaves of brown and white breads, bowls of fruit, plates of green and yellow string beans, pyramids of biscuits, cookies, and small pink cakes. The eight expert witnesses had had the whole day to settle in and get to know one another, and now they were digging into this feast with more than casual enthusiasm.

George, the person with whom they'd had the most contact, arrived soon after I did and was given a hero's welcome. The men shook his hand and patted his shoulder. If they were at all apprehensive about taking on Williams Jennings Bryan, they certainly didn't show it. They seemed downright giddy.

To be clear, this was 1925, and making and possessing liquor had been illegal in Tennessee since the Bone-Dry Bill eight years before. Moonshine, however, had been around as long as the mountains. Moonshine was what had fueled Walton Allen's rage. Even

George had long ago instructed me to keep a jug of grape juice around so it would ferment. On our first anniversary, he'd insisted I try it, but I hadn't liked the sour, sludgy taste of it. Now he was handed a glass by one of the men.

"Well, what on earth could this be?" he asked, and everyone laughed. He avoided my eye, and as he drank, I went to the kitchen to see what was needed.

When I came back just a few minutes later, carrying a heavy striped bowl filled with fresh potato salad, George Rappleyea was just arriving at the front door with another stranger. It had started to rain, and both of them were drenched. Rapp's usually electrified hair had been flattened down, and as the other man removed and tipped his hat, a small puddle dropped on the floor.

I ran to get some towels for them. Rapp took his wordlessly, but the visitor thanked me. He glanced down at the puddle.

"Looks like we're making plenty of work for you, young lady," he said.

"It's no trouble," I said.

Some of the men stood up to greet him. He was a short man, with very dark hair, and eyebrows that looked as if someone had drawn them on.

"I told you I'd bring you a rabbi," Rapp said to the lawyers and scholars, and he introduced the man to the others. I had heard about Jewish people, of course, but Rabbi Rosenwasser was the first one I'd ever met. In short order, that very night, he also became the first person to help me understand the deeper meaning of what Darrow's words that afternoon had already suggested. The Bible wasn't just one book, and even in English it didn't have just one translation.

I was gathering used dishes to take to the kitchen when Rabbi Rosenwasser asked if I'd mind putting them down a minute and helping out.

"Me?" I asked stupidly.

"If you don't mind," he said.

I looked nervously at George, who seemed just as nervous look-

ing back at me. The rabbi had taken up a spot next to Rapp in front
of the tall, wide stone fireplace, and as he started talking, he un-
furled a large banner the size of a schoolroom map and secured it
to the top of the mantel with some books. I could tell I wasn't the
only person puzzled by this object. The letters on the banner, written in large dark black ink, looked more like numbers than letters.

"Gentlemen, if you'll allow me," the rabbi said. With the fireplace poker, he touched the first words of the banner and moved it
over the words, like a pointer. But he went from right to left instead
of left to right. He read, as he pointed, in a language that sounded
as if he was trying to clear his throat.

He stopped after the first few lines and looked straight at me.

"What's your name, young lady?"

"It's Annabel," I said.

"Ah, Annabel," he said. "Did anyone ever tell you what your
name means?"

"Well," I said, probably blushing. "I'd guess 'beautiful Anna'
because doesn't *bel* mean *beautiful*?"

He nodded, and I felt a bit proud.

"It does," he said. "*Belle* is French for *beautiful*. But what about
Anna?"

I didn't have a guess.

"Well, as it happens, you know, the name *Anna* comes from the
name *Hannah*. Do you remember reading about her in your Bible?"

I shook my head no.

"You know, Hannah was a prophetess. She appears at the beginning of the first book of Samuel. Her name in Hebrew means
grace."

I nodded.

"Not to put you on the spot, Miss—"

"Mrs.," George said before I could say it myself. "Mrs. Craig."

"Not to put you on the spot, Mrs. Craig. But can I ask, did you
grow up in Tennessee?"

"Yes, sir. Here in Dayton."

"And can I assume you attended church?"

"Of course."

"And what church, if you don't mind my asking?"

"Methodist-Episcopal North."

"And what Bible do you read?"

"The Bible," I said.

"Yes. Which Bible?"

"Both the Old Testament and the New," I said proudly.

"Yes, Mrs. Craig. But which translation?"

I looked to George, who smiled just a whisper, then to Rapp and Precious, who were the only other people (not counting Professor Atkins) I knew in the room. Precious fiddled with the collar on her blouse. Rapp nodded reassuringly.

He said, "Isn't it the King James Version?"

"I suppose," I said.

"Ah," the rabbi said. "You know, the language of the King James Bible is beautiful—surpassingly beautiful—but when that translation was written, you know, not much was known yet of Hebrew language."

I don't remember the first time that my father took me into the fields to pick strawberries while he talked to the men doing the harvesting. But sometime early, wandering among the bushes and bees, I learned to tell the difference between a vine and a weed, between a berry that was ripe and one that was blighted, between soil that was rich and ready and soil that was too dry for planting.

I must have been four or five when my father first sat me on his lap to read to me from the Bible, and one of the first things I remember him reading was the Parable of the Sower: how seeds a farmer scattered on a path would be eaten by birds, and how seeds scattered on rocks would not be able to take root, and how seeds scattered in thorns would be choked by them, but how seeds scattered on fertile soil would grow into ample crops. I remember him explaining how the story wasn't about how we needed fertile soil in order to grow good strawberries, but about how we needed open hearts in order to let the word of God take root. I remember him letting me lean my head back against his chest; the feeling of his breath on the top of my head; the sound of the Bible pages crinkling slightly as his rough hands gently turned them over.

My father's Bible was well worn. It was bound in fine black leather with the words HOLY BIBLE embossed in faded gold letters on its cover, and a frayed white silk ribbon for marking pages dangling from its spine. There were colored maps of the Holy Land on the last pages. And every word Jesus had said was printed in bright red ink. I knew this as the family Bible, though it had always irked me that at the front, where there were pages labeled for a family tree, no one had ever filled in a name.

My father's Bible may have been extra nice on the outside, but it had the same words inside it as the ones at Sunday School. The ones at Sunday School in the church basement had been a motley collection: different sizes, ages, bindings. Some of them were relatively new, others inscribed with fragmented family trees or the names of successive owners. They all held the same claylike smell of dampness and age, but they also all held the same holy words. The Bible was the Bible. Why had no one ever suggested to me that not all Bibles were the same?

Rabbi Rosenwasser said the King James Bible's translation had a lot of mistakes in it.

"Again, if you don't mind, Mrs. Craig. How does Genesis begin?" he asked me.

"In the beginning, God created the heaven and the earth, and the—"

"Yes," he said. "Already there is a question about translation. That word, *create,* is supposed to be the translation of the Hebrew word *bara. Bara* does not mean to create. The correct translation of *bara* is *to set in motion.* Do you see the difference? For God to set something in motion means that a thing already exists." He went on to explain that the word *Adam* was neither a name nor a simple translation of the word *man.* He said in Hebrew the word *Adam* could mean just *earth* or *red* or *blood* and thus any red-blooded living thing. There were also many different words in the Bible that meant *man* in different ways, he said. "Do you understand?" he asked me.

I understood what he was saying, but I chafed against it, and I would learn in time that the specific "corrections" the rabbi put forth were questionable at best. But his assertion of them that night was enough to make me realize that any translation of ancient Hebrew was bound to be subject to interpretation and debate.

"Why is it so important that *I* understand?" I asked.

"Because if you weren't a woman, you could be on the jury, and the jury needs to understand. If we are the descendants of Adam and Adam is any living thing containing blood," he said, "then there is no reason that the Bible and evolution cannot be reconciled."

The first flash of lightning came just after sunset, brightening the bare windows on the main floor. The men looked out and then around at each other, some startled, some already smiling. I assumed everyone was thinking the same thing, but it was the geologist from Tennessee who said it.

"If God's angry at us just for coming to town and eating some biscuits, what's He going to do when we testify in court?"

There was genial laughter, and then the lights went out. A stunned silence followed, something I already understood to be unusual for this particular group of men. Even more startling was a thump on the door, then the sound of the rabbi's banner falling to the floor. Precious had the good sense to grab one of the candles from the mantel and somehow find a match.

"Let there be light!" one of the men shouted as the others chuckled.

She opened the door, and I could just make out Clarence Darrow himself, shaking out a ragged shawl that someone must have given him.

"Well, fellas," he said. "Looks like we're in for it now."

George was the first one at his side.

"That you, Craig?" I heard Darrow ask as, following Precious, I went running to the shed to fetch the kerosene lanterns we'd stored there just in case.

We carried two in each hand, ducking through the rain. A huge blast of thunder hit just as we reached the kitchen. It shook me.

"No stopping now, girl," Precious said. "Your George and my George still have a long row to hoe."

We lit the lanterns and began to pass them around. "When I was growing up," Darrow was saying, "all of us boys had a weird idea about darkness. The night was peopled with ghosts and wandering spirits, and you couldn't catch any of us lingering by the fences that went along two sides of the graveyard. We always ran when we passed the white stones after dusk. Fable and superstition," he said, shaking his large head. "Who can guess what the world would be like if it wasn't plagued by superstition?" He paused, leaving his question in the semidarkness. "Is there a perch here for me somewhere? I can't see a thing."

I stayed at the Mansion until about ten o'clock, listening to Darrow and George debate the potential order and relative impact of the experts' testimony: the age of the earth, the striations of the rock, the way of dating fossils, the bone structure of the mammal, the brain size of the chimpanzee. George, in these conversations, seemed to be, if not Darrow's equal, then in certain respects his guide. George. G.

In that hour, standing just outside that circle of eager, intense men, I was thrilled and confused, tempted and angry. I wanted my love of God to be as easy and natural as my love for my parents had been. I didn't want to lose any part of that love, to question my own faith, but the men's ideas seemed to glitter in that dark room, and it was impossible not to be dazzled by them.

I believed that in the experts' testimony there would be so much evidence that man had evolved that it could not be ignored. I wished that Mercy could be here, and the major as well, to see how decent and warm and kind these men were, how committed they were to the task at hand, and how—unlike Mercy and the major and Bryan especially—they were ready, even eager, to admit there were things they didn't know. Yes, as the Fundamentalists liked to point out, there were gaps in the evolutionary chain. But that didn't mean the gaps couldn't someday be filled. And it didn't make what had already been discovered any less true. Several of the scientists—Professor Atkins included—even talked about God, even said that He had given us minds with the power to ask new questions and discover new answers all the time. Professor Atkins said we did a disservice when we confused the power of God with the process of evolution. Dr. Metcalf, who was a zoologist, said it was insulting to God to suggest that He was not, even through the discoveries of science, perpetually revealing Himself.

I understood why George was thrilled to be in the company of these men. He seemed especially excited to be called upon by Darrow, but he managed to look casual about it, at least to the others. I was aware that his hands were busier than usual, though—gesturing whenever he spoke, forcefully pushing a pipe cleaner through the stem of his pipe, emptying the bowl, then filling it, lighting it. Darrow was a cigar smoker, so George wasn't able to offer him his tobacco pouch, but he offered it to others. His steady, smiling self was, beside Darrow's and perhaps the rabbi's, the dominant personality in that room that night.

"And what if the judge allows us just one expert witness?" Darrow asked the group.

"Oh, it has to be archaeology or genetics," said Professor Atkins.

"I wouldn't think so, sir," George said—not combatively, just confidently.

Darrow said, "Craig?"

"I think we'd be better served by leading with Wilbur Nelson, here."

"Geology's not exactly on the mark for the descent of man," Professor Atkins said.

"True," George agreed. "But it does get us to the age of the earth, and Nelson is our state geologist. Tennessee means a lot to Tennesseans."

Darrow nodded and smiled.

"You hear that, Nelson?" he asked. "How much twang can you put in your voice?"

Slim Andrews, who was making some spare change trotting people around town in his wagon, gave me a lift back home. Once there, I was happy to hear Lottie's typewriter. I needed to make some food for the next day, and I wanted a moment alone. I tied on an apron and set three big sweet potatoes to boil. I mixed up butter, cinnamon, milk, sugar, and eggs, and I rolled out dough for a pie crust. I didn't want to see Lottie. I wanted to think about all the things I'd heard. I wanted to revel in George's importance. Waiting for the potatoes to cook, I wondered if the men were all still talking at the Mansion, still throwing their ideas around and drinking, still calling George *Craig*. Eventually, though, the smell of the sweet potatoes wafted upstairs, and Lottie's typing stopped. A few moments later, she appeared beside me at the kitchen table.

"So?" she said. "How was it at the Mansion?"

"Busy," I said.

"Who was there?"

"You know," I said. "The scientists. The lawyers."

"Was Darrow there?"

"Yes," I said.

"Who else?"

I got up to take the potatoes from the stove.

"George Rapp and Precious. A rabbi. A geologist from Tennessee. A zoologist. I don't know them all," I said. "The storm knocked the lights out."

I stripped the potatoes of their skins.

I wanted Lottie to go away. Too many people had been asking me too many questions today.

"So, what was the conversation like?" she asked.

"Lottie," I finally said. "I'm trying to concentrate on this."

She seemed to notice for the first time that I was doing something, and for at least a few minutes, she watched as I lined the pie plate with dough.

"What kind of mood were they in?" she asked.

"Lottie!" I scolded. "If you were so curious—"

"I wasn't invited," she said.

I added the sweet potatoes to the bowl and started to stir.

Lottie shook her head, then asked: "After this whole day, what with court and then the Mansion, you've made a sweet potato pie?"

I crimped the edges of the crust, then picked up a fork and started to stamp the edge with the tines.

"People need to eat," I said.

She shrugged, then looked heavenward.

"Someday, when you're married, you'll understand," I said, feeling it was my turn to dispense a little wisdom.

Lottie laughed. "What makes you think I'll ever want to get married?" she asked.

I put down the fork.

"Why wouldn't you want to get married?" I asked.

"I don't think I like men all that much," she said. "Especially this week, with all of them spouting all the time, and all so loud about everything, no matter what side they're on."

"But that's different," I said.

"Different from what?"

"Different from love. Different from one man alone."

"Oh, I've had one man alone," she said with a grin. "More than a few, in fact. That was fun."

"That's not what I meant," I said in a whisper.

"I know."

She picked up the fork I had put down and started to work it around the edge of the pie.

"Am I doing this right?" she asked.

A sinner, I thought. *A perfectly proud sinner.*

"Annabel? Is this the right way?"

"A little less pressure," I said. "You don't want the dough to separate."

She followed my instructions.

"You mean all you ever want to do is work?" I asked her.

"Don't you think women should work?"

She had made her way around the pie and put down the fork.

"I *do* work," I said. "You ever tried to run a household? Or look at Mercy, with all those children. The cleaning and the cooking and the planning. Do you know how to make jam?" I asked. "Do you know how to bake even a simple loaf of bread? Do you know how to weed a garden? Do you know how to can tomatoes?"

"Just this week," Lottie said, ignoring my questions, "I read in *Reader's Digest* that there are five women bank presidents in this country, and a dozen women are making thousands of dollars a year running post offices, and something like fifty cities have women police. There are women working everywhere."

The police thing surprised me, but I didn't let on. "You know, Lottie," I said, "I worked at the Aqua Hotel for nearly four years after my parents died."

"I don't mean working because they have to. Working because they want to. Because they have ambition."

I put the pie in the oven and closed the door.

"Are you ambitious?" she asked.

"I don't know," I said. "It's hard to think ahead."

"Try."

"I don't want to," I said, and then all I could think of adding was "So you don't ever want to get married?"

Lottie fixed me with a stare. "You've got *The Awakening* on your bookshelf," she said. "A pretty well-thumbed copy, it seems."

Shocked, I asked, "Have you been through my dresser drawers too?"

Lottie just smiled noncommittally.

"The heroine of that novel realized she was living a life she didn't want to live."

"Right," I said, "and she drowned."

"Annabel," she said. "People are allowed to want what they want."

"I know that."

"And, Annabel," she added softly. "What a person wants can change."

Did she mean it to sound like an invitation? I wasn't ready for that.

But I thought about my mother, about whether what she wanted had ever changed. Had she always wanted the canning clubs, or were they simply what she wanted when she realized she'd have no more children?

Maybe that was why my father had never objected to her traveling around.

"As long as the canning doesn't take you away from God and your family," I could imagine him telling her, and suddenly I remembered something I *had* heard him utter, a famous saying about how only God could know the future: "Bethany, love, go and count the number of seeds in a tomato if you will, but only God can count the number of tomatoes in a seed."

Lottie glanced at her wristwatch and reluctantly went upstairs to resume typing, and I sat on a kitchen chair, thinking about the unknowable future, and waiting for George to come home and for the pie to be done.

6

I was back in court the next morning, sitting beside Lottie as the packed room awaited the appearance of Bryan and Darrow. A number of the defense witnesses I'd met the night before were seated, jackets on, behind the still-empty jury box. Rabbi Rosenwasser looked my way and smiled. So did Professor Atkins.

Unlike on the previous days of the trial, I felt I had a sense of what was to come. In effect, I had seen a dress rehearsal the evening before. But first, Judge Raulston introduced Reverend Stribling, who stepped up to the bench and bowed his head.

"Lord—" he began, and Clarence Darrow immediately stood.

"Your Honor," he said. "I want to make an objection before the jury comes in."

It was clear that his patience with prayer in the courtroom had been used up.

Darrow spoke calmly, but his passion was evident in the way he repeatedly slammed his right hand down onto the palm of his left. "I object to prayer." Slam. "And I object . . ." Slam. "to the jury being present . . ." Slam. ". . . when the Court rules on the objection." Slam. The strange thing was that in between these smacks, his right hand was lifted high, as if he were taking an oath.

There were murmurs, and one man shouted: "See what I said? They want to be taking away our prayers!"

"Order!" one of the court officers shouted.

I was aware of currents moving through the courtroom all the time. Unspoken communication between the judge and Bryan, the judge and the press, even the judge and the jurors, in the rare times they were present. There were also silent conversations going on between H. L. Mencken and Clarence Darrow, Darrow and Neal, Neal and George. I imagined all this as a kind of web and knew we were each, in our own way, clinging to one of its threads. John Scopes, though supposedly the center of all this action, remained still and mostly expressionless. However sincere he was about the issues at hand, it was clear he had never bargained for all the attention.

Darrow waited for quiet. "Seeing that the very nature of this case is one in which the State claims a conflict between science and religion," he said, "I object to any attempt to influence the jury by means of prayer. It is bad enough that the town is festooned with signs urging every Daytonian to read his Bible."

Bryan stayed seated. "One thing has nothing to do with the other," he declared.

Judge Raulston readjusted the angle of his coveted desk fan. "Now, I do not want to be unreasonable about anything," he said, "but it has been my custom since I have been a judge to have prayers when it was convenient, and I know of no reason why I should not follow up this custom, so I will overrule the objection."

George, without warning, pushed his chair back noisily and got to his feet.

"But, Your Honor, can't you see—" he began.

Darrow cut him with a look that I knew George would remember for the rest of his life. George's sentence remained unfinished, his argument and his disbelief suspended in the humid air.

"Mr. Craig?" Judge Raulston said more than asked.

George looked to Darrow. Without moving a muscle, Darrow managed to say, *Sit the hell down right now.* "Begging your pardon, Your Honor," George said in a small voice, and sat.

"My colleague," Darrow said, regaining the floor and the room's attention, "was intending to support our cause."

There was faint laughter in the crowd. Then Bryan stirred and took to his feet, flapping a Robinson's Drugstore palm fan in front of his belly even as he spoke. "I believe there was a case that made it to your Supreme Court," he said to Judge Raulston. "A jury, being asked to deliberate on a man's guilt or innocence, asked for a minister to help them pray for divine guidance. The state's court saw nothing amiss with that."

"If it please the Court," Darrow said, "I do not object to the jury or anyone else having the right to pray in private or in secret, but I do object to the turning of the courtroom into a meeting-house." Again, he slapped his right hand into his left palm with every other word: "You *have* no *right* to *do* it."

The judge adjusted some papers on the bench and maintained an entirely even tone when he said, "What you have a right to do is put your objection into the record. That you have done. What I have a right to do is ask members of the ministry here to open the court with prayer. I've instructed them to make no reference to the issues involved in this case, and I see nothing that might influence the jurors. It will be the duty of the jury to investigate Mr. Scopes's alleged offense with open minds."

"You'd need a crowbar to open their minds," Lottie whispered to me.

"Or a cudgel," Mencken added.

Even as the members of the defense team shook their heads in disbelief, and Darrow stuck his thumbs under his suspenders, the judge glanced past them, in Bryan's direction. Apparently wanting to leave no doubt as to where he stood in relation to heaven, Raulston, the lay preacher, added, "I constantly invoke divine guidance myself."

As Reverend Stribling began his prayer, I saw George look to

Darrow, as if expecting another objection, but Darrow, at this point anyway, seemed to have far more control of his feelings than George did. I saw Professor Neal extend a comforting, or perhaps just a governing, hand to George's forearm.

After Reverend Stribling said *amen,* it was Neal's turn to stand. His suspenders were frayed, his hair greasy, but his voice, though almost apologetic, was firm.

"Please the Court," he said, "we have here a petition from representatives of various religious denominations, that if you continue your custom of opening the daily sessions with prayer, then we might hear prayers from other faiths—"

Tom Stewart was our district attorney, officially leading the prosecution in fact if not in fame. He leapt from his seat as if there were springs beneath it. "Your Honor, just a minute. I submit that is *absolutely* out of order."

"Will you hear the petition?" Neal asked the judge, ignoring Stewart.

Stewart was red-faced, though to be fair, most people were because of the heat. "Your Honor, this is not an assembly met for hearing the prayers of other people. I object to it," he said.

Neal was unruffled. "Will Your Honor hear the petition?" he asked again.

"Who are the signatories on this petition?"

Neal turned to George. "Mr. Craig?"

Newly composed, George stood up with a legal pad in hand.

"Your Honor," he said. "These four men have petitioned the Court to be heard. The Reverend Charles Potter of New York City, Rabbi Herman Rosenwasser of San Francisco, the Reverend Fred Huntington of—"

Stewart stood again. "I repeat my objection with all the vehemence of my nature."

The judge cast his eyes around the courtroom. "I have already overruled the defense objection to prayer," he said. "I will however refer the selection of other clergymen to the pastors' association of this town."

At that, there was full-out laughter in the courtroom, but George looked entirely unamused.

"Your Honor knows that this town's pastors' association is made up almost entirely of Fundamentalists and does not include clergymen of the sort who have signed this petition," George said.

"Be that as it may," Judge Raulston said. "Let us bring the jury back in."

Glaring, George sat back beside Darrow, who didn't move. The heat pressed down and around us all.

Things got even more inflamed in the afternoon. "Keep your mouth shut!" Stewart barked at Neal at one point. At another, Stewart said he wanted to remind Malone that he was in a God-fearing country, and Malone said it was no more God-fearing than the country he came from. It seemed the trial, like polish on wood, was bringing out people's deeper colors, deeper passions, and deeper flaws.

The judge called a short recess around three o'clock, so I rushed home, warmed the pie I'd made the night before, and brought it over to Mercy's.

Usually, her back door was open, and I'd been in the habit—a habit she'd encouraged—of just walking into her kitchen. Now, I knocked, waited, and knocked again. I knew she had to be home because I heard the Puppies' voices, but it was another few minutes until she opened the door.

"I brought you a sweet potato pie," I said, which was stating the obvious but was all I could think to say.

She didn't look at it, though I knew she wanted to.

I raised the pie plate higher and hoped the scent would soften her.

"I know what you're trying to do," she said.

"I didn't think it would be a secret," I said. "I'm trying to lure you back into our regular ways by tempting you with a sweet potato pie."

"I'm praying for you," she said.

"I appreciate that," I said. "But I miss you, and I just know if you would listen to the men talk about evolution, you'd realize it's not what you think it is."

"Whatever it is," she said, "you can keep it to yourself. You can keep the potato pie too."

I stared at her in disbelief, and she stared back from a zealous height, but then we both broke out laughing.

"Oh, all right, Lamb," she said at last. She took the pie. "And thank you."

She shut her kitchen door again, a barrier still between us, but I figured I'd made a start.

Following the afternoon session, I went with Lottie to the make-shift pressroom that had been set up on the second floor of the hardware store. It was jammed with desks and phones, typewriters and telegraph machines, and there were even cots set up along the back wall, where, Lottie told me, some of the men had been sleep-ing. The room was full of cigarette smoke and crowded with desks and men, and it looked the way I'd always imagined a newspaper room would look, but the walls were still covered with pegboard holding tools of all sorts, packages of nails and screws and drill bits. Like the scientists at the Mansion the night before, the reporters seemed genial and pleasant, though there was an obvious under-current of competition among them. I had read a lot of their stories by now, and to me it seemed that all the men in the newsroom had the same goal, which was to prove that whoever didn't believe in evolution was destined to be left behind in the darkness of the past, with horses and steam engines and long skirts and shame. In their stories, it seemed, only the fearless could meet the future, and being fearless meant you might not even fear God.

Lottie introduced me to a reporter named Paul from St. Louis, and someone named Ray from Atlanta, and a man named Hutchin-son, who worked for one of the wire services.

"Hutchinson is John Scopes's shadow," she told me, teasing him.

"I'm not his shadow; he's mine," Hutchinson said.

The noise was constant: the men seemed able to type and banter simultaneously, and the fact that Lottie and I were women didn't seem to bother or impress anyone. Lottie took a seat at a desk, and when I looked around for a chair and couldn't find one, she said, "Hop up," and she meant that I should sit on her desk.

I laughed.

"What?"

"When I was growing up, I heard a girl would never catch a husband if she sat on a table."

Lottie smiled wryly. "Well, that isn't a problem today, is it?"

For at least ten minutes, I sat on the desk while she typed, and I took in the bustle around me.

"What was it Hicks said about the jury?"

"Which Hicks, Sue or Herb?"

"Does it matter?"

They were laughing as if it was all a lark, as if the outcome was preordained and it was only a matter of how well each of them could put it into words.

Every time one of them finished with a page, he would rip it off the typewriter carriage with gusto and roll in another piece of paper before the ink on the last one had dried. Absorbed in her typing, Lottie just nodded when I slid off her desk and said goodbye. I rushed home and, using just about everything left in the refrigerator, I managed to whip up a squash casserole. While it was in the oven, I went upstairs. I just wanted to take off my dress and change into something lighter, but I woke to the smell of burning food. In my slip, I ran downstairs to pull the casserole from the oven and drop it on the stove.

Only then did I realize that Lottie and George were sitting at the kitchen table. I don't know who was more surprised: them for seeing me in my slip, or me for seeing that whatever conversation they'd been having was so engrossing that they'd let the casserole burn.

I still had a pot holder in each hand and instinctively—if ridiculously—crossed them over my top.

"Couldn't you smell this was burning?" I asked.

"Sorry."

"Sorry."

"George," I said.

"I'm sorry."

"Honestly," I said.

"I'm certain it'll be just delicious anyway," Lottie said, all Southern manners and syrup.

"Don't be ridiculous," I said. "It's burnt."

"Still smells delicious," George said.

I tossed the pot holders onto the counter, shrugged, and went back upstairs to get dressed.

I really hadn't seen them talk before—at least not to each other, or at least not through me. From the start it had seemed that, despite their shared understanding of what was at stake in the trial, George and Lottie had a natural antipathy. I suspected George would have been much more respectful of a reporter who was a man. Even though it was clear that Lottie was sure-footed, George still seemed to think she was here to cover the women in the drama: Mrs. Bryan, for example, or Judge Raulston's daughters. As for Lottie's view of George, she had already made it clear to me, by inference, that she thought he was too overbearing—or perhaps just too willing for me to welcome his authority.

When I came back downstairs, though, he and Lottie were still deep in talk.

"No one's hungry?" I asked.

They both apologized again and thanked me when I handed them each a plate of whatever I could dig out from under the burnt top.

"He's a fool," George was saying.

"Who's a fool?" I asked.

"Raulston," George said. "Overruling the objection to prayer. As if this whole case wasn't about the Bible and Darwin. If there was any justice, Raulston would open court tomorrow by having someone read from *The Origin of Species.*"

"The spectators certainly didn't seem to mind about the prayer," Lottie said.

"Why would they?" George scoffed. "As far as they know, not only is Darrow out to steal the Bible, but he wants God and Jesus too."

"Is that what they think?" Lottie asked me.

"Some of them," I said. "But it's not like they're those hill people we saw the other night rolling around on the ground."

"They're worse," George cut in before I could answer.

"How so?" Lottie asked, ever so casually.

She finally took a delicate bite of the casserole and said a perfunctory "Delicious" to me.

"If you've spent your whole life on a mountain," George said, "then you can be forgiven for giving yourself over to superstition. You need God to make sense of the weather, and you need to feel there's a better life waiting for you beyond the desolate one you're living."

He had not yet tasted his food. He was getting excited. I had the sense he was being possessed by a different kind of spirit, perhaps the spirit of Clarence Darrow.

"But if you've lived in a town," George went on, "if you've had some education, read the newspapers, listened to the radio, you should have some sense in you, some ability to discern what's religion from what's science. Unless you're a complete idiot. Or you're so under Bryan's spell that you'll believe anything he says just because he's Bryan. These people won't take their noses out of their Bibles long enough just to hear some scientific facts."

"What was it like going to school here?" Lottie asked suddenly, turning back to me.

"What do you mean?"

"I mean, when you got to science class, did your classmates have a problem with the way science explained the world?"

Before I could answer Lottie, George broke in again.

"Annie isn't like the rest," he said.

"Yes I am."

"No you're not."

"I went to school here, just like everyone else," I said. "And I went to church, just like everyone else. I don't think we thought about it," I said to Lottie. "School was school, and church was church."

Through this conversation, Lottie continued to eat politely, a lady dabbing the corners of her lips with one of our good napkins. We'd been using them since she'd first come to town. I hadn't had time to launder them, and we were down to just four. I decided at that moment that I didn't care whether the napkins would need to be reused. Certainly neither Lottie nor George would notice. The judges inside me—my mother, Mercy, even the tidiest version of George I'd first known—put up a distant argument: wife, housekeeper, homemaker. But somehow whatever objections they might have had didn't hold much water.

I tested this theory by looking around the kitchen. On the painted shelves, a layer of dust was visible; I could have drawn on it with my fingertips. I hadn't cleaned the counters after I'd put the casserole in the oven. Spitfire jumped down from her windowsill perch and seemed to stare at me condescendingly before scooting into the parlor. I marveled at her at that moment. She knew how to be free.

"Annie," George was continuing, "had to educate herself because she spent so much time alone after her parents died. She read everything she could get her hands on, and—"

"George," I said. "I can speak for myself."

He looked abashed.

"Of course you can," he said. "I'm sorry. I think the lawyer in me is just itching to give a speech."

Lottie chuckled.

"If you weren't going to say it, I was," she told him.

"It's this myopic judge," George went on. "When he isn't posing for photographs or sending the jury out of the room or asking questions of our team as if he cares about the answers, he's just looking over at Bryan to see if he's impressed."

"Eat something, George," I said, and eventually he picked up his fork and tasted the now-tepid casserole.

I stood up to make coffee and to clean the countertops, and Lottie went upstairs to write.

I was used to her typewriter by now. In my mind its sounds had just replaced the ones that used to come from George's ham radio. The typewriter was only slightly less annoying. The clatter of the keys and the ringing of the bell when she reached the end of each line was one thing, but you never knew, when the typing stopped, whether she was thinking (between words or sentences or paragraphs) or whether she was just putting in a new sheet of paper or whether she was done for the night. Tonight, she was typing as I fell asleep, and when I woke up, she was still typing. I guessed that her story would be exceptionally long. I didn't guess that it would also be exceptionally destructive.

It wasn't until the next day—the fourth day of the trial—that the first witnesses were finally called.

Leading the prosecution, Tom Stewart questioned the school superintendent, making it sound as if on that May day in Robinson's, John Scopes had had to be wrestled to the ground and led away in handcuffs for breaking the anti-evolution law. A part of me wanted to leap up in protest. This was the part of me that had still not entirely embraced the idea that it wasn't really John on trial but the Butler Act. Though his name was then and would remain famous, no one paid a lot of attention to him. No one on the defense was going to argue that he hadn't done what he'd done. The argument was entirely about whether he and teachers all over the state of Tennessee should reclaim the right to do it.

Naturally, the students who were called to the stand hadn't really remembered what the biology textbook said, let alone whether John had taught it to them. Not even John could remember if he had. Still, Darrow had to establish, for the purpose of future appeals, that Scopes had indeed taught evolution. So, wearing their cleanest shirts, and with fresh comb marks striping their still-wet hair, each of the three well-coached boys swore to tell the truth, and they each did a fine job of pretending to do so.

I had just gotten home when I found Mercy striding toward me with a rolled-up newspaper in her hand. This time, she launched it across the yard at me.

"What is it?" I asked.

She said nothing.

"What?" I asked again, going to fetch the paper.

"Shame on your husband!" she said. "Shame, shame! Y'all can all go chase yourselves."

I picked up the paper with dread.

"Mercy—" I began again. "What does it—"

"Read it yourself," she said.

She turned, as crisply as her large body permitted, to go back to her house, but just then two of her children came running out, so her exit wasn't quite as effective as she probably wanted it to be. But the second I saw the headline, I understood her rage.

DEFENSE ATTORNEY CALLS JUDGE A FOOL
BY LOTTIE NELSON

Dayton (Special) Monkey trial defense lawyer George Craig called judge John T. Raulston a "fool" in an exclusive interview with the Times on Wednesday.

Mr. Craig, a local co-counsel to famed Chicago attorney Clarence Darrow, went on to accuse Judge Raulston of grandstanding in the closely watched trial of John T. Scopes for allegedly violating the state's law against teaching evolution. "When he isn't posing for pictures or asking questions of Darrow as if he cares about the answers, he's just looking over to see if Bryan's impressed," Mr. Craig said, referring to the celebrated chief prosecutor, three-time Democratic presidential candidate William Jennings Bryan.

Tuesday's proceedings were the third day of the trial, and also the third day on which Judge Raulston had invited a visiting pastor to open the court with prayer. Mr. Darrow, for the defense, didn't waste a moment before objecting to what he characterized as an official endorsement of religion, and the judge's decision to overrule him appears to have triggered Mr. Craig's caustic remarks later that evening.

"This fool says starting court with a prayer is not relevant. But this whole trial is about the Bible versus Darwin. He should either keep the Bible out or allow someone to read from *The Origin of Species*," Mr. Craig said.

Mr. Craig, at whose Dayton home this reporter has been staying, is the youngest member of the seven-man defense team. In court Tuesday, he responded to the ruling allowing prayer in the courtroom by requesting that members of a variety of denominations and religions—including a rabbi—be given the chance to pray as well. The judge's answer—to refer the selection of the clergymen to the town's pastors' association—prompted laughter in the courtroom and later outrage from Mr. Craig.

"Raulston knows damn well that every single member of that council is a dyed-in-the-wool Fundamentalist," the local defense lawyer said, "and won't take their noses out of their Bibles long enough to hear some science. Might as well have Bryan preaching in a Chautauqua tent. Raulston and the spectators and the jury are eating up every word."

The judge could not be reached for comment.

In an instant, I found myself sitting flat on the front lawn, despite the fact that it was still wet and muddy from midday showers. I was shocked. I could remember my father saying that watching his first picture show, he'd been knocked into the middle of next week. Those words suddenly made sense to me.

I didn't know whether I was angrier at Lottie for having tricked George into talking, or at George for having been so smug and insulting to the judge and Bryan and the jury and all those people in the courtroom. How could it ever be that smart to call other people that stupid?

Sitting there on the lawn, clutching the newspaper, I didn't blame Mercy at all for throwing it at me. I would have loved to throw it at George or Lottie—both if possible. Even more, I would have loved just to be with Mercy in her kitchen, watching her cook, hearing her children, and seeing the world the way she did.

Eventually, though, I went back to the house and straight up to the spare room. Normally, I would never have intruded into a person's privacy, but this was not a normal moment, and, anyway, Lottie had intruded into our lives.

The room was surprisingly messy, given how few things Lottie had brought with her. All of them seemed to be spread out. The bed held her several dresses. She had hung a pair of her white stockings to dry over the back of the desk chair. Stacks of newspapers—one stack for each day of the trial—surrounded the table. Beside the wastebasket was her leather typewriter case. I unzipped it and put it on the bed, then accidentally jammed my fingers between the keys of her machine as I lifted it to put it into its case. It wasn't an easy fit. There were levers meant to hold it in place, but I ignored them and zipped the case shut. Then I grabbed her suitcase from the closet and threw that open on the bed too.

When I first started working at the Aqua after my parents died, a chambermaid named Velma had taught me how to fold sheets, towels, and clothing. In another life, I think she would have been a geometry professor. The precision of her movements was a thing of beauty, and I'd never come near that perfection, but Lord knows I had mastered the arts of filling a dresser drawer—or packing a suitcase.

I used no skill at all in packing Lottie's clothes. I grabbed her few dresses, her two hats, her hose, and one after another pushed them into her suitcase, not trying to make things tidy. If anything, I was trying to make them as messy as possible. On the table, she had a stack of typing paper and her bouquet of souvenir pencils. I

threw them into the suitcase too, and then, without exactly thinking it through, I took the Dayton pencil out of that bundle, broke
it in half, then tucked the pieces back in. Rage, betrayal, the smoldering remnants of three weeks' worth of trust and novelty, sat inside my gut. I slammed her suitcase shut and, for a moment, perched
on the bed beside it.

Then I carried her typewriter and suitcase downstairs and put
them by the front door.

George got to the house before Lottie did. He was so calm it was
eerie. Often, people don't recognize the turning points in their lives
until long after they've taken place. That was apparently not the
case with George, who quietly walked to the kitchen, reached for
the bottle of fermented grape juice from the top of the cabinet, took
a tumbler, filled it, and drank it in one gulp.

"So, I guess you saw the paper," I said.

By way of answering me, he put the glass down with a thud,
then filled it again and drank again.

"What do you think the judge is going to do?" I asked.

"Oh, to hell with the judge. It's Darrow I care about."

"But the judge—"

"No, Annie!" he shouted at me. "You're not seeing it straight!"

"I guess I'm just a fool, like the judge, and all the other fools,"
I said.

"No!" George nearly wailed. "It's Darrow!"

"Of course it's Darrow," a deep voice said. George and I both
turned to see H. L. Mencken standing in our kitchen.

"Oh, wonderful," George said to him. "Look, I'm not going to
say a damned word to you."

"I'm not asking you to," Mencken said. "I just wanted to offer
my congratulations to Lottie."

George glowered.

"Is she here?"

"She is not," I said before George could answer.

"And young Mrs. Craig here seems to be aggrieved," he said.

The words were clearly sarcastic, and yet there was some unexpected kindness behind them. I wasn't sure how to react.

"Young Mrs. Craig," George said, "finds it confounding that the woman we've been boarding for three weeks could have written what she wrote."

"Did you say those things?" he asked George.

George's eyes looked flat. He didn't answer the question.

"Were you there?" Mencken asked me.

I nodded.

"Your husband say those things?"

"Yes," I said.

"Did you tell her not to print what you were saying?" Mencken asked George.

"We were having a conversation," George said. "In my home."

"Never have a conversation with a reporter," Mencken said, "unless you're willing to read it in the next day's paper. And if you don't want it to be in the paper, then you have to say that straight out and get her to agree. Even then you can never be sure."

"That sounds like you're saying the rules of Snakes and Ladders," I said.

"It's not exactly a game," Mencken said. "But it does have rules."

Lottie walked in. I couldn't help noticing that she looked weary. Even the flower on her hat looked wilted.

"Why didn't you tell George the rules?" I demanded. "How could you take advantage of us like that?"

She removed her hat and sighed. She rested a hand on the kitchen table.

"I saw my things at the front door," she said softly. "I know you want me to leave. I'll go. But please, can you give me a glass of water or lemonade first? It's so hot. I'm feeling faint."

I didn't move. George pulled out a chair for her and poured her a glass of lemonade. Maybe he was still hoping to undo, or some-how correct, what had happened. Or maybe his Southern manners were kicking in for Mencken's benefit.

She drank the whole glass in just two gulps. Mencken was look-ing on admiringly.

Lottie put the glass down and flattered me by ignoring the men in the room.

"Can I talk to you alone a minute before I go?" she asked me.

"I don't much see the point," I said. I was trying to be steel.

She tugged at the sleeve of my shirt.

"Come on," she said. "Just a moment or two."

Reluctantly, I walked with her out the back door.

"What?" I said, my hand on my hip.

"I want to explain."

"There's nothing to explain," I said. "You just wrote gossip."

She shook her head. "This wasn't just gossip, Annabel," she said. "Don't you realize? George is the only lawyer on either side who said what everyone else was thinking about this judge. He's been colossally biased against the defense."

"I still think it wasn't fair for you to use what he said without asking him."

She surprised me by putting a hand on my shoulder.

"I thought we were friends," I said.

She sighed.

"Remember I told you about when I hid in those haunted woods and got that possum bite and they had to stitch me up?" Lottie asked.

I nodded.

"Well, you have to take lots of risks when you're a reporter. All kinds of risks, you know. Last year, I talked the mail carrier into letting me go up in his airplane with him."

"You flew in a plane?" I asked, intrigued despite myself.

"I did," she said proudly. "Saw all of Chattanooga—and all of Dayton and Knoxville—from two thousand feet up."

"I don't know what that's got to do with anything," I said. I started to walk back toward the kitchen door. I needed her to leave.

"I saw how big the world is," she said. "I mean, really got a view."

"Well, I don't want to fly anywhere," I told her.

She smiled a little sadly.

"Not today, Annabel," she said. "But you might want to someday."

The thought that she might be right was still something to fight. George was my husband, my other half, even if he was no longer the man I'd married. Even if I was no longer the woman he'd married. I shuttered the thought from my mind.

In the kitchen, Mencken was waiting for Lottie.

"I'll find you a place," he said.

At the Mansion, I had heard the geologist talk about evolution in the earth itself: how there was a difference between weathering and erosion, how some types of rocks lasted longer than others, but how when water got into crevices and froze, it could, over time, break any rock apart.

Part Four

1

Before Lottie's and Mencken's voices had even faded, I saw George take the stairs two by two. I went back to the kitchen, wondering whether he shouldn't at least try to make sure Neal and Darrow understood that he hadn't known he'd be quoted. I couldn't stand what Lottie had done, and it would take me time to fathom it, if never entirely to forgive it. Still, the house felt empty without her. She had brought so much of the future with her, and now that she was gone, I could see myself being shut back into the past.

I heard a crash from upstairs and somehow knew before I reached the landing what it was that had broken. When I opened the spare room door, I saw George looking down at the scattered shards of the rosy glass of my pink etched lamp. The pieces lay—flat, dark, and common—across the hearth and the floor beside it.

"Did you mean to do that?" I asked him.

"It was an accident," George said, seemingly wounded by the question. His eyes narrowed. "How could you think I was trying to hurt you?"

The year of his ignoring me. The condescending explanations. The insults about my education. Even the fact that he had never apologized for any of these.

All I said was "Because you've hurt me before."

"When?" he said, the single syllable launched at me like an arrow.

Hold your tongue, I could hear Mercy whisper to me.

Answer him! I could hear Lottie shout.

But I wasn't Mercy or Lottie. I wanted neither to retreat nor to attack, at least not now—at least not yet.

"Clean that up," I said to George instead, which Mercy would have found too disrespectful and Lottie too respectful.

Still, it surprised him. Anger. Anger from Annie. Flossie. Busy Bee. Even if his breaking the lamp had been an accident, I wasn't inclined to pick up those pieces. The many vacant nights after my parents' deaths had been little more than misery, but they'd held the seeds of my strength. It would be one thing to know the symbol of those times was gone, quite another to sweep the pieces up and throw them into the trash.

I left George standing in the bare room, and as I went downstairs, I prayed he hadn't gone there to resurrect his radio rig.

In the parlor, I turned on the Westinghouse, tuning the dial away from the news and welcoming the company of boisterous singers on a nearby station. But just minutes later, John Neal knocked on the front door.

"Sorry to trouble you this evening, Mrs. Craig," he said.

I offered him sweet tea or coffee, but he said he just needed a moment with George.

I called to George, and he came to the landing, eyes cast down at his feet and hands fiddling with some metal piece of something. He looked guilty. By the time he had reached the bottom step, though, he had squared his shoulders.

"Are you here to reprimand me?" he asked the professor.

"Shall we talk somewhere else?" Neal asked, with a glance at me.

"No need to keep anything from my wife," George said. "She

spent so much time with that reporter she's probably learned how to eavesdrop anyway."

His tone was light, but the professor seemed embarrassed that I'd been insulted. The three of us sat in the parlor, though it was clear Professor Neal had no desire, or perhaps no ability, to get comfortable. Like an overstrung child, he rubbed his hands forward and back over his thighs.

"It won't be helpful to John Scopes to keep you on the team now," he told George.

George didn't look angry or surprised. He just looked frozen. I waited for him to speak or move. He did neither.

"Oh, Lord," I said without intending to say anything.

Neal draped one of his huge hands over mine but waited for George to speak.

Absurdly, the radio started playing "Nothing Could Be Finer Than to Be in Carolina in the Morning."

I stood up to turn it off.

The ensuing silence was worse.

"So that means my services are no longer required at all," George said. He had unfrozen.

"I'm afraid that is the state of the thing," Neal said.

"Where is he?" George asked.

"Darrow? At the Mansion, I suppose," Neal said. "But there's little point—"

"Don't go, George," I said, though he was already checking that his shirt was tucked.

"Your wife is right, Craig," Neal said.

George pondered this a moment, then shook his head.

"No," he said.

In a flash, he had run upstairs, grabbed a tie, and returned. He was putting on his seersucker jacket even as he headed out the front door, followed by Neal. I raced after them and squeezed into the car beside the professor.

I tried to stay calm as George took the wheel, tried to keep my fear from showing.

Neal tried again: "George, I really don't think there's any point—"

George wasn't driving that fast, but his fingers were curled tight around the wheel, and I wasn't sure he had taken a breath since he'd turned the engine over. He said nothing, just seemed to focus intently on the road, where our dim headlights allowed us only the shortest glimpse of what was ahead.

Inside the Mansion, Clarence Darrow was seated in front of the tall stone fireplace. He was apparently in the midst of telling a story, because he was talking in a gentle, relaxed voice. He did seem strangely at home for someone who'd come from a life in Chicago.

He smiled kindly when he saw me walk in, but then glowered when he saw George. Darrow's huge forehead suddenly looked like a jutting cliff, and as Neal came in behind us, Darrow said to him: "I had hoped you'd be a more emphatic messenger."

"Professor Neal was perfectly clear," George said, "but I had to hear it from you myself."

I understood now that, in the car, George had been silent because he'd been preparing his argument to Darrow. But before Darrow could say anything, we heard voices and laughter coming from the kitchen, and together, Lottie and Mencken emerged carrying trays of mismatched glasses, each filled with an inch or so of brown liquor.

"Ah," Darrow said to them. "So that's what you two were cooking up."

"There's food, too, plenty of food," a nervous Precious Rappleyea said as she followed the two reporters, wiping her hands on her apron.

"We'll bring it all out," George Rappleyea said.

Mencken in particular was ever so jolly. The line was that he had come to town with four bottles of scotch and a typewriter. Now, apparently, he had decided to share. Along with Lottie, he began to take the trays of liquor around. When Lottie's and my eyes met, she showed neither regret nor embarrassment, as if we were meeting for the first time and she was sizing me up in her journalistic way. It was chilling to think I'd meant nothing to her except as a conduit to George, or to whatever other insights she could find that eluded others. I wondered if there was anyone in her life she didn't treat that way. I would have asked her, but I didn't want her to think I cared.

She offered the tray of drinks to Darrow, ignoring George completely now, but George was so focused on Darrow that he didn't acknowledge her either. Darrow took a glass for himself and handed one to George. George stared at the contents of the glass for a moment and then, when Darrow said, "Drink, Craig," George downed the liquor in one motion.

"You made the judge look ridiculous," Darrow said evenly to George. "You made the jurors look ridiculous. And you made us look like the worst kind of snobs. If you'd set out to do it, you couldn't have done a better job confirming everything the people in this town think we godless elite Northerners believe about them."

"I never meant—" George began, with a lethal glance at Lottie—"I never meant for a single one of my words to see print."

"I'm sure you didn't," Darrow said. "But that's neither here nor there now."

"We've all said as much about Raulston," George said.

"Craig, I can't have you sitting at the defense table again. I can't even have you in the courtroom."

George looked stricken. Instinctively, I went to his side and took his hand. He twisted it away from mine and stared back at Darrow.

"George," I said softly.

"Mr. Darrow," George said.

"Craig, you're too good a lawyer not to know that if you care about this case at all—if you care about what it stands for—then you have to walk out of this room right now."

I took George's hand again, meaning to lead him toward the door. But he turned sharply, this time swatting my hand away.

"Don't come with me," he said, his mouth set hard.

Without a hint of hesitation, Lottie put down the drinks tray, uncapped her pen, and started after him.

I grabbed her arm.

"Don't you dare," I said. "You've already done enough to him."

"If you're so concerned about him," she said, "then why aren't *you* following him?"

"Because he asked me not to," I said.

"He *told* you," Lottie said. "He didn't ask you."

With some noticeable effort, Lottie stopped moving, and I let her arm go.

Precious quickly was at my side. "Also, Annabel promised to help me," she said and added somewhat pointedly, "and she's a woman who keeps her word."

Back at the kitchen sink, I washed my hands but then let the water keep beating down on them. I was just trying to compose myself, staring at my hands, staring at the faucet, just letting the feel of the water overwhelm any of my thoughts. But then Precious was at my side, putting a stack of dishes on the counter.

"Lickety-split," she said.

As I washed the dishes, I remembered a church social where George and I had run into each other just a week or so after we'd met. About half an hour in, he had gotten a fierce headache. He'd apologized and told me he was going to have to leave, and I'd gone with him, just as naturally as anything, and I'd realized as I walked him home that in that simple moment, we had become a couple. If he was leaving the dance, then I was leaving the dance. It had made no sense to stay. *Whither thou goest,* I'd thought. Now, it was the reverse. I hadn't wanted to go with him. He hadn't wanted me to come. I'd stayed behind at the Mansion House while my mortified, rejected, guilty husband left to go raise hell.

It was past midnight when I decided I couldn't wash another dish. George Rappleyea drove me to the corner of Walnut Street and thanked me for my help. I could see our car parked just outside our house, but I walked toward the front door with dread, expecting to find George shut away in the spare room, hustling to reassemble his rig or, worse, already tapping out Morse code to some stranger who lived who knew where.

But I quickly realized that there were no lights on in the windows, a more alarming discovery. I prayed that George was upstairs in bed, even though I knew he'd be too agitated to sleep. Now, as I opened the front door, I prayed he hadn't had an accident or harmed himself. With every room I entered, I half expected to find him lying on the floor.

When I went back downstairs, Mercy—having heard Rapp drop me off—was just letting herself into the kitchen.

"Come, Lamb," she said, opening her wide, loving, forgiving arms.

"I've got to go find him," I said inside her embrace.

She put her hands on my shoulders and gave me her sternest look.

"You can't go by yourself," she said. "Especially what with all this riffraff here from all over kingdom come."

"I have to," I said again.

She shut her eyes tight, and I knew she was silently asking the Lord for guidance.

"Then I'm coming with you," she said at last.

2

The life of a farm begins before dawn and ends just after sunset. When I was growing up, I don't think my parents and I ever passed through the center of Dayton after dark. There'd never have been a reason. Nighttime had meant washing up and doing homework and sometimes stepping out to look at the stars. Nighttime had been peaceful. The only sounds beyond my bedroom window had been the chatter of tree frogs and katydids and the calls of whippoorwills. When my parents died and I had to move to Bailey's Boardinghouse, I eventually got used to the noises of laughter and shouts from the street and the sputter of the occasional car. Now, however, with the carnival atmosphere of the trial, the town felt almost menacing. I was happy that Mercy was with me.

Wednesday had been the hottest day of the trial yet, and even now, past midnight, the air was still a burden. Mercy fanned herself with a palm leaf stamped with the words IT STARTED HERE. Little puffs of the sultry air came my way each time she waved it, the puffs scented by tobacco whenever we passed a group of men.

"Where's he gonna be?" Mercy asked me.

"That's just it," I said. "I don't know."

"He can't have gone far without that car."

It was a delicate reference to the week after Walton Allen, and it was exactly what I was thinking.

As we reached the corner of Market and Main, we found a cluster of men gesturing boldly and talking at high volume, and it was clear that something had happened, or perhaps was about to happen. They didn't seem in any way approachable, but that didn't stop Mercy. "Have you seen her husband?" she barked at them.

Their answers were useless. The men were drunk.

"Who's her husband?"

"Haven't seen him."

"Want a drink, ladies?"

Then we reached the Aqua and found Fred Whittle sitting on one of the iron benches outside his hotel, leaning his head back against the garish yellow façade. His eyes were half closed, but he was tapping a restless foot.

"I figured as you'd come looking," he said when he saw me.

"Is he here?" I asked.

" 'Fraid not."

"But you've seen him?"

Fred nodded.

"Which way was he heading?"

Fred took a deep breath and pointed at the courthouse.

"I don't see any lights," I said.

"Look again."

The Rhea County Jail was a wide, low brick building with one high arched entryway. I had never been inside it, and I'd always imagined it as a fearsome place. Whether it had been cleaned up, like the rest of the town, in anticipation of visitors, I had no idea. But when I entered, I found it bright and clean, even at this late hour. Sam Wilkins, the same police officer who had strapped the Monkeyville Police sign to the department's motorcycle a few weeks back, was sitting on a high stool behind a wooden desk, reading the late edition of the *Chattanooga News,* where Lottie's story about George was still a front-page headline. Quickly and kindly, he tried to cover it with his forearm.

"That's okay, Sam," I said. "I've read it. Everyone's read it. Where is he?"

The jail was built with three cells extending on either side of the front room.

Sam pointed to his left.

The cells were each about ten feet square, and there were rounded metal bars running from the ceiling to the floor. I had never been to a zoo, but I knew from books and newspapers what zoo cages looked like, and these were no different. In the first cell, a town hothead named Luther Mudrow was pacing and mumbling, his shirt darkened with sweat everywhere but the very front. I walked past the second cell without looking in. In the third, George was sitting in the far back corner—squatting, actually, when I first saw him, his elbows on his knees.

I had seen George happy and I'd seen him stone-faced. I had seen him ill, once with a fever so high that we'd worried what he had was worse than grippe. Obviously, I had seen him angry and disappointed, and I'd seen the way his mouth could set, seemingly unopenable by a smile. But I had never seen him drunk.

When he realized that Mercy and I were standing there, he lost his balance, toppling over like a toy.

"Excuse me," he said to the leg of the metal cot he'd brushed on his brief fall to the floor.

Leaning on his knuckles, he pushed himself back up to his knees. I could see brown stains on his white shirt, and his lips looked puffy and red, so I knew that he'd been sick.

"So, you found me," he said.

"Where have you been, George?"

"Knocking around," he said. "Knocking around."

His eyes were bleary, nothing at all like the sharp, clear windows in which I'd once seen myself and our future reflected. He pointed a rude finger at Mercy.

"You brought your protector with you, I see," he said. "I see." Then, more softly, embarrassed, he added, "I wished you hadn't done that."

"I'm not here to judge you, George," Mercy said quietly.

"That's good, that's good," he said. "'Cause I think Clarence Darrow already took care of that."

"Knocking around where?" I asked him.

"We had a meeting. A meeting."

I wondered if there was something about being drunk that made people say things twice.

"Who had a meeting?" I asked.

"Luther and Cedrick and Billy and Dennis and me."

"What kind of meeting?"

"It was about running a certain journalist out of town on a rail."

"You wouldn't—" I started to say, but he cut me off.

"No, it had nothing to do with your pal Lottie," he said. "Different journalist altogether. Luther and them are not all that keen about what Henry Louis Mencken has been writing."

I wasn't exactly happy about it either. In recent days, Mencken had upped his attacks. He was now calling us peasants, rabble, imbeciles, and morons; Bryan was a hatred-filled, mangy, and flea-bitten mountebank.

"So, they got a rail to run him out of town," George said. "A big old one-by-four."

Then he burped. A nasty, unpleasant burp. I felt disgusted by him. That was another first.

"And we decided to go and find the bastard," George continued. Needlessly, he was trying to do up the button on the top of his shirt, as if he was preparing to go somewhere. But his fingers weren't behaving.

"I told them he was at the Mansion," he went on, "and I knew he'd be leaving there to find your pal Lottie a place to stay. So we went to Bailey's Boardinghouse, and when neither of them showed up, then we tried the Aqua, and then Luther decided we should go to his house and get some fortifications in the form of glasses of whiskey. You were still at the Mansion. The Mansion," he added. It was clearly intended as a reproach, as if nothing bad would have happened if I'd left along with him—no matter that he'd told me not to.

He gave up on his collar button and, in frustration, ripped his shirt open further, popping the button off.

"That's going to need mending," Mercy said unnecessarily.

George looked mournfully at the button as it rolled across the concrete floor, and he seemed to consider the futility of bending over to fetch it.

"Well, you know how things go when someone takes a bottle out," he said.

"No, I don't, George," I said. "I don't know how things go when someone takes a bottle out."

"Of course you don't." And he said that as if I was some terrible prig, instead of an everyday citizen abiding by an everyday law.

He sat heavily on the cot. The springs squeaked, and the sides of the thin mattress nearly lifted up around him.

"It sure took you a while to find me," he said.

"This wasn't the first place I thought to go looking for my husband," I said.

His eyes narrowed. "Well, it sure took you a while!" he shouted. Now he was furious. He pulled himself up and managed to start pacing. He seemed to be looking for something to throw, but there was only the mattress. "Maybe you're not that quick!" he bellowed.

"You can barely stand," I said, "and you're in a jail cell, and you're mortified, and you're raising your voice to me?"

"What do you want from me, Annie?"

"I'm not sure I want anything from you, George."

He stared at me. We were strangers.

"I can stand," he said—a delayed reaction—but he sat back down again.

"Come, Lamb," Mercy said. Together we turned and started back down the corridor.

"I can stand!" George shouted after me. "Get me out of here!"

I didn't turn back. I called: "You got in all by yourself."

I didn't want my husband to come home.

It had been just a little over a year since the last time I'd slept alone in the house, but I felt so much older now. All I had wanted then was to be a wife and a mother, to have a house full of children the way that Mercy did and Caroline would, to have mornings and evenings with George the way my mother had had with my father.

Tonight, coming back to find neither Lottie nor George, the lights off, the quiet oppressive, I almost felt as if I were trespassing in my own home.

It was nearly two in the morning. I was exhausted. Lying in bed and trying to sleep, I could swear I heard the sound of Lottie's typewriter. Shouldn't I have guessed what that story of hers was going to say? Shouldn't George? Eventually I gave up on sleeping and wandered into the extra room. I turned on the light. George had already removed the tablecloth that I'd used to cover his workbench. He'd brought back a few of his boxes, and the stack of cryptic postcards poked out from one of them. So did a bundle of newspaper clippings:

DON'T ASSUME IT'S YOUR WIFE'S FAULT!
YOU MAY NEED A MANLY BOOST!

and

HOW GOOD IS YOUR SEED?

and

ARE YOU AS VITAL AS YOU WANT TO BE?

They were all advertisements for a patent medicine called Dr. Bloom's Curative Liquid. In George's way, he had, despite all appearances, been trying to give me what he knew I wanted. It made my heart hurt to think about it. But I was still too angry and disgusted with the drunk man I'd just seen in jail to let any emotion overcome those feelings.

I turned the light off and went back to our room and slept, still dressed, in the bed that was still ours. When I woke the next morning, I had no dream to remember.

George had been standing in a courtroom as a lawyer not twenty-four hours earlier, and I'd left him squatting in a jail cell. How had we gotten here?

In the beginning, that miracle of our marriage had been formed in a single bold act: George lifting me into Oak Tree Pond. But however beastly his behavior had been last night, the shift wasn't really that sudden. Even this morning, some part of me understood that we had gotten here small step by small step.

But I didn't want to think about George. I wanted to go back to court. This was the day when William Jennings Bryan himself was finally going to speak for the prosecution. I wanted to be there for myself—neither as Lottie's sidekick nor as George's wife.

3

The entrance to the courtroom was jammed with even more would-be spectators than usual, and I didn't have Lottie to lead the way. Instead, I just raised my camera, like a banner, above my head, as if I'd been sent on a special mission, and I made my way through the crowd. Perhaps I was no longer Lottie's photographer, but I was still a photographer.

Once through the door, I saw the familiar main players, as well as a young man I assumed was a clerk who was sitting in what had been George's chair. If anyone on the defense team was angry with Lottie, it certainly didn't show: Still in her front-row seat, she waved to me gaily, as if nothing between us had happened.

I looked away.

"Annabel!" she shouted above the buzz.

She waved again, indicating that she'd saved a seat for me. It was so hot and crowded that I was tempted to join her. But I wasn't going to forgive her—not today, anyway. I found my own spot, standing on the side, close to the jury seats, and like everyone else I turned toward William Jennings Bryan: After four days of the other lawyers preparing the way, it was finally his turn to speak.

Though Judge Raulston asked for quiet, that wasn't necessary. Bryan's voice could have been heard over a furious waterfall, and as he spoke, his thin smile seemed to show both confidence in his own righteousness and pity for those who didn't share it.

He began by attacking Darrow's background, professional history, godlessness, and motives, then repeated the argument that none of the defense's scientific witnesses should be allowed to testify because the law against teaching evolution was clear, and no expert could defeat it by defending or explaining what evolution was. He made fun of the chart in Hunter's textbook, how it didn't draw man in any way separate from other mammals. "This is the great game they want to put in the public schools," he said jovially. " 'Go and find man among the animals, if you can!' Talk about putting Daniel in the lions' den!" He feigned horror—or perhaps he really felt it. "How dare those scientists put man in a little ring like that with lions and tigers and everything that is bad!"

The crowd in the courtroom was rapt. Bryan turned to face them directly, his back to Judge Raulston, who didn't seem to mind.

"Shall man be detached from the throne of God and be compelled to link their ancestors with the jungle? Tell *that* to your children!"

I was here, in a Tennessee courtroom, witnessing the man I'd only heard on the radio, seeing the starched face and the big belly and the raised hand that I'd only imagined as I'd listened to the rise and fall of his voice. It was thrilling, but a little less thrilling than I'd thought it would be. His voice faltered at times. He called Robinson's "Robertson's." He forgot the name of a student. He repeated himself. But at the end, his voice rising, he declared: "The Bible is the word of God; the Bible is the only expression of man's hope of salvation. The Bible is not going to be driven out of this court by experts who come hundreds of miles to testify that they can reconcile evolution, with its ancestor in the jungle, with man made by God in His image. The parents of Tennessee have a right to say that no teacher paid by their money shall rob their children of faith in God and send them back to their homes skeptical, infidels, or agnostics, or atheists!"

In a way, I realized, that was the crux of it. It was the fear of another kind of evolution, not species to species but generation to generation. What would happen if the young people—with their red ties, short skirts, and street corner conversations—lost their respect for their parents and started to think themselves better? If they didn't have the Bible, how could they learn to be good?

Bryan finished to resonant applause and amens. I thought of all the letters George had written, his entreaties to all those professors to come and give their testimony. If he were here in the courtroom and not, as I suspected, still in jail, what would he have done now, with the arguments against those experts set out so forcefully?

People were looking toward Clarence Darrow, but it was Dudley Field Malone who rose to speak. In four days of infernal heat, unlike every other man in the courtroom, he had still not removed his black suit jacket. Therefore, all he had to do in order to silence the courtroom was to rise, slowly remove the jacket, and drape it across the back of his chair. He might as well have stripped naked. Going into battle against the man once dubbed "the Silver Knight of the West," Dudley Field Malone had not secured his own armor but had removed it. It was somehow thrilling.

He started by expressing confusion about how Bryan could, on the one hand, say the case was merely about whether John had taught evolution and, on the other, give a stirring speech—nearly a sermon—about the absolute authority of God and the Bible. "What I don't understand is this, Your Honor," he said. "If the issue is as broad as Mr. Bryan himself has made it, why the fear of meeting the issue? I feel that the prosecution here is filled with a needless fear. I believe that if they withdraw their objection and hear the evidence of our experts, their minds would not only be improved but their souls would be purified."

Gathering speed, Malone asked why we should discard what

we've learned of the world in the last century and depend solely on a book written at a time when men believed the sun revolved around the earth.

Bryan, intently flapping his palm-leaf fan, seemed unable to look at Malone, whose voice began to rise, forming words that would soon find their way into newspapers and magazines and eventually into countless anthologies of the world's greatest courtroom speeches.

"We have come in here ready for a battle," Malone said. "We have come in here for what Mr. Bryan has called a duel. Does the opposition mean by *duel* that our defendant shall be strapped to a board and that they alone shall carry the sword? That isn't my idea of a duel. Moreover, it isn't going to be a duel. There is never a duel with the truth. The truth always wins, and we are not afraid of it. The truth is no coward. The truth does not need the law. The truth does not need the forces of government. The truth does not need Mr. Bryan. The truth is imperishable, eternal, and immortal and needs no human agency to support it."

The spectators started clapping. Malone, with increasing confidence, eased his voice into bolder and grander declarations. "We are ready to tell the truth as we understand it," he said. "We do not fear all the truth that they can present as facts. We are ready. We feel we stand with progress. We feel we stand with science. We feel we stand with intelligence. We feel we stand with fundamental freedom in America. We are not afraid. Where is the fear? We meet it! Where is the fear? We defy it! We ask your honor to admit the evidence as a matter of correct law, as a matter of sound procedure, and as a matter of justice to the defense in this case."

It wasn't clear whether the spectators were rewarding Malone's eloquence and passion or his reasoning, but almost to a person they rose and offered the most sustained and emphatic applause I had yet heard in the courtroom or outside of it. The response shocked and stirred me. The people in the courtroom who had clapped for Bryan were now cheering for Malone. The bailiff broke a corner off a tabletop by rapping his stick in enthusiasm. The reporters stood and applauded. John Scopes patted Malone on his back. And then William Jennings Bryan himself stepped forward. "Dudley," he said, "that was one of the finest speeches I ever heard."

I assumed that after all that, the judge would of course allow the scientists to testify. But he adjourned the trial for the day and said he would give his decision in the morning. I took my time walking home. I guessed George was out of jail by now, but I was in no rush to find out how sober—or sorry—he might or might not be.

Instead, I stopped to take pictures of Joe Mendi, the chimp. I had seen Joe from a distance on the first day of the trial, just arriving in town with his handler, already enveloped by children. But I hadn't photographed him yet, and doing so allowed me to stall. He was right on the corner of Main and Market, seated at a miniature piano. Only Bryan had so far drawn a larger crowd. But when the children seemed to be getting too close, Joe Mendi opened his mouth, bared his huge yellow teeth, and screeched like a wounded bird.

"I don't like people getting close up when I'm fixing to play," his handler said.

She was a buxom woman in a navy blue linen dress and city shoes, and she apparently was speaking in the imagined voice of Joe Mendi, because Joe Mendi, naturally, couldn't speak for himself. If he could, I suspect he would have said, "Could someone please get me away from this woman in the navy blue linen dress?"

Joe Mendi was wearing a child-size suit, complete with a vest, a bow tie, and a flower in his lapel. He had been taught to hold a cane and a pipe, I guessed so that he could look even more like a sophisticated gentleman. He also wore a bowler hat, but despite his handler's best efforts, he kept taking the hat off and throwing it away. The youngsters squealed and went racing after the hat each time.

"Now, Joe," the handler said again and again, returning the hat to the chimp's head.

Down the street just a little ways, some boys were singing a new ditty:

> *You can't make a monkey out of me*
> *You can't make a monkey out of me*
> *I am human through and through,*
> *All my aunts and uncles too.*
> *You can't make a monkey out of me . . .*

I took photographs. Joe sitting at the piano. Joe standing with his cane. Joe holding a book, his fingers long and graceful, ending in ridged, pointed dark gray nails. His enormous ears seemed to flap on either side of his face, nearly as wide as palm-leaf fans. But the cloudy brown eyes between them seemed sad and wounded. I had seen that exact expression in old people and lost children. I looked and looked at his eyes until, for a moment, he seemed to look right back at me, as if pleading for rescue.

George was indeed out of jail. He was in the backyard, wearing dungarees and an undershirt. He had a pile of lumber near my clothesline, which he was in the process of taking down. When he saw me, he glared.

"Thanks a heap for getting me out," he said. His words were precise, but he didn't sound entirely sober.

"You were so mean to me," I said.

"And thanks for having Mercy there to be a witness. That was extra fine."

"She was worried about me," I said.

I waited for him to apologize. He didn't.

"George, do you remember what you said to me last night? Do you remember what you called me?"

He didn't answer.

I tried a different approach. "George, I know you're unhappy," I said.

"I'm fine."

"I know this isn't what you wanted."

"It's fine."

"And, you know, I found those ads," I said.

He straightened up. "What ads?" he asked, though it was clear he knew.

I took a step closer and touched him on the arm, wrongly thinking he was embarrassed and would welcome reassurance. "That was such a sweet surprise," I said. "I guess I didn't know you still wanted us to have a family."

"I clipped those out before," he said brusquely.

I withdrew my hand. I didn't ask him *before what*. Would it have been before Walton Allen killed his son? Before George built his radio shack? Before he got on John's defense team? Before Clarence Darrow kicked him off? In any case, he was clearly saying that he wouldn't have clipped those ads out now.

Maybe I would have asked him those questions out loud if he had asked me something at all, if he hadn't assumed that I was just fine, if he'd wanted to know how I felt about Lottie, about Mencken, about Bryan—even about him. But he asked none of those questions, and I knew he wouldn't have answered mine. I didn't feel like begging for his attention or respect. Perhaps there had been a time when I wouldn't have thought I deserved either. That time had passed.

From Mercy's backyard, I could hear the Puppies pleading with her for more time to play before supper. When she saw me, she took Caleb by his skinny shoulders, bent down, and whispered to him. He came to the fence.

"Mama says you should come to supper," he said quietly.

"I'm not hungry," George said, though he hadn't been asked—and doubtless understood, especially after last night, that Mercy wouldn't have invited him. I decided to go. I walked through our house and around to Mercy and Tim's front door.

Mercy's kitchen table was everything mine was not: crowded with children and bumping elbows, laden with all sorts of food, noisy with chatter. After Tim had us hold hands while he said grace, Mercy served up mashed potatoes and ham and advice.

"We all of us hit a rough patch, isn't that right, Big Dog?"

The Big Dog nodded like a man who had been trained to nod.

Over the clamor of the kids, she whispered to me: "George will come knocking. You'll see."

"I don't think I want him to," I said.

"Can't say as I blame you," Mercy said. "But remember you made a promise before God when you promised to be George's wife."

"Let me ask you this," I whispered. "What would you do if the Big Dog stopped talking to you? Stopped going to church? Stopped respecting you?"

"I'd pray for him."

"What if he took to drinking? Landed in jail?"

"Same answer."

"What if he didn't love you? What if he tried to hurt you?"

"With his fists, you mean?" Mercy sat up straighter. "Did that man hit you?"

"There are other ways to get hurt," I said. "Cruel ways that can make you feel worthless, you know, and so alone."

"Whither thou goest," she said for the umpteenth time. But I figured she didn't really understand that whatever place George had gone to, it was, woefully, well beyond my reach.

I shook my head. The table had suddenly grown quiet.

"You just settle in here with us tonight, Lamb. He'll come knocking," she said again. "You'll see."

I was exhausted. The pillows on Mercy's parlor sofa were decorated with handprints and footprints of all sizes, but the cushions were very soft and comfortable, and I watched sleepily as Mercy and Tim attended to their evening ritual, corralling one child at a time to go upstairs and say their prayers and get into bed.

"We used to try to do them all at once," Mercy explained, her hands squarely on Caleb's shoulders as she started him up the stairs. "That ended up taking longer. There's probably math for that."

I was all but asleep by the time the last child was being steered away. I had already drifted in and out, trying to find the strength and the will to go back to my own home. I didn't have enough of either. I slept straight through till morning, and I awakened refreshed and ready.

Not so George, who was facedown on our own sofa when I got home, one arm hanging over the side, as if it had become unhinged from his body. I crept upstairs, washed, changed my clothes, and got to the courthouse just in time to see people leaving. I assumed it was only another recess, but I quickly learned that the judge had delivered his ruling on the admission of expert witnesses. There would not be a single one.

So after all the work George and others had done to get them involved; the work Rapp had done to arrange their travels; the work Precious had done to make the Mansion House livable; and after those evenings of ideas and strategies and nights that were steamy and uncomfortable, they would not be allowed to take the stand. The judge's only concession was that the statements the experts had planned to give could be typed into the record for the purposes of future appeals.

It seemed the drama was over. There would be no counterargument; no second act, and on the lawn, I sensed general deflation, even among the people who'd been cursing the scientists. Apparently, they *did* want a duel with the truth. And the men hawking the pamphlets, souvenirs, and food were still hoping to make money. But the scientists were going back to the Mansion to have their statements typed up, and even without Precious asking me to, I went to help them pack their things.

I was somehow still hoping that George would have gathered himself together to go thank the men he had coaxed into coming. But he was, once again, absent. In a way, that seemed the starkest proof of just how thoroughly he had given up.

After I took photographs of the scientists gathered on the steps of the Mansion, Professor Atkins asked me if he would see one in the newspaper.

"Oh, I doubt it," I said, wondering despite myself where Lottie was. "But maybe."

"Don't you lose that photograph, then," he said.

"Sir?"

"Someday, this will be part of history, even if we're not allowed to testify right now."

I was confused. "Did you know the judge wasn't going to let you be called?" I asked.

"I had that suspicion, yes."

"Then why did you come?"

"Because the fact that he wouldn't let me speak is probably what will win this case in the end, even if it takes years."

I couldn't help noticing how much more graceful than George the professor was being about his exclusion from the case.

By Friday evening, people were acting as if the trial was over. Getting the scientists before the jury had been the defense's best strategy for making the case that no one should reject the teaching of evolution without understanding what evolution was. Old Eva Jenkins, back during her reign over the Aqua kitchen, had made a similar point when she saw me pulling a face as she dropped a handful of bloody oxtails into the huge soup pot. "How can you know you don't like oxtail soup unless you try it?" Evolutionary theory was the oxtail soup of the Scopes trial. The chance for people to try it had been offered by the many scholars who were even now on trains and in automobiles heading away from Dayton. But the judge had not let anyone in the courtroom have a taste.

Most of the journalists were leaving too, giddy with the prospect of escaping the punishing heat, the heavy meals, the cramped courtroom, and—for some of them—the folding cots in their makeshift hardware store headquarters. They had lost their hope of watching Clarence Darrow do what he'd come to do, which was to show, through the testimony of the experts, that if there was a devil, his name was not Charles Darwin, and if there was a sin, it wasn't science. But it was Friday, after all, and the weekend beckoned. Some of the reporters drove over to Chattanooga. Others went hiking in the Tennessee hills. Still others boarded a northbound train decked out with a banner saying, PROTOPLASM EXPRESS. All of them would curse themselves later on for what they missed.

Even H. L. Mencken left, to his everlasting regret. "All that remains of the great cause of the State of Tennessee against the infidel Scopes," he wrote before he departed, "is the final business of bumping off the defendant. There may be some legal jousting on Monday and some gaudy oratory on Tuesday, but the main battle is over, with Genesis completely triumphant."

He was wrong.

I heard hammering as soon as I reached our front door, and I found George in the backyard, exactly where I'd seen him last, except that now he was standing beside a wooden base, already about three feet tall.

He held up his hammer when he saw me. "Where were you last night?" he demanded.

"I fell asleep next door," I said.

"That's the first time I've ever spent a night here alone," he said. "How'd it feel?"

"Lots better than jail."

That was not the answer I was hoping for, which must have shown on my face.

"And I missed you," he added, unconvincingly.

"You did not miss me."

"I was busy."

"George. I know you feel bad about the trial," I said. "But everyone's saying it was over today. The judge didn't allow the scientists to testify—"

He cut me off.

"I *know* what happened, Annabel," he said.

Even the simplest words in a marriage can be wounding. That afternoon, it was just my full first name that came as a reproach. *Annabel,* he had said. None of the nicknames, none of the endearments, none of the casual ways of calling to me, not even *Annie.*

"You weren't at the Mansion to see them off," I said. "I didn't know if you knew."

"It was broadcast. We do have a radio, remember?" he said.

"All right, then. So do you know that most of the reporters have left too?"

He bent over an old wooden stool, where he'd lined up several boxes of nails.

"Does that include your friend?" he asked.

"You know she's not my friend anymore," I said, although a part of me was hurt that if she had left, she hadn't said goodbye.

"George," I said. "Why don't we go inside and have some coffee?"

"I'm busy."

He picked up a set of instructions. On the cover was the same picture that had been in his radio magazine:

NOW YOU CAN BUILD YOUR OWN RADIO TOWER

"You're really going to do this?" I said.

"I want to reach all forty-eight states."

"Why?"

He paused a moment, then said, "You wouldn't understand."

Three words this time. The exact opposite of the three words that had begun our courtship and sustained the first part of our marriage: "I've got you."

"What else can't I understand, George?" I asked.

His eyes narrowed. He scratched his scruffy, unshaven cheek.

"Geology," he said. "Embryology. Paleontology. Zoology."

"All right, George."

"How do we know how old a rock is? What are a fish's gill slits and what's their significance to man? Why do we have an appendix? Why do we have wisdom teeth?"

"All right, George," I said again, my eyes tearing up. "I don't know those things."

He scoffed. "Why is it so hard for you people to say that you don't know?"

You people.

"But we *do* know," I said. "We know about the Garden, and Jesus, Mary, and Joseph. We know about the Sermon on the Mount and Christ feeding five thousand people. Why does it bother *you* so much that we know things you don't know? Do you really expect me to unlearn what I know?"

"What you know," he said, "is nonsense."

Something inside me slipped out of place.

I'd once thought he respected me. He'd had his book learning and his kind of smarts, but I'd been the one to get things done, to keep the household clean and warm, to cook and bake and sew and polish and mend and do the marketing. I had read books—maybe not his science books or his law books—but I'd read plenty. In the last two weeks, I'd learned so much of his world. In nearly three years, he'd learned almost nothing of mine.

Once again it seemed that without a light shining on him, he would retreat into this rigid, solitary man. For the first time ever, I was glad we didn't have children. I wouldn't have wanted them growing up with a father whose goodness could be degraded and whose distance would be likely whenever things got difficult. Since Walton Allen's death, I had been mourning the George I'd first met, but it wasn't until this conversation that I realized he had never been only that man. He had always been this man too. Like the people who refused to acknowledge the contradictions in Genesis, I had seen only the parts of George that confirmed what I wanted to believe.

I left him in the yard and went upstairs. Once again, I knew I couldn't spend the night in this house, and even Mercy's felt too close. I had to go somewhere else.

4

In the previous two weeks, Bailey's Boardinghouse had been overrun by reporters, but now that so many had left town, there were a few vacancies, and Mr. Bailey told me I could have a small room at the back. Naturally, he gave me the once-over. Why was this married woman alone again? I didn't let that bother me. I figured there would be plenty of people asking plenty of questions in the days to come, and in time I'd be able to answer them.

For now, I settled, more happily than I would have imagined possible, into the modest, tidy room. A bed, a washbasin, a table, and a chair. Nothing that needed tending. The last time I had lived here, I'd essentially been an abandoned child with much more attachment to the past than to the present or future. I hadn't known adult love yet, and I hadn't been sure I ever would.

By ten o'clock, I was lying in bed under a pale yellow chenille cover, a slow but steady ceiling fan turning overhead. There was a painting of a grove of trees on one wall and, across from it, a window framed by faded calico curtains that were exactly like the ones I'd had in the room where I'd lived before. I could hear sounds from the street I hadn't realized I'd learned to love—the sputter of engines, the knock of horses' hooves, the laughter of men relaxing and the chatter of them planning how they were going to spend their days.

The fact that I didn't know yet exactly how I would spend mine somehow didn't bother me at all.

I went to Caroline's first thing in the morning and, over a hastily brewed pot of coffee and with the baby in his playpen, I told her where I had spent the night. Whether distracted by the baby or just unsurprised by my story, she seemed to take my news in stride. She asked if I was all right and if I wanted to spend the day with her. She had cousins coming for lunch, she said, but after that we could go to Oak Tree Pond.

I hadn't even thought about going there, but I'd already heard at Bailey's that a bunch of folks, including John Scopes, were planning to go and cool off. I told Caroline I might see her there later, but in the meantime, I borrowed a bathing suit, a frock, and a towel. Alone, I walked up to the pond.

I could hear the shouts and laughter from a quarter mile away, and I almost decided to turn back. I wasn't sure I was in the mood for the kind of revelry I was hearing. On the other hand, if the previous weeks had taught me anything, it was that how people acted and what people felt were often very different things.

Standing for a moment in the shadow of the trees, I tried to fix on one swimmer after another. Which of them had secretly wanted to hear what the experts would have said? Which of them had simply found they liked Clarence Darrow? Which of them had gotten close enough to William Jennings Bryan to smell the sour breath that came from those radishes he kept in his pockets and munched on all day long?

I knew many of these people from church or the Aqua. Others were strangers. Maybe even the most devout among them yearned to consider other explanations of how the world worked than "God, in mysterious ways." Maybe the least religious among them

yearned for fewer books and simpler answers. Maybe all of them
were so enmeshed in whichever side they were on that the expression of any uncertainty would risk their being cast out.

I took a few steps closer to the shore, looking for John. Instead
I saw Lottie. Though I was still furious at her, I had hoped to see
her here. She must have borrowed a bathing suit, too, because as
she swam to shore, I saw no billowing slip. But when she emerged
from the water, her possum-bite scar shimmered as it had the first
time we'd come here.

She didn't hesitate, walking toward me as if we'd made a date.

"I was hoping you'd come," she said. "If you hadn't, I would
have gone looking for you. I have something for you."

"I didn't come because of you," I said.

"I know that."

She was soaked. She shook her head, like a dog, and the water
went flying from her short brown hair.

"Don't you have a towel?" I asked, solicitous without meaning
to be.

"Back over there."

She pointed to a young couple who were sitting on a blanket on
the bank of the pond. I didn't recognize them, but they waved to
her, and despite myself I felt a twinge of envy. Someone else had
taken her in. Someone else was getting to relish her liveliness and
maybe even receiving some of her affection.

I handed her my towel. "You staying with them?" I asked.

She nodded. "Just the last two nights. I'm leaving today."

"Before it's over?"

"It *is* over," she said. "No defense witnesses. Even Mencken
left." She draped the towel, cape-like, over her shoulders.

"But how is it really over? Won't there be closing arguments?
What about the verdict?"

Lottie shook her head. "The wires will all report the verdict,
and we all know what it's going to be. And Darrow's going to
change John's plea to guilty so Bryan won't even get to give a closing speech."

"Really?" I asked.

She nodded. "It's cruel, and Bryan will hate it, but it's brilliant."

"Brilliant," I repeated bitterly. "You're pretty good at confusing *brilliant* with *devious*."

"Annabel," she said. "I hate you being so angry with me."

"You'd be angry too," I said.

"Fit to be tied," she said. "But let's just have a little time before I go."

"What do you want?"

She looked around for inspiration.

"I want you to swim," she said.

She didn't drag me into the water, so I must have gone willingly, and I know there was some part of me that had always wanted to learn. This was, after all, the very place where George had first scooped me up, and I was enough of a dreamer to imagine I could claim my independence in this very specific, symbolic way.

She told me to put my face in the water, just to get a sense of what it was like.

Splashing all around us were fearless children and old people bobbing up and diving under.

"You can do this," Lottie said to me, and for that moment I had as much to prove to her as I did to George or to myself.

I took a deep breath and intentionally plunged my whole body underwater for the first time in my life.

Here is the thing about taking a deep breath and plunging underwater for the first time in your life—when you're twenty-three years old. You have to know that the deep breath needs to be held, and that if you let it out as soon as you go under, your instinct will be to take another breath immediately, and that means you will be swallowing about a gallon of water, and that means you will panic.

I would love to say—to know, to remember—that at that precise moment in my life I plunged underwater and discovered how wonderful it felt, how easily I floated, how naturally I swam.

Instead, I thrashed and choked, came up to the surface, slapped the water, went under again, swallowed more water, and reemerged, blinded by my own hair.

"Put your feet down!" I heard Lottie shout. But I was too panicked to understand what she meant.

"Annabel!" she shouted. "Put your blessed feet down! Stand up! You can stand!"

Turned out I could.

My soles touched the muddy bottom, and when I finally stopped coughing and got the hair out of my eyes, I realized that a lot of the action around me had stopped, and people, including children, were pointing at me and laughing.

"Try again," Lottie said, "but this time, keep holding your breath when you go under."

I gave her a deathly stare and trudged past her to the shore.

"Annabel, come on!"

I grabbed the towel and sat on a rock with my arms on my knees and my head in my arms.

I didn't cry, but I didn't look up until I saw Lottie's toes in the sand before me and felt her shadow blocking the sun.

"You have to try again," she said.

"I don't want to."

"You'll be proud of yourself if you do."

"I'll be prouder if I do it sometime when no one's telling me I have to."

I stood up, looking around for my shoes, dizzy enough that for a moment, the sparkling flecks in the rock seemed to flicker past my eyes.

"Are you all right?" Lottie asked.

"Fine. Where are my shoes?"

"I don't know."

"I was sure I left them here."

"Want some help finding them?" she asked. She extended a

hand, and it was only then that I realized she had my shoes on her hands, and that was it. I had to laugh.

She put her skinny arms around me, my shoes clicking together behind my back. She hugged me. I shouldn't have been surprised that her physical strength matched the rest of her. She was all sinew.

I fought it for only a moment but then I put my arms around her too.

She whispered into my neck. "Annabel, I'm so sorry. I was just trying to do my job."

I broke away from her embrace.

"Great job," I said.

"Look, you saw all those fellows in the pressroom, didn't you? Any one of them would have jumped at the chance to print what the defense was really thinking about the judge. It *matters* that he wasn't being impartial. It might matter on appeal."

"You could have warned George," I said. "You realize he got kicked off the case? Or you could have warned me to warn him. Even a hint would have been enough. For heaven's sake, you were a guest in our home."

"What Henry Mencken said is true. Unless you tell a reporter that they're not allowed to print something, you've got to assume they will."

"Shouldn't you tell someone that rule in advance? Doesn't seem very fair if you're playing a game where only one side knows the rules."

"You've got a point," she said. "And I'm sorry it was your husband who didn't know the rules."

I took my shoes from her hands, sat back on the rock, and pulled them on.

"Before I go," she said, "I've got something to give you."

"I don't want another swimming lesson."

She laughed, for once not a closed-mouth chuckle but a lovely waterfall. "No, not that," she said. "Wait here."

She went over to the blanket where her new hosts were sitting and came back with an envelope in her hand. My name was written on it in a lovely, surprising script.

"What is it?"

"I stayed with you for over a month," she said.

"I know."

"I—" She hesitated.

"What?"

"My paper wants me to pay you for the room and board."

I eyed her suspiciously.

"That was never our understanding," I said.

"You fed me and you housed me," she said. "A hotel would have cost more than this."

Naturally, I was curious to know how much was inside the envelope, but I didn't want her to see me look.

"Whatever it is, I can't take it," I said.

"You can't not," she said.

She shoved the envelope into my hand as if launching both it and me from shore. Quickly she gave me one more embrace, and then she walked away.

"If you're ever in Chattanooga," she said over her shoulder.

Back at Bailey's, on the porch, rocking chairs were lined up straight as fence posts, as if no chaos had ever come to town, and in two of them, facing the gravelly patch behind the boardinghouse, sat John Scopes and his father, Tom. Their feet were resting on mail sacks, which seemed to give their rocking added momentum, and as I approached, I could see that John's hair and the back of his shirt collar were wet.

"Were you swimming?" I asked him. "I didn't see you at the pond."

He said they'd driven up to Walden's Ridge.

"So, you *really* wanted to get away," I said.

Both men chuckled.

"Pretty much since that first day in the drugstore," John said.

We all turned at the sound of gravel crunching as two boys from the boardinghouse, one in bare feet, rolled a cart filled with wood scraps next to the burn barrel.

"Thank you kindly," John called to them.

"Want us to get 'er started?" the one who had shoes on asked.

"Much obliged," John's father said.

In the yard, the boys began pitching wood scraps into the burn barrel.

"You going to light that thing?" Tom asked them.

"Yessir."

The shorter boy took a small can from the cart and sprinkled gasoline into the barrel as if he were seasoning a stew.

The taller one lit a match.

"Stand back, boy!" Tom shouted, just as a plume of fire shot up from the barrel.

John reached into the mail sack at his feet and grabbed a dozen envelopes.

"What, you're going to burn those? Have you even read them?" I asked.

"Enough of them," John added. "They're all pretty much the same."

"Can I see one?" I asked.

"Take your pick," John said, and he fanned out a dozen envelopes like playing cards.

I chose a pale blue envelope, with tidy writing, addressed to "John Scopes, Tennessee." The postmark was Mississippi. "Dear Scoundrel Scopes," it began. "No good yer thinking we are apes though maybe you don't have more sense than one."

John took the letter back from me and fanned out the letters again. "Try another," he said.

Dear Dr. Scopes

If you manage to make everyone think the way you do, the children will never learn that they were born in sin. And if they never learn that, they will never learn that Jesus Christ our Lord died to save them from hell. And if they never learn about Jesus Christ, they will never learn all that is decent and virtuous. Then what will stop them from fornicating and blaspheming?"

"Well, at least this one calls you "doctor," I said.

"Dear Sir," another letter said. "You will surely burn in hell for all of eternity."

I handed the letters back to John. He crumpled them one by one and shot them at the burn barrel. Each one missed.

He shook his head.

"Well, you were always better at coaching, Son," Tom said.

Sighing, but amused, John grabbed an armful of the letters and headed down the back porch steps.

The boys had gathered up the envelopes John had thrown down.

"Go ahead, fellas," he told them, and they shot the letters in. Then John dumped his armful on top of those. It took less than a minute for them to catch, and though the flames didn't shoot up above the rim, I could see the light of the fire reflected in John's glasses.

"You can watch," he called up to me, "or you can give us a hand."

I looked to his father to make sure that he'd have no objection.

"Go ahead, lass," he said. "We could use the help."

I dragged John's mailbag, still almost full, and bumped it down the porch steps.

"Grab a handful," he said.

It took a full hour for us to burn all the letters. Every once in a while, I stopped and opened one, wanting to make sure that they really were as hateful as the others I'd read. They were.

About Bryan, Mencken had written: "The fellow is full of such bitter, implacable hatreds that they radiate from him like heat from a stove. He hates the learning that he cannot grasp. He hates those who sneer at him. He hates, in general, all who stand apart from his pathetic commonness. And the yokels hate with him, some of them almost as bitterly as he does himself."

Reading the letters, I saw this hate on the pages—the paper actually ripped at times with the force of pencil or pen—exclamation points like little daggers, launched at John Scopes by good Christians from all over the country.

Sunday morning, I put on the dress I'd grabbed two nights before, but somehow, I'd forgotten that there would be no service at our church. The doors were once again closed. On the street outside, Reverend Byrd's wife, Sylvia, had their baby in a sling across her chest and was holding a bag of oats for a horse hitched to a wagon. The wagon was half full, and just as I approached, Reverend Byrd himself emerged from the little house he'd built. Clara was on his shoulders, and he was carrying two standing lamps.

"Howard!" Sylvia shouted. "Be careful!"

"She's fine, Sylvie," Reverend Byrd said, but he put the lamps down, lifted Clara from his shoulders, and settled her into the wagon on a rolled-up rug. Then he lay the lamps beside the rug.

"Where will you go?" I asked him.

"Kentucky. I have friends in Evansville who'll put us up for a bit. We'll find our way."

"Who's going to lead the church?" I asked.

He looked at me with those dark, intense eyes. "The council is sending someone," he said. "He should be here in a week or so."

"It won't be the same without you," I said.

He started back toward the house.

"Reverend Byrd—" I began.

He turned back expectantly.

"You were there when I said, 'until we are parted by death.'"

He knew I was asking a question. He placed a hand on my shoulder and kept it there while he held my gaze.

"Yes," he said. "It was the same day your husband promised to love and comfort and honor you. Has he done those things?"

"Does one broken promise make another one all right?" I asked.

He patted my shoulder. "I believe in a God who understands

that there are times humans can't keep all their promises. I think you should pray on whether this has to be one of those times for you."

"Darlin'," Sylvia called just then. "I can't feed the horse and hold the baby and watch out for Clara all at the same time."

"I'll do it," I said.

"Which one?"

But I was already standing beside Clara, looking at her thin reddish curls and wondering what her hair would be like when she grew up. And where she would grow up. And if she'd have both her parents. One thing I did know was that she had absolutely no interest in sitting still, so there was good reason to keep an eye on her. With her rose-petal hands on the rough wood of the cart, she pulled herself up, then started to climb around, first balancing on the rug, then getting a foot up on one of the crates. Just as she was about to topple, I tucked my hands under her armpits and pulled her back toward me. Unexpectedly, she hugged me.

"We're going bye-bye," she said.

"I know."

When Reverend Byrd came back outside, he was carrying a box of books, which he hoisted into the cart.

"Do you believe in evolution?" I asked him.

"Evolution isn't a belief," he said. "And the Bible isn't science."

"You never said that in church."

"In church, I can tell you what I know of the Father, the Son, and the Holy Spirit. That's not the place where I should tell you what I know of science."

"Do you think God created Adam?"

"Annabel," he said, "I believe that God created man, but I can't give you an easy answer about how or when that happened, even if the major and Mr. Bryan and all the Fundamentalists in the world would want me to. I'm saying I know the Bible holds truth, but that doesn't mean it necessarily holds facts."

Sylvia came down the steps, carrying a box filled with kitchen things.

"Howard Byrd, you'd best be saving room for my pots and pans, or I'll be taking those books out one by one," she said. She was teasing him. I marveled at the fact that their lives were coming apart and yet they seemed so serene.

They had their faith.

They had their children.

They had each other.

I didn't want to go home.

5

On Monday morning, with so many of the scientists and journalists gone, I was expecting it would be easy to find a place in the courtroom, but it seemed even more crowded than it had on Friday, and the judge said he had been told that the courtroom floor was in danger of collapsing from all our weight. The rest of the proceedings would take place outside, he said. The real reason may just have been that it was the hottest day yet on record. Or perhaps Judge Raulston had an inkling that the final parts of the trial would feature less law and more theater, so it belonged not in a courtroom but on something more like a stage.

The platform was already there. It was where an old-time band had played just the evening before. It was where Dr. Potter had given his talk. It was where Wilbur Glenn Voliva had put forth his theory that the world was flat and had offered a five-thousand-dollar reward for anyone who could prove otherwise—at least to his satisfaction. Now the members of the defense and prosecution teams awkwardly carried ladder-back chairs and tables down the stairs and outside to settle them on the platform. Once both teams were in place, Clarence Darrow made it clear that he intended to make one more argument for the defense, which was to call Bryan himself—as an expert on the Bible.

"Your Honor," Darrow said, "we recognize that what Mr. Bryan says as a witness would not be very valuable as far as the question of what Mr. Scopes taught. But we think there are other questions involved, and we should want to take Mr. Bryan's testimony for the purposes of our record."

The judge looked utterly baffled.

But Bryan, possibly seeing an opportunity to regain the supremacy that Dudley Field Malone had challenged the previous week, simply turned to Darrow and asked, "Where do you want me to sit?"

In later years a myth would grow that the idea to examine Bryan had come to Darrow in a flash of inspiration once he'd run through all other avenues to present the case for science. But Darrow had rehearsed it all at the Mansion the previous night; even a few years before, in an open letter to the *Chicago Daily Times,* he had challenged Bryan to answer many of the questions he was about to ask. In a sense this was what the trial had been heading for the whole time: the contest between two men who had spent much of their lives fighting for their beliefs but had never had this good a chance to fight each other.

Now, in the July sun, with spectators surrounding the raised platform and shielding their eyes from the glare, the two men finally had their moment. I couldn't believe that Lottie and Mencken were going to miss this. Around the town, however, news traveled quickly about what was happening, and within five minutes, the crowd outside the courthouse had doubled; in another five, it had doubled again. There were babies in mothers' arms, and men lying on the grass. There were children looking down on us from the vacated courtroom, leaning over the windowsills as if they were watching a parade. On the platform, there were only about ten reporters, and I was the only photographer. In my whole career, my greatest regret would remain my failure to have extra film with me that day. I was able to take just eight pictures. The best known is of Darrow on his feet with his thumbs under his suspenders while Bryan looks up at him, smiling; two policemen stand by, and the crowd is a blur of white shirts and hats. The two famous men are divided in the photograph by a large maple tree in the distance, with one large arm arced over Darrow, as if to shelter and protect him from whatever wrath he might provoke.

From his very first questions, Darrow made it clear that his intention was to find the flaws and contradictions in Bryan's beliefs.

"Do you claim everything in the Bible should be literally interpreted?"

"I believe," Bryan said, with a cheerful smile, "that everything in the Bible should be accepted as it is given there."

Darrow seemed equally cheerful. "So, when you read that a whale swallowed Jonah, how do you literally interpret that?"

"The Bible doesn't say 'a whale.' It says, 'a big fish.'"

The onlookers laughed. Darrow nodded patiently.

"Now you say the big fish swallowed Jonah, and he there remained three days, and then he spewed him upon the land. You believe that the big fish was made to swallow Jonah?"

"I believe in a God who can make a whale and can make a man and can make both do as he pleases."

Just then I saw George, still in his dirty clothes, still unshaven, serpentining his way through the many people in faded denim and gingham. His face had been ashen the last time I'd seen him, but now his cheeks were red. I guessed he must have run all the way from Walnut Street. In two days and three nights, as far as I knew, he had made no excursions from his hiding place in the backyard—and he certainly hadn't gone anywhere in search of me. This, obviously, was entirely different.

Darrow took a step closer to Bryan. "You don't know," he asked, "whether it was the ordinary run of fish?"

George hadn't gotten any closer to the platform than a hundred feet, but I could see him smile when he heard the question.

"You may guess at that," Bryan sneered. "You evolutionists guess."

Darrow, aloft on a cloud of sarcasm, asked: "You don't know whether that fish was fixed up specially for that purpose?"

George was hardly the only person who laughed along with this question, but his was the loudest laughter I heard.

"But you believe," Darrow said, smacking his right hand onto his left, "that God made such a fish and that it was big enough to swallow Jonah?"

"Yes, sir," Bryan said, and for the first time, he turned toward the crowd—the audience, as I came to think of them. "And let me add that one miracle is just as easy to believe as another."

"Easy for you, perhaps," Darrow said, and again I could hear George's laughter.

But this was the point that many people present—and so many newsmen and other writers—would miss when they came to write about Darrow's famous duel with Bryan. If you believe in an all-powerful God, you believe He can do anything. You believe it's His choice whether to abide by the laws of nature that He Himself created. He is, by definition, above nature. Supernatural. And so, yes, when Darrow tested Bryan with a string of "do you believes," Bryan had no difficulty answering each question with an unflinching yes.

Was Eve really made from Adam's rib? Did the serpent really have legs before it was punished? Did Joshua really command the sun to stand still?

"Now, Mr. Bryan," Darrow said, "have you ever pondered that if the sun stood still, the earth would have been converted into a molten mass of matter?"

"You can testify to that when I get you on the stand. I will give you a chance," Bryan said.

"Don't you believe it?" Darrow asked.

"I have never thought about it."

"Never?"

"No."

Again, George's was the laughter that seemed loudest, most heartless. Ironically, ever since he had joined the hapless, drunken crew looking to harass Mencken, his reactions were just what I imagined Mencken's would have been. Mencken would have pounced on the same apparent foibles with this same evident glee.

An hour in, Bryan's black bow tie had wilted, and Darrow's lavender suspenders were dimpled halfway up his chest from all the times he'd tucked his thumbs beneath them. The cheerful nature of the questions had given way to a battle of wills and pride. Tom Stewart, the district attorney, tried several times to stop the show.

"This has gone beyond the pale of any issue that could possibly be injected in this lawsuit!" he said.

But Bryan, as if to mollify Stewart, replied, "These gentlemen did not come here to try this case. They came here to try revealed religion. I am here to defend it. And they can ask me any question they please."

The crowd cheered at that.

"Great applause from the bleachers," Darrow noted.

"From those you call 'yokels,' " Bryan responded.

"I have *never* called them yokels," Darrow insisted.

"I mean those people whom you insult."

Darrow smacked his right hand onto his left.

"You insult every man of science and learning in the world because he does not believe in your fool religion."

Over the course of the next hour, the heat of the afternoon and the heat of the questioning grew even more intense. I got the sense that the crowd around the platform was leaning in, creating a swelling sea. Members of both the prosecution and defense teams seemed alternately delighted and concerned. John looked interested but numb. Even from this distance, I could see George's eyes gleaming.

Each time Darrow asked a biting question or made a particularly forceful statement, George slapped one hand onto the other, just the way Darrow did. It wasn't exactly applause; it was more like emphasis, as if whatever point Darrow was making needed an added physical demonstration. I had no idea if Darrow was aware that there was a shadow version of himself out in the crowd, but when George caught me looking at him, he paused. I was expecting a sheepish shrug, but instead, he hit his hand again, this time with his eyes not on Darrow but on me. It felt like a blow.

"Mr. Bryan, the Bible says only Adam and Eve and their two sons were on the earth. Did you ever discover where Cain got his wife?"

"No, sir. I leave the agnostics to hunt for her," Bryan replied, delighted—as the spectators were—with his answer.

But Darrow pressed on, turning from Bryan's confidence about the Bible and making his limited knowledge of and curiosity about the real world seem preposterous. This was where Bryan struggled—and failed—and deeply disappointed me. "Don't you know," Darrow said, "that there are thousands of people who profess to be Christians who believe the earth is much more ancient and that the human race is much more ancient than you say?"

"I think there may be," Bryan said.

"And you never have investigated to find out how long man has been on the earth?"

"I have never found it necessary."

"You have never in *all* your life made *any* attempt to find out about the *other* peoples of the earth—the ancient civilizations of China and Egypt—how long *they* had existed on the earth, have you?"

"No, sir," said Bryan. "I have been so well satisfied with the Christian religion that I have spent no time trying to find arguments against it."

"You don't care how old the earth is, how old man is, and how long the animals have been here?"

"I am not so much interested in that."

"Do you *ever* think about that?" Darrow asked, his right hand smacking his left.

By now rattled, Bryan declared: "I do not think about things that—I don't think about."

Darrow pounced. "Do you ever think about things you *do* think about?"

As laughter swelled, Stewart was on his feet again, his face contorted by anger and concern. "I want to interpose another objection," he said. "What is the purpose of this examination?"

"The purpose," Bryan declared, turning his whole body to face the crowd, "is to cast ridicule on everybody who believes in the Bible."

"We have the purpose," Darrow responded with equal passion, "of preventing bigots and ignoramuses from controlling the education of the United States, and you know it, and that is all."

It was a statement that Darrow's admirers would repeat and revel in for years. But the true damage Darrow did to Bryan's argument—the Fundamentalist argument that the Bible was literally true—came a little later, when Darrow asked Bryan if he believed the earth had been made in six days.

"Not six days of twenty-four hours," Bryan answered, and for the first time, the crowd was almost entirely silent.

"Doesn't it say so in the Bible?" Darrow asked.

"No, sir, not twenty-four hours. I would not attempt to argue as against anybody who wanted to believe that, but I think it would be just as easy for the kind of God we believe in to make the earth in six days as in six years or in six million years or in six hundred thousand years."

It was a huge, an almost incomprehensible, misstep, perhaps explainable only by the fact that Darrow had worn Bryan down with his relentless questioning. If the word *day* could be open to interpretation, then what else might be?

Everything, I thought. Everything could be open to interpretation. That much was undeniable. But I didn't want Darrow to win.

I didn't want George to win. I didn't want Bryan to lose; I was heartbroken for him—not because he clung to miracles, but because his total rejection of what man could learn made him seem so fearful and so foolish.

The remaining reporters in the crowd were alternately scribbling and flexing their sore hands. From time to time, I could see them exchanging delighted looks—as if by staying through the trial's disappointing second act they had been rewarded with a brilliant third. Even as the judge rapped the gavel, they started toward the hardware store pressroom, and I was following them.

It was then that George came up behind me and grabbed me by the elbow—not to see if I was all right, not to ask me to come home, not even to say he was sorry. Simply to gloat, as if he was still thinking of me as "you people."

"How the mighty have fallen," he said.

I looked at his angry, flat eyes and said, "Who are the mighty who've fallen, George?"

"Are you coming home?" he asked.

"No. I'm going to the pressroom."

Only six of the many desks were taken, though a few more newsmen came in after me, skimming their straw hats onto the floor. It seemed they started typing before they even sat down.

The desk where Lottie had worked was empty, and so I took her chair, listening to the typewriters and the men calling back and forth to each other.

"What color were his suspenders today?"

"What was that part about Bishop Ussher?"

"I'm out of smokes. Bill, can you spare me a smoke?"

A pack of cigarettes went arcing through the air.

"Mencken's going to have apoplexy!" one of them shouted. "Imagine him being scooped by us!"

There was a torn green blotter on Lottie's otherwise empty desk, and it was covered with notes I assume she'd made:

Malone taking off his jacket
Sweat stains under Darrow's armpits
Bryan's breath!
Fan on Raulston's desk
Mencken standing next to newsreel camera
George Craig

I watched and listened while the men excitedly typed and talked. The plan was that each of them would make five carbon copies of his article, hand them around, and then allow other people to change them just enough so they could be filed by friends at other newspapers who'd missed the show. It was kind and collegial, although naturally the "real" stories were filed and would be printed first.

As soon as the teletype machine started transmitting, Paul Anderson from the *St. Louis Dispatch* gave me one of his copies.

"Use all the facts you want," he said, "just leave me the poetry."

The poetry was beautiful. Anderson wrote: "It was magnificent and tragic, stirring and pathetic, and above all it was pervaded by the atmosphere of grandeur which befitted a death grapple between two great ideas."

At the top of his teletype, though, in capital letters, he had written: BRYAN HYSTERICAL/DARROW PITILESS.

"Hysterical?" I said to Paul.

He was knocking a cigarette out of a pack of Luckies, relaxing, happy that his story was done.

"When was Mr. Bryan hysterical?" I asked.

Anderson laughed at me and took a seat on one of the cots.

"You don't think he was hysterical?"

"He was defending the faith," I said.

"Did you count how many things he said he didn't know?"

"Did you count how many things he did?"

"Didn't you notice that whenever he was losing, he started giving his answers to the crowd?"

"He wanted to be heard," I said.

"Annabel," Paul said, leaning back on his elbows. "You'd better get to work, or Lottie's paper will be the last one to get the story."

Just then, John Scopes came in. He barely got any notice, which was nothing new. But when Paul handed him another of the copies to rewrite, the other men laughed.

"You're sure you want me to do this?" John asked.

"Aw, give it a try, Professor."

Sheepishly, John used his shirttail to polish his glasses, then reached into his front pocket for his ever-ready smokes and his pencil.

"Is there a sharpener?" he asked the room in general.

"Not a classroom, John," one of them said and handed him a penknife.

Smiling, he whittled the pencil into a sharper point, then sat down with the carbon copy of the story.

Meanwhile, I dialed the operator and asked to be connected to the *Chattanooga News*. After a few minutes, a gruff man's voice asked what I wanted, and when I said I wanted to talk to Lottie Nelson, I was asked what it was about, and when he said she wasn't in, I told him it was about the Scopes trial.

"Are you in Dayton?" he asked.

"Yes."

"Are you a reporter?"

"Photographer. But I'm sitting in the pressroom. Clarence Darrow just put William Jennings Bryan on the stand."

"Hot damn!" he said. He told me to write what I could as fast as I could, and he hung up.

I read through Paul's story. "Let there be no doubt," he had written. "Bryan was broken, if ever a man was broken. Darrow never spared him. It was masterful, but it was pitiful."

I crossed out those words. Bryan certainly hadn't triumphed, but I didn't think he'd been broken. Instead, I wrote, "Let there be no doubt. Bryan was shaken, and Darrow never spared him. But Bryan's head remained unbowed."

Then I crossed those words out too.

I wrote: "Let there be no doubt. Bryan was shaken, and Darrow never spared him, but the only jurors present were the crowd around the courthouse, and many of them believed Bryan had held his own in the face of a faithless attack on the Bible."

A version of my story would appear the next day, but I barely recognized it. My words about Darrow and Bryan did not tell the version of the event that the *Chattanooga News*—and almost every other newspaper—wanted to tell. The narrative of that famous day would remain—around the state, the country, the world—that Darrow's examination of Bryan had utterly destroyed him.

By the next morning, the judge seemed rueful about having allowed the drama of the previous day to unfold, and he ordered that Bryan's testimony be struck. There was a long discussion about which objections should and shouldn't be put in the record, and then Darrow landed the blow that Lottie had predicted.

"Let me suggest this," he said. "I think to save time we will ask the Court to bring in the jury and instruct the jury to find the defendant guilty. We make no objection to that, and it will save a lot of time."

The prosecution looked stricken. Before his testimony on the lawn, Bryan had been promised an equal chance to question Darrow. Even without that, he had been writing his summation for weeks. Everyone, including the judge, seemed disappointed that they wouldn't get to hear the master orator deliver his masterstroke. But there was no legal or logical reason for a summation to be given. Bryan, almost meekly, suggested he would have to trust the press to report what he had planned to say.

I was disappointed too. I think some part of me still hoped

Bryan would find a way to come out on top. I had no wish to imagine a world—or a life—that had not been created by God, or a world in which no miracles had happened, or ever could. But Bryan's viewpoint seemed to demand that we remain hamstrung—even spellbound—by mystery. The contest was over, though. The judge took half an hour to read his charge to the jury; the lawyers took another fifteen minutes to discuss future appeals; and the jurors took just nine minutes, standing in a crowded hallway, to find Scopes guilty. The hundred-dollar fine was the minimum for a misdemeanor.

In answer to the judge's invitation, John, speaking for the first and only time in the trial, said he'd been found guilty of an unjust statute that he would continue to fight. Then Raulston asked Parson Charlie Jones to give a closing prayer.

It had been quite a while since I'd gone to visit my parents' graves, but despite the heat, which made the metal parts of my camera sting my skin, I decided that that was where I needed to be. A mile or so out of town, the farms were still thriving: fields stretching into the wide, rolling distance as they always had, with row beside row of leafy, low green bushes, set just far enough apart so that mother plants could send their runners out to make daughter plants.

At the cemetery, I picked two wild daisies and laid them across my parents' footstones, and then I wandered about, looking for a perch out of the sun. Near the crest of one hillock, I saw an ancient tombstone that was split nearly in half, and I was reminded of what I'd learned about how ice, over time, could change rock.

In the distance, cottonwood and dogwood trees bowed toward one another. I watched as a squirrel ran up and around a tree trunk as if following the lines of a barbershop pole. A butterfly, colored more perfectly than any of the cards made by the women in the school lunchroom, lit on a moss-covered stone. I remembered the pale yellow and deep purple tomatoes on the long-ago day with my mother. I thought of the different strains of strawberries my father had planted, and the seed catalogues he'd pored over, looking for new blends of grass. No one seemed to have a problem believing that other things in nature had altered over time. Only man was supposed to have been perfect from the start.

I looked out on white and red wild rosebushes, and the bees and small white butterflies that darted among them. Farther on there were orange nasturtiums and large red poppies. Did it matter how long it had taken for a flower to become a flower? Did it matter if it was a day or a million years? Either way, life was improbable, miraculous.

Turning to leave, I nearly stumbled over Walton Allen's footstone—and his son's. I stared down at the twin markers, wondering what would and wouldn't have happened if George had never taken this man's case in the first place, or if the "unwritten law" had not been the universal way people perceived a husband's rights—and a woman's helplessness? What if Walton Allen had been thrown in jail and kept from doing further harm? For that matter, what if Mary Sue Allen had never had relations with Burch Gardenhire?

These were all links in the chain of events that had led both Walton Allen and his son to lie in this place—and my husband to be so racked with guilt that, despite the brief respite when the Scopes trial had seemed to restore him, he could no longer love himself or me or even God.

And what if John Scopes hadn't, back in May, decided to hang around Dayton on the chance of seeing that girl at the box social? Would George Rapp have found a different teacher? Would Clarence Darrow have come to town?

And what if I hadn't lost the baby? Would I now be capable of seeing myself as Lottie saw herself: a woman who had choices? I had not forgotten how, in *The Awakening*, Kate Chopin had written about Edna's resolve never to take another step backwards.

.   .   .

As I headed for Walnut Street, I steeled myself against that temptation, the impulse to try to return to some version of what I'd always thought George and I could have. I was sad, but I was determined. It finally seemed horribly real to me that the bed, the chairs, the stove, and the hearth were the least of what I would no longer share. I would no longer have even the hope of sharing the stories of what happened each day, at least not with George. I would no longer have George's love—if that's what it had ever been—as the simplest way to make sense of my life.

But I had to get Spitfire and the rest of my things.

I thought I was prepared for what I'd meet on Walnut Street. Twice I had found George in the backyard; twice I had found him rude, unwashed, and unreachable. And his sneering on the courthouse lawn the day before had made me certain that he would be gloating now over the way the papers had described the scene, and over the fact that Bryan had been denied the chance to give his big speech.

But as it turned out, when I opened the front door, I found no sound of hammering, no sound of a radio, no sound at all.

I called George's name, and there was no answer.

In the kitchen, the sink and table were empty, clean dishes neatly laid out on the counter to dry. In the backyard, the wood had been stacked in tidy piles, and the base of the radio tower George had been building was only a bit higher than it had been just a few days before. There were no tools or nails scattered about. Everything had been tucked away.

I had been ready to answer whatever questions he'd have for me. I had been ready to tell him that even if he thought he was still the man I'd married, I was no longer the woman he'd married. I was ready to remind him that I was only twenty-three years old, and that nothing that had happened between us in the last three years had made me feel as full of life as what had happened in the last three weeks.

But he was gone. Rushing back out to the street, I realized the car was gone too. In a flash, I remembered how George had driven away after the murder and suicide. Once again, he probably hadn't gone far. His books were still on the parlor shelves, his extra tobacco still in the side table drawer.

But what about Spitfire? I called her name—not that she'd ever answered to it. Had George fed her, even once? Had he let her curl up in the sun on the back steps, as she loved to do? As I climbed the stairs, a terrible thought went through my mind: that he had hurt her. Worse, that I no longer trusted the man I'd married not to hurt a cat. I took the stairs two by two and checked each of the bedrooms and the bathroom. Then I pulled down the attic stairs and climbed up. She was there, under the rafters, clutching a dead mouse by its neck. She settled down, holding the thing proudly between her paws, then looked at me as if I'd just interrupted a lunch at the Aqua Hotel. I cried with relief but left her to finish her meal as I went to pack my things.

Unlike the last time I'd been upstairs, the bed was perfectly made. The things on my dresser were neatly lined up. I took down the valise that George had bought me for our honeymoon, remembering how he had assured me I should have my own because of all the places we'd go. But my travels had been in my mind and heart, and the valise was exactly where I'd left it three long years before.

When I opened it, I was hit with a mist of perfume that I quickly realized came from a bar of soap in a little box that I'd taken from the Read House as a souvenir. I held the soap up to my nose and closed my eyes, and I was in our honeymoon room, wearing only a towel, which George was unwrapping oh so delicately before lifting me onto the bed. I opened my eyes and hurled the soap into the wastebasket. Then, almost immediately, I retrieved it. No matter what anyone will tell you, there is rarely a clear line between your past and your future.

I took my parents' wedding rings and wondered what I would do with my own. I took the SEE HOW WE CAN banner and wondered if, in my situation, my mother would have left my father or whether the times were just stricter enough then that she wouldn't have dreamed of it.

From the bureau, I gathered my underclothes and my blouses, and when I turned to put them into the bag, I saw that Spitfire had come downstairs and already curled up inside it. The thin black diamonds in her yellow-green eyes seemed set, and for a moment we seemed to stare at each other, and I imagined we had the same thought, as if she had made up her mind too.

I left.

6

I still had no idea where George was when the news came, so I never knew how he reacted when he found out that William Jennings Bryan had died. For my part, I heard the news in the lobby of the Aqua Hotel. I can't remember who told me. Probably Fred, since the lobby was nearly deserted, compared to the way it had been just a week before. I do remember walking down Market Street, looking from one person to another, trying to meet their eyes, as if hoping I could find just one person to reassure me that this was a prank or at least a false rumor. But everyone looked at me with the same plea. He had just been here. He was the most important person any of us had ever met, or likely ever would. He had smelled of radishes and sweat. To some people, it seemed that he had triumphed in this last drama, and to others that he had failed. But it had seemed reasonable to think he would do all he could to go on spreading his message.

In time, some people would say that he died right after Darrow cross-examined him, that in a sense he died of a broken heart. Others said his gluttony had been the reason. In reality, he died a busy five days after the end of the trial, five days in which he polished and rewrote and arranged for the publication of the speech that would have been his summation. He had seen his doctor the week before and had been told he had a heart condition and to take it easy. He didn't. Planning to take the speech on a public tour, he was driven to Jasper, and then again to Winchester, where he tried the speech out on crowds of several hundred. He didn't even rest on Sunday morning but led prayers back in Dayton at the Southern Methodist Church.

He died a few hours after that while napping at the Rogerses' home on Market Street. Mary, his wife, had been on the porch, just outside his window, and had not heard a thing.

Eventually, with crowds of thousands looking on, a train would carry him in a brass coffin through Tennessee and Virginia and finally to Washington, where he'd be buried in Arlington National Cemetery. But first—starting the morning after his death—there was the chance for Daytonians to pay our respects on the Rogerses' own front lawn, where Bryan was laid out under the green-and-white-striped awnings that were draped with baskets of moss.

The line of people who'd come to see him was long and wide, and cars and wagons kept arriving. Every third or fourth person held a palm-leaf fan or a rolled-up newspaper and flapped it against the hot, moist air, so the whole mass looked like a strange insect trying to take flight. People wept. They cursed Clarence Darrow. They said God had called Bryan home. They said his death as a martyr would help spread his message forevermore. They talked about creating a college in his honor. They railed against the newspapers, which had treated him so cruelly. And they complained most bitterly about Mencken, who in the morning's vicious obituary had written that Bryan "was born with a roaring voice, and it had the trick of inflaming half-wits."

"Half-wits!" people around me repeated in protest.

As I got closer to the casket, I could hear talk giving way to tears and lamentations. I saw people bend low over the casket. When I reached it, I realized why: The part of the casket above Bryan's face was made of glass.

William Jennings Bryan was the first dead person I had ever seen. The people from the funeral home had clearly done their best to achieve a state of dignified, if not wise, repose. But he was colorless, barely flesh toned. His lips, though sculpted into a smile, were as gray as weathered shingles. To me, he looked like one of the thousands of cartoons that had accompanied countless newspaper columns, long before the Scopes trial, as if his face had been outlined in ink.

After I had seen him, I joined the other mourners who had crossed to the neighbors' lawns to form an impromptu chorus, singing hymn after hymn. For a while I listened. "Nearer My God to Thee." "Amazing Grace." I was just about to join in when I saw George, bobbing his way through the crowd, his eyes intent, his face now fresh and clean. There was a spark in his eyes, and a smile I knew he meant just for me.

He was newly shaved. He was wearing a shirt that he must have pressed himself, because even the collar was crisp. He smelled of shaving cream, and the corners of his eyes creased when he saw me. He had tidied himself up the way he'd tidied the house, but by now I understood that the tidiness was only surface deep.

"Annie," he said.

I looked at him warily. I didn't know what had happened to make him realize that he had lost me, but he looked almost afraid.

"Why did you come?" I asked.

"To comfort you," he said, putting his arms around me in an embrace I didn't return.

"And to pay my respects," he added.

"Not to pay your respects," I said. "You didn't have those for him."

"I want you to come back," George said. "It's so lonely there without you."

I was trying not to cry.

"Cat's Pajamas," he said hoarsely. "Flapjack. Butternut."

Around us, people were singing:

> Shall we gather at the river,
> Where bright angel feet have trod;
> With its crystal tide forever
> Flowing by the throne of God?

George looked around at the singers, and then to the ever-longer line of people waiting to file past Bryan's body.

"You don't belong here," I said. "You only want me to think you do."

I meant here, with the mourners, but as I said it, it struck me that he didn't belong in Dayton, either. Maybe neither of us did.

I had a fleeting image of a happy family living in our house someday. I didn't know how long George would stay there. But I knew that, like a snake shedding its skin, the house had no more use for us.

"Do you think he died from disappointment?" George asked me.

"I don't think he was disappointed."

"You were, though. By me," he said.

Beside us the singers were continuing:

> Yes, we'll gather at the river,
> The beautiful, the beautiful river,
> Gather with the saints at the river
> That flows by the throne of God.

"I'm sorry I disappointed you, June Bug. First there was Walton Allen. And then I said those things to Lottie. And then Darrow kicked me off—"

"No, George," I said. "None of that mattered to me. What mattered was how you took it."

"Shutterbug," he said. "Let it be about us now."

"It's not about us. It hasn't been about us for a really long time."

"It could be, couldn't it?" he said.

He grabbed my hand as I took another step toward the singers.

"I want us to go to church," he said, and that made me stop.

I turned around.

"Church is closed," I said. "Remember? Our pastor had to quit."

He paused, and I could see him thinking it through.

"Are you really going to leave me?"

"I'm really going to leave you," I said. "I'm really going to leave."

"Do you know where you're going to go?" he asked me.

"Not yet," I said, though I assumed I'd start in Chattanooga.

Then I turned away from him and joined the chorus of voices, which lifted and buoyed me. Along with them I sang:

> As I went down to the river to pray,
> Studying about that good ole way
> And who shall wear the starry crown,
> Good Lord, show me the way.

Clouds were moving in swiftly above us, one of those strange Tennessee skies that seem to have meaning but only mean rain. On the Rogerses' lawn, a number of tall men struggled to lift Bryan's casket and bring it inside the house.

George's brown eyes were unaccepting.

> O sisters, let's go down,
> Let's go down, come on down.
> Come on, sisters, let's go down,
> Down to the river to pray.

"Don't you think things can change between us?" he asked.

"Don't you know they already have?"

"Don't you think we can change back?"

"I don't think that's how change works," I said.

I took a step back from him, and then another. I let the crowd absorb me, and I watched George recede. Some changes cannot be missed: the vivid flowerings of summer, the fallow fields of winter. Others require a keen eye: the color of a strawberry when it's nearly too ripe; the confidence of a small child conquering her first staircase; a man who's lost his faith in himself; a woman who's gained hers. I did not know, in the robust heat of that summer of 1925, which changes mattered most. I simply wanted to fear none of them. "Behold," the Lord said to Isaiah. "I will do a new thing."

AFTERWORD

Ninety-nine years after the summer of Scopes, you can stand on the courthouse lawn in Dayton, Tennessee, and easily conjure the crowds that gathered to witness the epic battle between Clarence Darrow and William Jennings Bryan. You can walk down Market Street along what's called the "Scopes Trial Trail" and find a plaque identifying the former hardware store where reporters wrote and filed their stories.

For several days in July, you can also take part in the annual Scopes Trial Festival, listening to bluegrass bands, buying strawberry jam, or paying a small fee to see a reenactment of the trial based on the original transcript. Logos for past festivals have featured monkeys eating hotdogs; T-shirts have shown jaunty chimps playing banjos; a local watering hole called the Monkey Town Brewing Company has been in business since 2014.

But it took a while for Dayton to make peace with its past. The trial, which was really conceived to put the town on the map, did attract publicity, but not the kind the town's boosters had envisioned. The crowds weren't as large as expected, the desired boom in business was modest, and much of the press coverage was not just snooty but ecstatically condescending. Dayton came across as backwards and foolish, and never more so than in the blistering descriptions by H. L. Mencken, whose dispatches to the *Baltimore Sun* took on not only the "yokels" of Dayton but also all "inferior orders of men," whom he accused of embracing Genesis because they feared the science they couldn't understand.

In 1955, a play by Jerome Lawrence and Robert E. Lee did even more to make the trial seem like a battle between the enlightened and the ludicrous. Though *Inherit the Wind* was written as a cautionary tale about McCarthyism—and it renamed the town and main characters—it was unmistakably based on the Scopes trial. When a film version premiered in Dayton in 1960, it left residents mortified and angry. At the movie's climax, the character based on Bryan is so humiliated by the questioning that he is reduced to a sputtering, defeated man who expires right there on the courtroom floor. (For people of a certain generation, that version of history—and Bryan—is hard to erase.)

What really happened after the nine minutes the jury took to find John Scopes guilty?

William Jennings Bryan died not during the trial or even during an argument but five days later and in his sleep. He had been a national figure for forty years, a force of conviction, bombast, and righteousness, a hero to everyday people. His death would have been front-page news no matter when it had happened. But the obituaries written about him invariably began or ended with the Scopes trial and the evolution controversy. Some papers suggested that the trial's exertions had led to his death. But by many accounts, Bryan had been galvanized by the case. Despite the fact that his ignorance of science and history had been surgically exposed, he was more convinced than ever that the country needed him to continue the fight against the teaching of evolution. He was preparing to embark on a speaking tour of the South, using the closing argument that Darrow's maneuvering had prevented him from giving in the courtroom. The timing of Bryan's death conferred an aspect of martyrdom on him, and among its many expressions was Dayton's

1930 founding of Bryan College, a Fundamentalist institution whose motto is "Christ Above All."

As for Clarence Darrow, no college bears his name, but a number of the trials where he led the defense have made their way into law books—and legend. Both his 1924 defense of Chicago "thrill killers" Leopold and Loeb and his 1925 defense of Scopes are often cited among the most famous and important cases in American history. Just months after the Scopes trial, Darrow joined the defense—ultimately successful—of a Black physician named Ossian Sweet. Along with ten other men, Sweet had been charged with murder when protecting his Detroit house from white rioters, one of whom was shot. Darrow made a passionate plea for racial tolerance, at one point saying: "I know that if these defendants had been a white group defending themselves from a colored mob, they never would have been arrested or tried. My clients are charged with murder, but they are really charged with being black." Up until his death in 1938 at the age of eighty, Darrow continued to take on cases and to write and lecture.

Both Bryan and Darrow have been the subject of multiple biographies, the best of which delve into the complexities and contradictions of their personalities and politics. Bryan, the Populist, the supporter of labor unions and women's suffrage, was also often accused of belonging to the Ku Klux Klan, some of whose members burned crosses in tribute after his death. Though his son and wife vehemently denied his membership, it is true that amid countless opportunities to decry the Klan's horrific acts, Bryan chose not to do so. Darrow's life was also complex. He married several times and, as a proponent of what was then called "free love," he was apparently a serial philanderer. His legal career had been nearly derailed in 1911 when he was twice accused, though not convicted, of having arranged to bribe a juror in a labor case. Yet Darrow's image has remained largely untainted.

And what of the man whose name will forever be linked with Dayton? John Scopes moved to Chicago after the trial and, as much as possible, tried to stay out of the limelight he had never sought.

300 AFTERWORD

He gave up teaching. He studied geology and worked, over the course of a lifetime, for a number of oil companies. He married, had two children, and eventually wrote a memoir called *The Center of the Storm,* in which he gave a modest and compelling first-hand account of the momentous days in Dayton.

The debate about evolution has outlived all three men. Although the Scopes verdict was overturned (on the technicality that the fine was set by the judge, not the jury), the Butler Act was not repealed until 1967. As of this writing, no statewide bans on teaching evolution remain, but twenty of our fifty states permit or encourage the teaching of a Biblical version of creation alongside evolution. Sometimes the Biblical version is called *creationism,* sometimes *intelligent design,* most perniciously *creation science.* In some science classrooms, students are explicitly given a choice between versions of man's origins, as if faith and fact must always be at war—as if to be a Christian means to reject wholly the discoveries of biologists, geologists, geneticists, and archaeologists.

I started to write this novel during the era that brought us "fake news" and "alternative facts." Along the way, the rancor about what public schools should and shouldn't teach has intensified, with ferocious battles erupting over everything from climate science to the history of race relations, from human sexuality to human anatomy. Censorship—and censoriousness—have made a comeback across the political landscape. Amid such bitter and corrosive divisions, I wanted to write about another time in American life when, in the face of competing orthodoxies, one young woman could find a way to think for herself.

ACKNOWLEDGMENTS

Four years ago, I met in person with my agent, Julie Barer, and my editor, Kara Cesare, to discuss my plans for this novel. These were the days before Covid and Zoom, but there was another way of meeting virtually, which was called the telephone. Into Kara's office came the warm, confident voice of Susan Kamil, then head of Random House. She paused for a moment after my long and somewhat disorganized pitch, and then she said: "I get it. It's a modern retelling of *The Awakening,* but it's set during the Scopes trial."

As she had with previous books of mine, she had zeroed in on the heart of what I wanted to write. I thanked her profusely. I didn't know that it would be the last time. She died just two months later, at a ridiculously young age. She will forever have my gratitude and my love.

So will the other two women who were in that meeting. Sometimes I think that, like surgeons, agents and editors often spare authors knowing about the less pleasant tasks they perform. So, when I express my gratitude to Julie and Kara, it's not just for what I know they do, but for what I don't know. In the case of Julie, what I *do* get to see is a passionate and relentless advocate with exquisite judgment. Kara is the editor a writer dreams of having. She doesn't just get my writing, characters, settings, and stories; she also gets *me*. In addition to improving the novel in immeasurable ways, she appears to have pulled off a magic act by reassembling the team that launched my last novel with such brio and success.

It can be daunting to read a friend's work. My friends are apparently dauntless. Sharon DeLevie, Darrel Frost, Peter Lurye, and Dan Okrent each read different sections and drafts of this novel and offered their comments, encouragement, and—most valuably—criticisms. I will, as a consequence, do anything any of them ever asks of me in return. As always, Betsy Carter was deep in the weeds of this book— endlessly patient and giving, taking time away from her own newest novel to read drafts of mine. She knows what this means to me.

I'm grateful, too, to Georgia Channing and her parents for doing some legwork in Dayton that I couldn't. David Gilmour gave me in-depth tutorials on the world of ham radio. Phillip Blumberg, Richard Cohen, Marcus Forman, Jon LaPook, and Saud Sadiq have tirelessly tended to my health. And I will forever be thankful to Debbie Fields, who had the grace and generosity to try to educate a Jewish woman from New York City about what it means to be a Fundamentalist Baptist from North Carolina. Debbie and I had the kinds of conversations I would wish for anyone: two people of vastly different beliefs and backgrounds intent on understanding, rather than converting, each other. I couldn't have written this book without the insights she gave me about her faith.

When you have children, you hope they'll grow up to be decent people and to be useful in the world. Elizabeth Grunwald Adler and Jonathan Grunwald Adler have turned out to be both, and to an extraordinary degree. But they've also turned out to be invaluable sounding boards and insightful readers. It's not necessarily a picnic to be asked to comment on a parent's work, and I've relied on them a lot. If they weren't so smart, I wouldn't ask for their help, so they only have themselves to blame.

Stephen Adler is married to a woman with a chronic illness and a chronic need to write. Somehow, he understands both these things—usually better than I do. He is my friend, editor, partner, and the love of my life.

SOURCE NOTES

The line between fact and fiction is blurry by design in historical novels. But ample resources abound for anyone wanting to delve into the historical record of Dayton, Tennessee, in the summer of 1925. Books by and about the most famous players, contemporaneous newspaper and magazine articles, speeches, and trial transcripts are all readily available. Much of what's said in public settings in this novel is taken verbatim or condensed from these sources. The same is true for lesser-known historical figures: the "drugstore conspirators," the Rappleyeas, the lawyers, the judge, Howard Byrd, Reverend Charles Potter, and some of the expert witnesses.

The crimes involving Burch Gardenhire, Walton Allen, and Walton Allen's son actually happened, but several years earlier than I've had them appear. Howard Byrd did quit the Methodist-Episcopal Church when congregants objected to Potter speaking about evolution.

Lottie Nelson is very loosely based on an extraordinary woman named Nellie Kenyon, a reporter for the *Chattanooga News* who was indeed the first journalist to get a press pass to the Scopes trial.

The articles that Lottie writes in this book are not Nellie's, and all other aspects of her character and actions are fiction.

There are dozens of books and documentaries about the trial, and no shortage of contradictions among and between them. For the most comprehensive overviews, I relied on Edward Larson's Pulitzer Prize–winning *Summer for Gods,* Marvin Olasky and John Perry's *Monkey Business,* as well as documentaries and original footage from PBS, the Smithsonian, and the History Channel. Bryan College produced a kind of Fundamentalist rebuttal to the Hollywood version of events with a reenactment of the trial called *Inherit the Truth.* Going back to earlier sources, I frequently consulted Scopes's 1967 autobiography; the 1939 Federal Works Agency's *Tennessee: A Guide to the State;* as well as a 1959 Master's thesis written by Warren Allen and available online from the University of Tennessee, Knoxville.

ABOUT THE AUTHOR

LISA GRUNWALD is the author of the novels *Time After Time, The Irresistible Henry House, Whatever Makes You Happy, New Year's Eve, The Theory of Everything,* and *Summer.* Along with her husband, former Reuters editor in chief Stephen J. Adler, she edited the anthologies *The Marriage Book, Women's Letters,* and *Letters of the Century.* Grunwald is a former contributing editor to *Life* and former features editor of *Esquire.* She lives in New York City and Weston, Connecticut.

lisagrunwald.com
Facebook.com/lisagrunwaldauthor
Instagram: @lisagrunwald

ABOUT THE TYPE

This book was set in Sabon, a typeface designed by the well-known German typographer Jan Tschichold (1902–74). Sabon's design is based upon the original letterforms of sixteenth-century French type designer Claude Garamond and was created specifically to be used for three sources: foundry type for hand composition, Linotype, and Monotype. Tschichold named his typeface for the famous Frankfurt typefounder Jacques Sabon (c. 1520–80).